The Cowboy Meets His Match

The Cowboy Meets His Match

His Match

A 79th Copper Mountain Rodeo Romance

Sarah Mayberry

TULE
PUBLISHING

Chapter One

CASSIDY JANE COOPER sat a little straighter behind the wheel as she spotted the sign on the side of the highway. "Welcome to Marietta, Montana, home of the Copper Mountain Rodeo." Her pickup sped past the tall billboard and the knowledge that she was only minutes from her destination sent her heart into overdrive.

Dumbass, she told herself. *No point getting wound up yet. Save it for tomorrow.*

It didn't make any difference—her pulse continued to pound in her throat as she spotted the motel she'd booked for the next three nights. A faded sixties' complex, it was located on the outskirts of Marietta, its No Vacancy sign indicating they had a full house. A lot of visitors would prefer accommodation in town, she suspected, but this place was perfect for her, since it was just five minutes from the rodeo grounds.

She pulled into the driveway and parked, taking a moment to wipe her suddenly damp palms down the sides of her jeans before making her way into reception to collect her room key. Five minutes later she was driving past rows of dusty pickups, most of them plastered with bumper stickers extolling the virtues of cowboys in general and rodeos in particular. She pulled into a spot in front of her room, then got out and spent the next few minutes calming herself with the mundane act of unloading her gear.

Only when her saddle, riding gear and luggage were safely in the room did she let herself sink onto the end of the bed and flop onto her back. Pulling her phone from her pocket, she punched in a quick text home: Arrived safe and sound. All good.

Her mother's reply was almost instant: Thanks for letting us know. Make sure you eat something and get a good night's sleep. I'll try to call tomorrow. xxx.

Duty done, CJ let her hand fall to her side and closed her eyes. It had been a long drive from Plentywood in the state's northeast, but she was finally here.

This was really happening.

Her stomach gave a nervous-excited lurch and she sat up abruptly. If she stayed in this room staring at the ceiling, she was going to think too much and start second-guessing herself. Her decisions had all been made weeks ago. Now all that was left was for her to ride her best and show the world—well, Marietta, at least—what she was made of.

She went into the tiny bathroom and washed her face. Her hair was too kinked from being tied up in a ponytail to leave it down, so she tied it back up again and grabbed her car keys. There were a bunch of cowboys leaning against one of the trucks a few doors up when she exited her room, and she felt more than one of them give her the once-over as she made her way to her truck. She kept her gaze straight ahead, having learned the hard way that giving some of these rodeo-circuit cowboys even the minimal encouragement of eye contact or a polite smile was considered a resounding invitation to much more.

The last thing she needed was that kind of noise this weekend.

GPS took her to the rodeo grounds by a direct route and she parked among the scattering of other cars and trucks. This place wouldn't get busy until tomorrow, when the rodeo kicked off, but she wanted to do a bit of re-con so she could hit the ground running. Plus she needed to pay her entry fees, and collect a schedule.

Dust kicked up from the dry gravel lot as she walked toward the low cinder block building emblazoned with a large Ticket Office sign. Behind it rose the concrete-and-steel bleachers, fresh paint gleaming in the afternoon sun. There had been a fire here not so long ago, CJ had heard, and the town had pulled together to rebuild the rodeo grounds.

From what she could see, the people of Marietta had done a great job—everything looked neat, bright and ready to accommodate the many thousands of people due to attend the Copper Mountain Rodeo this weekend.

The gate was pulled down on the ticket window, but the

door marked Office was open, so CJ put on her big girl panties and went in. It was dim inside and it took a moment for her eyes to adjust. A middle-aged woman sat behind a high counter directly in front of her, and a doorway led into what looked like another office. The woman offered CJ a smile, her bright blue eyes friendly.

"Afternoon. How can I help you? I'm afraid if you're after tickets they won't be on sale until after ten tomorrow."

"Afternoon. I'm here to pay my fees. I'm a contestant," CJ explained.

"Wonderful. Let me just find your details." CJ watched as the woman automatically reached for a folder marked Barrel Racing and started flicking through a series of forms. "What's your name?"

CJ shifted her weight. "CJ Cooper. Short for Cassidy Jane. But I'm competing in saddle bronc, not barrel racing."

"Oh." The woman gave a long, slow blink. "Well. All right, then."

She was frowning now, and CJ knew exactly what she was thinking. *Are you* allowed *to do that?* She'd been asked the same question half a dozen times since she'd started riding in the traditionally all-male saddle bronc competition twelve months ago.

A shadow in her peripheral vision alerted her to the fact that someone was standing in the doorway to the adjacent office. She flicked a glance toward the tall, grizzled cowboy propped there. His keen gray eyes took her in for a long, drawn-out beat, his expression inscrutable.

CJ straightened her shoulders. *Here we go.*

But he surprised her by stepping forward, his hand extended in greeting.

"Travis McMahon. I'm responsible for this dog and pony show," he said in a deep rumbling baritone. His hand was rough and dry when he shook hers.

"CJ Cooper. We spoke on the phone," she said, recognizing both his name and voice.

"We did indeed. Just wanted to welcome you on board. Good to have fresh blood," he said.

There was no judgment in his tone, but there was reserve behind his gray eyes. No doubt he was wondering if she was up to the challenge she'd set herself.

She was, but he'd find that out soon enough.

"Thanks, appreciate it," she said.

"Let me know if you've got any questions. Laurie here'll hook you up with all the information you need."

"I was thinking of having a bit of a walk around, if that's okay. Get myself familiar with the layout."

"You help yourself to whatever. Chutes are other side of the arena, opposite the bleachers. Locker rooms out the back here. Pretty proud of them—they're part of the rebuild, so you definitely want to check them out. And you can just follow your nose to the stockyards."

CJ smiled at the small joke. "Thanks, I will."

She turned back to Laurie, who was waiting patiently

with CJ's paperwork.

"Is cash okay?" CJ asked.

"It certainly is," Laurie said brightly.

They made polite chitchat while Laurie processed the transaction and offered further directions to help CJ navigate the grounds.

"Appreciate all your help, Laurie," CJ said as she tucked her wallet into the back pocket of her jeans.

"I'll keep an eye out for you tomorrow," Laurie said. "Good luck."

It wasn't until CJ was outside in the warm afternoon sunshine that she registered how tight her shoulders were. She gave them a roll as she headed toward the bleachers. It wasn't that she'd come here expecting resistance or trouble exactly, but she *had* been prepared for it.

Almost exactly a month ago now, she'd become only the second woman in the world to qualify to ride saddle bronc on the professional rodeo circuit, competing head to head with the men. She was well aware that there were plenty of people who were not cool with her ambition to ride among the best of the best. The reasons for their resistance varied. Some were merely traditionalists and didn't like change. Others viewed women as too delicate, fragile, emotional or physically weak to take on such a demanding and dangerous sport. And yet others felt that the arrival of fierce female competitors signaled a threat to their place in the world. They were right, too—she wanted to win. She wanted to be the best, just like her fellow competitors did. The fact that they were all men and she was a woman was beside the point as far as she was concerned.

As she'd worked her way toward achieving professional status—a process that had involved accruing a certain amount of prize money at smaller, non-pro rodeos—CJ had quickly learned to ignore the looks and barely heard comments. To engage or give the doubters and haters any of her energy meant taking her eye off the prize. And there had been enough vocal supporters—as many of them men as women—who stood and cheered for her, for her to feel encouraged. She might be a curiosity to a lot of folks, but she was confident that with time she would earn their respect.

Her strategy for her first outing as a professional contestant here at Copper Mountain was simple—keep her head down and concentrate on what she wanted, what she was here for: to win.

With that goal in mind, she headed for the fancy new locker rooms Travis McMahon had mentioned, first stop on her re-con tour.

GUILT BIT AT Jesse Carmody the moment he was within the town limits of Marietta. It bit harder still when he blew past the turnoff to head west, toward the Carmody family ranch. He hadn't seen his family in more than a year, and he knew his siblings were anticipating his arrival, especially his younger sister, Sierra, but he needed to stable his horse out at the rodeo grounds before he did anything else. He'd been on the road for nearly three hours and his sorrel gelding, Major, needed out of the combination living-quarters horse-trailer hitched to the back of his pickup.

It was as good an excuse as any to delay his arrival, he figured. And if avoiding the inevitable awkwardness of a homecoming by a few hours made him a coward…well, so be it. He could live with that.

He pulled into the rodeo grounds and did a quick survey of what he could see of the newly rebuilt arena from the truck before driving around back to where the outdoor stalls were. Major gave him an eye roll and an impatient snort as Jesse released him from the trailer, backing him down the ramp. His hand light on the leading rein, Jesse took the gelding on a few slow laps of the yard before leading him to the outdoor stall they'd been assigned. As usual, he'd made arrangements ahead of time to make sure Major's favorite feed and familiar bedding were on hand, and he was pleased to see both in evidence. He spent twenty minutes massaging the horse's major muscles to help dissipate any travel fatigue. Only when Major had shown interest in both water and feed did he leave his four-legged buddy, carefully shutting the gate behind him.

About half the other corrals were empty, which meant there'd be a lot of arrivals later this afternoon and into the evening. He checked his watch as he walked back to his truck. He should probably unhitch and park his trailer in the lot set aside for competitors, then head out to the ranch. Get the big homecoming out of the way.

Instead, he veered off toward the stockyard. He'd been assigned one of the newer broncs in the competition in the draw yesterday, and he was keen to check the animal out.

He made his way to the nearest corral and rested his forearms on the top rail. He could see the tour's vet busy inspecting bulls in one of the distant pens, checking the animals for injuries and health, part of the rodeo's strict rules around animal welfare. Major would get a going-over, too, before being cleared for tomorrow's exertions, as would all the other competitors' horses.

He was looking for the distinctive gray and white coat of Buckmaster, the bronc he'd drawn, when movement drew his gaze to a cowboy leaning against a corral further along the run. He started to lift his hand in greeting, assuming it was someone he knew, when the cowboy shifted and he realized it was a she, not a he, the generous curves of her hips and chest giving the game away now that she was facing him. She flicked a glance his way, catching him with his hand midair, and he felt more than a little foolish. He changed the gesture into a casual adjustment of the brim of his hat, but he wasn't sure he'd gotten away with it.

He hadn't seen her around before. She wasn't staff, and she definitely wasn't one of the barrel-racing competitors— after months of touring together, he was more than familiar with all the regular faces. Maybe she was with one of the rough-stock suppliers? Or just a curious local?

He told himself it was none of his business, either way, and went back to looking for Buckmaster. Still, he was conscious of her pushing away from the rail and heading in his direction, and he couldn't resist the impulse to check her out again. She was tall for a woman, with an athletic, long-legged stride. Despite her curves, she had the toned physique of the very fit, her thigh muscles visible through the soft denim of her jeans, her shoulders broad and strong. A thick, dark ponytail hung down her back, and her black straw cowboy hat cast her face in shadows, revealing only a stubborn-looking chin and a full-lipped mouth.

She lifted her chin as she moved closer and their eyes locked. Hers were dark brown and steady on his. She nodded her head in silent acknowledgment. He nodded in return.

"Afternoon," he said.

She drew abreast of him, and just as she was about to pass by, there was a small hitch in her stride, and she stopped and turned on her heel.

"Excuse me. I don't suppose you could tell me which one of these broncs is Hellion Boy?" she asked.

"In theory. Not sure where they've put him, though…" Jesse turned to scan the corrals, spotting the gelding in question after a few seconds. "There he is. Back corner, chestnut with the irregular blaze."

She followed his pointing finger, eyes narrowed.

"Thanks."

She started to move off.

"You with the stock contractor?" he asked, turning to face her more fully. She was almost as tall as him, and up close he could see she had a light scattering of freckles across her nose and cheeks beneath her tan. She was pretty rather than beautiful, but there was something about the way she held herself and her steady gaze that spoke to him.

"I'm a contestant," she said.

"Yeah? You'll have your work cut out for you, catching up with Lena Martinez, coming in late on the tour like this. She's really racking up the points this year," he said.

Her gaze slipped over his shoulder, focusing, he guessed, on the horse he'd just pointed out to her.

"Yeah, I heard the barrel racing was competitive this year," she said, and there was something about the way she said it and the way she seemed to be distancing herself from him while still standing in front of him that piqued his curiosity.

That, and the way she filled out her jeans.

"So—"

"Carmody. Not wasting any time, are you?"

Jesse glanced over his shoulder to see a trio of cowboys approaching, all three his competitors in steer roping and saddle bronc. The speaker, Dean, was wearing a shit-eating grin, his gaze traveling up and down the woman in front of Jesse like she was on sale in a shop window.

Subtlety wasn't exactly Dean's strong suit, with women or life in general. In his mid-twenties, he was pretty boy good-looking and full of swagger, with a reputation for partying hard.

"Did you boys just get in?" Jesse asked easily, shaking the hand Dean offered him, along with a slap on the shoulder.

"Came in yesterday. Just about to head into town and meet up with some of the boys. You in?" Dean asked.

"Probably gonna head out to the ranch," Jesse said.

"That's right. Forgot Marietta is home for you." Dean's gaze shifted away from Jesse. "Going to introduce us to your friend here?"

Jesse glanced at the woman. "We hadn't gotten to names yet."

The moment the words were out his mouth he realized how they sounded—as though he'd had a whole plan of attack where she was concerned.

"I take it back, Carmody—you *are* wasting time." Dean turned up the dial on his smile. "Name's Dean Maynard. Pleased to meet you."

He offered the woman his hand.

"CJ Cooper," she said.

"CJ. That short for something?" Dean asked.

"Cassidy Jane."

"Cassidy Jane. That's real pretty." Dean waved a hand at Jesse and the other riders. "This dumb lug here is Jesse Carmody, and these two are Billy and Bobby Miller."

CJ smiled politely. "Nice to meet you all."

"So, CJ. You a local girl?" Dean asked, his big, easy grin inviting CJ to confess her sins so he could reward her for them.

Jesse had seen Dean turn on the charm like this in too many cities to count, but his gut told him the other man was about to crash and burn, big-time. Jesse had only known CJ Cooper for two minutes, but there was a determined set to her jaw and a challenging glint in her eye he was pretty sure he wasn't imagining. Crossing his arms over his chest, Jesse leaned back against the rail.

This was going to be good.

"I'm not a local. I'm a contestant," CJ said.

"Yeah? You joining the tour with us, huh?" Dean said, clearly pleased by the prospect. He hooked his thumbs into the front belt loops on his jeans, playing the cowboy to the hilt. "Lot of competition in the barrel racing this year. Hope you're a good rider, sweetheart."

Billy and Bobby both smirked at the clumsy double entendre.

"I'm not competing in the barrel racing," CJ said. "I'm riding saddle bronc."

Dean cocked his head, a frown pleating his forehead. "They doing some kind of exhibition program for the ladies this time around?"

"Nope. I'll be competing with the men. Against you guys, actually. You all ride saddle bronc, don't you? I recognize your names." Her gaze took them all in, direct and quietly confident, and Jesse wondered if his surprise showed on his face.

"You can't ride in the men's comp," Dean said, letting out an incredulous crack of laughter. "That ain't gonna work, sweetheart."

"It's worked okay so far, well enough for me to qualify for my pro ticket," CJ said with a modest shrug.

Jesse swept a gaze down her body again, seeing her athletic build in a new light. Strength-to-weight ratio was important in saddle bronc, but flexibility and having a low center of gravity played a part, too.

Theoretically there was no reason a woman wouldn't be as good as a man. In fact, she might even have an advantage when it came to flexibility—if she had the guts to get on the back of a wild, bucking animal who was determined to throw her off.

"This is a men's competition," Dean said. "Always has been, always will be."

"I'm not the only female saddle bronc rider. Kaila Mussell's been riding broncs for years now," CJ pointed out.

Dean's face flushed an ugly red and he took a step closer to CJ, anger in every line of his wiry body. Jesse pushed away from the rail, surprised by the heat of the other man's reaction and how quickly things had escalated.

"You listen here, *sweetheart*," Dean said, turning the endearment into an insult. "You women might think you own the world now, but some things are sacred. Some kind of mistake has been made, and I'm gonna go sort it out right now."

He swiveled on his heel, stalking off in the direction of the office, leaving a trail of dust in his wake. It took a moment for Jesse's brain to catch up with events. One second Dean had been laughing, turning on the charm, hoping to get lucky, the next he'd been snarling like a cornered dog.

Jesse had never seen the other man so riled before.

"Gentlemen, it's been a pleasure," CJ said, her dry tone at odds with her words. Then she headed around the back of the bleachers, head high, shoulders back.

"Je-sus," Bobby Miller said the moment she was out of earshot. "Thought Dean was gonna burst a vessel for a moment there."

"He's right, though. This ain't no women's sport. They got no business letting one into the comp without running it past the rest of us," Billy said.

Jesse threw the other man a look. "Come on, Billy. You really want to get into a situation where competitors can blackball new blood?"

"But she's not just new blood. She's a woman," Billy said, as if that fact alone was enough to make his point for him.

Jesse shook his head. "As far as I'm concerned, if she qualified like the rest of us, then she should be able to compete. Unless you guys are scared of going up against a woman?"

"Fuck off, Carmody," Bobby said, half annoyed, half amused. "I bet she doesn't even make it out of the chute. I bet this is just some bullshit PR stunt they're pulling to try to get some media attention."

"She must have placed or won plenty of times to get the prize money to qualify," Jesse pointed out. "Pretty sure they didn't bend the rules for her."

"Want to bet?" Billy said darkly.

Jesse shook his head again. "Don't go starting any stupid conspiracy theories, for God's sake."

Billy frowned at him. "You telling me you're really cool with this?" His tone said he thought Jesse was mad, as well as some kind of traitor to his gender.

"I don't care what a rider's got between his or her legs— if they can last eight seconds, I'll compete against 'em," Jesse said. "It's as simple as that."

"You got rocks in your head, man," Bobby said, looking genuinely bewildered by Jesse's take.

Jesse made a rude noise. If this conversation lasted much longer, he was going to say something he'd regret. Like it or not, he spent a lot of time with these men. "I've got to get out to the ranch, see my family. I'll catch you boys later."

He didn't hang around to wait for their response.

Chapter Two

CJ MADE A point of continuing her self-guided tour of the grounds after her encounter with the cowboys. She'd anticipated some resistance to her inclusion in the saddle bronc event, but those cowboys were just going to have to suck it up. There was nothing in the rules that said she couldn't compete, and she'd qualified for her pro ticket the same as any other contestant. Nothing was going to stop her from getting out there and taking her best shot at the prize money, least of all a loudmouth cowboy with a ridiculously fragile sense of his place in the world.

She kept telling herself as much as she inspected the practice ring and checked out the catering facilities. At the moment there was just a single shuttered kiosk, but she knew from past experience that there would likely be a bunch of food trucks and other outdoor eateries set up to cater to tomorrow's crowds, so no one would be at risk of going hungry. Lastly, she climbed into the stands and stood in the front row. Staring out across the dusty arena, she took a couple of deep breaths, letting the quiet and emptiness work on her.

Tomorrow, these bleachers would be full of people—cowboys, families, young and old. The smell of popcorn and chili and nachos would be floating in the air, along with the occasional whiff of more earthy odors from the stockyard. The sun would be high overhead, and the PA system would be blaring music in between filling the audience in on contestant stats and standings.

It would be chaotic and festive and electric, and she couldn't wait to feel the solid muscle of a bronc between her thighs, couldn't wait to give the nod to release the gate. The thought alone was enough to send a wave of anticipatory adrenaline surging through her, and she couldn't hold back a big, dumb grin.

It didn't matter what anyone else thought or wanted. She was a good bronc rider, and she loved it, loved the way it made her feel so alive, loved the primal battle between woman and beast, loved the pageantry and showy clothes and earthy smells of leather and dirt and manure.

Turning away from the arena, she made her way down the concrete steps and found the exit to the parking lot. She noticed a bronze and copper statue near the entrance on the way out—for some reason she'd missed it the first time around—a life-sized cowboy riding a bronco, mounted on a granite plinth. She studied the cowboy's face for a few seconds, admiring the detail in the work, before reading the plaque commemorating the opening of the new stadium.

The rodeo was obviously a big deal to the people of Marietta.

She headed for her truck, but the sound of a door slamming made her glance over her shoulder toward the ticket office. Her stomach dipped when she saw Dean Maynard powering away from the building, a deep scowl creasing his forehead, frustration and anger evident in every long, jerky step he took. That he'd gotten nowhere with his dumbass complaint about her was plain—he looked like he wanted to hurt someone or something. She felt a thump of unease as he looked up and met her gaze. For a second he hesitated, then he changed direction, heading straight for her. She shot a glance toward her pickup, which was still some twenty or thirty feet away. She could make it, if she hustled, but she wasn't going to run from this man.

Not in a million years.

She turned to face him, schooling her expression into a calm, neutral mask that belied the hard thud-thud of her heart against her rib cage.

She spent a couple of hours a week in the boxing ring at the local gym as part of her workout routine, practicing a combination of traditional boxing and kickboxing moves, but she'd never had to call on those skills to defend herself in a real fight.

If she had to, she would, though.

"You might have pulled some bullshit with the organizers, but no one wants you here, lady," Maynard said, the tendons standing out in his neck as he stopped in front of her. When he wasn't red-faced and angry, some women would probably find his blond pretty boy looks attractive, but all CJ saw was ignorance and petty defensiveness. "You think the crowd is going to cheer you on when you're stealing a spot from a man doing his best to support his family?"

"What makes you think I don't have a family to support?" she asked.

What century was this guy living in, anyway?

"Got a wife and kids back home, have you?" he asked, raking her with a contemptuous head-to-toe that told her how he felt about same-sex-attracted people.

"That's none of your business."

Maynard's eyes got flinty and he jabbed an angry finger at her chest, stopping just short of touching her. "You're stealing a man's dreams, all for nothing. There's no way you're going to be able to hold your own out there."

"Women have dreams, too, believe it or not," she said.

There was nothing more to say, so she turned and walked to her truck. The door handle was solid and warm beneath her hand as she opened it, and she slid quickly behind the wheel. Maynard stood where she'd left him, tension evident in every line of his body. Putting her car in gear, she drove out of the parking spot and turned toward the exit, a route that necessarily took her past Maynard. For a second she contemplated reversing back into the spot and making a longer loop to avoid him, but again she pressed forward. The moment she took a step backward, she was beaten. The only way to get through this weekend with her integrity and pride intact was to put her head down and keep moving forward.

She could feel him watching her as she drew closer, and she wasn't entirely surprised when he stepped into her path. She braked to a halt, eyeing him steadily through the windshield. He spat on the ground, not taking his gaze off hers.

The anger and scorn in his eyes triggered the stubbornness in her. She'd grown up working her parents' ranch with her brothers and father. She'd fallen off her first horse when she was four years old, stared down a deadly massasauga rattlesnake when she was seven, and wrestled with more ornery cattle than she'd had hot dinners. This man didn't know her, and he wasn't going to intimidate her.

She eased her foot onto the gas, edging the car slowly but inexorably forward. He had a choice—step out of the way, or get nudged out of the way by her beaten-up Ford F-150. She saw the shock in his too-handsome face when he understood she was serious. He broke eye contact with her to assess the height and width of her truck. Then, at almost the last possible moment, he stepped to one side.

She drove past him, eyes straight ahead. A loud bang made her start and she realized he'd slapped his hand against the side of her truck. The jerk.

She put her foot down and seconds later was pulling onto the road back to the motel. Her breath came out in a shudder as the rodeo grounds shrunk to a dot in her rearview mirror. Which was about when she registered her hands were shaking, too.

She reached for the radio, punching it on, needing the company and the distraction. The familiar sounds of the Dixie Chicks's "Wide Open Spaces" filled the truck and she sent up a prayer of thanks to the universe. She sang the lyrics at the top of her lungs for the duration of the short drive back to the motel, but she was still feeling rattled when she parked and let herself into her room. There was no solace to be found in the neutral, no-nonsense decor of her accommodation, and she slipped her hand into her back pocket and palmed her phone.

It was so tempting to call home, but it would only worry her mother unnecessarily, and her father was more likely to say "What did you expect?" than sympathize with her. From the moment she'd signaled her intention to achieve pro status, he'd shaken his head and prophesied she'd regret her decision. *Why do you need to rock the boat?* he'd asked on more than one occasion. He'd been worried there'd be talk locally, that she'd ruffle feathers, trying to muscle in on traditional male territory. It had hurt that he'd been more worried about what other people in their small, conservative community thought than her hopes and ambitions, but she'd never been brave enough to ask him the question in her heart: why teach her she could do or be anything and then not encourage her to fly as high as she could?

She shoved the phone back into her pocket. As much as she wanted to hear the voice of someone who loved her right now, she'd always known she'd be doing this on her own. And that was okay. Not ideal, but okay.

She checked the time. The program she'd perused while doing her self-guided tour of the rodeo grounds had mentioned some kind of street party in town this afternoon and evening, complete with a sidewalk sale, food, live bands and dancing. Apparently everything kicked off at four, and it was past that now.

Perfect.

She'd go check it out, see if she couldn't find something cute and unique for her mother's birthday, which was coming up next month. And if the noise and color of other people having fun helped drown out the echo of Maynard's ugly words in her head, all the better.

JESSE'S TRUCK BOUNCED out of a rut as he rounded the final corner in the drive to the family ranch, making him rock in his seat. Up ahead was the modest, single-level brick and timber house that had been home to the Carmodys for thirty-five years. To the right was the red-painted barn, and beyond that the home paddock, host at present to a handful of grazing horses.

Everything looked the same as it always had, down to the roses marching in a row along the front of the porch and the huge yellow pine that cast its shadow over the rear of the house. He pulled up near the barn and was just switching off the ignition when the front door of the house opened and his older brother, Jed, stepped out onto the porch. Their gazes met across twenty-five feet of dusty yard, and for a long beat his brother simply looked at him. Then Jed nodded, a small, quiet smile pulling at his mouth, and Jesse felt a twin kick of relief and resentment.

He freaking hated that he still felt nervous coming home. He really hated that his brother's approval—or, more accurately, *dis*approval—still had the power to affect him. It had been eleven years since his brother had issued the ultimatum that had led to Jesse leaving this place. He'd been home a handful of times since, but it was always the same— the wariness between him and Jed, Jesse's continuing resentment of the way things had played out, Jed's closed-mouthed, measured impenetrability.

Was it any wonder he never stayed for long, even though he loved his family and missed them when he let himself think about it too much?

Aware he'd lingered too long in the truck, Jesse pushed the door open and stood just as a blur erupted from the darkness of the barn. He had an impression of long, denim-clad legs and streaming dark hair before his sister was throwing herself at him, strong tanned arms pulling him close.

"You made it. I've been listening for your truck all afternoon and you still managed to sneak up on me," Sierra said, pulling back to laugh up into his face.

She was ridiculously cute, his sister, with a small, turned-up nose she'd inherited from their mom, a heart-shaped face and the Carmody green eyes. She was the baby of the family, cursed with being the only girl in a houseful of boys, and master of the art of strategizing to get her way.

"Had a stealth system installed so I could sneak past my nosy relatives," Jesse said.

She laughed and punched him on the pec, hard enough to make him wince. "You bet I'm nosy. I want to hear everything about everything. I haven't seen you for nearly a year and a half."

He was ready to dispute her claim, then did the math quickly in his head. She was right—the last Copper Mountain Rodeo had been canceled because of the fire, and he'd come up with an excuse not to travel home for Christmas. It had easily been eighteen months.

"Don't get too excited, not much to tell," he said.

Out of the corner of his eye he was aware of his brother approaching.

"Dropped Major off at the grounds already?" Jed asked, offering Jesse his hand in greeting.

The formality of the gesture—the arm's-length symbolism of it—wasn't lost on Jesse. He forced himself to smile easily as he shook his brother's work-callused hand.

"Wanted to give him as much time as possible to settle in

and find his legs," Jesse said.

Like Jesse, Jed's hair was dark, almost black, and he kept it short and neat. His face was tanned a deep nut brown by the Montana sun, but he'd lost weight since Jesse had seen him last and there were new creases at the corners of his eyes and bracketing his mouth. Perhaps it was the new age in his face or something else, but more than ever Jed looked like their father. The realization brought an unaccustomed lump to Jesse's throat and he focused on Sierra again.

"S'pose you've got my whole weekend planned out already?" he said.

"And next week," she said.

He frowned. He hadn't planned to stay in Marietta longer than the rodeo. But before he could speak the sound of a truck engine had them all turning to watch as his younger brother, Casey, pulled up behind Jesse's truck.

"Damn it. I wanted to be here when you arrived," Casey said, swinging out of his truck and grabbing Jesse in a fierce bear hug.

His brother smelled like fresh air, horses and clean sweat, and the fist he banged on Jesse's back was going to leave a bruise, but that was all good with Jesse.

His brother finally let him go and they pulled back to take a good look at each other. Casey had let his hair grow shaggy and wild, and his jaw was dark with beard scruff. Like Jed he looked lean and brown, his dark complexion making his eyes look even greener than usual.

"You 'bout to run off and start a cult or something?" Jesse asked, reaching out to ruffle his younger brother's unruly hair.

Like old times, Casey ducked out of the way, one hand lifting to block Jesse's arm. "Hey, hands off the merchandise."

The move brought back a flood of memories of the two of them practicing highly staged martial arts fights in the cool dimness of the barn, the choreography gleaned from obsessive repeat viewings of old Bruce Lee films.

"Crouching tiger, hidden Casey," Sierra said dryly. "Can you two wait a few hours before you start rolling in the dirt, trying to use the touch of death on each other? I don't want to drive two dusty idiots into town for the street party."

"Thought you might have wanted to skip it this year," Jesse said hopefully. "Maybe just have a quiet night here at home."

"Nope, but good try. The Whiskey Shots are part of the lineup, and I plan to be there to bask in my brother's reflected glory," Sierra said, flashing a big smile at Casey.

Casey had been the lead singer and guitarist in a four-member band for a couple of years now, picking up gigs locally.

"Hey, cool," Jesse said. "Don't want to miss out on that."

He'd yet to see his brother perform in public, although he'd heard him picking away at his guitar plenty when they'd been kids. In truth, Jesse had been a little surprised when he'd first learned about the band, since Casey was notoriously shy around people he didn't know well. The idea of his younger brother volunteering to stand on a stage with all eyes on him had seemed counterintuitive to Jesse, but Sierra had assured him many times that Casey more than held his own.

Casey eyed Sierra sternly. "No screaming this time, okay? Last time the Shots played, people thought someone was being mugged."

"That's because I am your number one fan," Sierra said, doing her best Kathy Bates-madwoman eyes.

Jesse laughed, tickled as always by his sister's sense of humor. Suddenly he felt like a huge dick for avoiding home for so long. Jed might be a stoic, taciturn bastard, but these people were his family and he loved them to death.

"Thought the Shots were playing last?" Jed asked.

"Sure, but we can find plenty to do until then," Sierra said.

"I was thinking more that Jesse won't want to be out all night when he's got to compete tomorrow," Jed said.

"Pretty sure I can handle a late night," Jesse said, resenting his brother's parental tone. He was twenty-nine years old to Jed's thirty-one, long past the age when his brother needed to look out for him.

There was a short pause following his too-sharp words. Jed's face was carefully blank as he nodded and took a step back, turning toward the house.

"Then I guess we're sorted," he said, already moving off.

Jesse watched him walk away, a lean, stiff-backed figure. If anyone else had made the same comment, Jesse would have taken it at face value, but with Jed every interaction always felt loaded with the weight of their personal history, and more often than not Jesse wound up overreacting—exactly like the resentful kid he'd been when he left home with his brother's boot up his ass all those years ago.

"I guess some things never change, huh?" Sierra said.

Jesse swallowed the urge to apologize. It wasn't like any of them were strangers to this shit. This was just the way it was.

"I'll grab your gear, help you get settled," Casey said.

"Thanks, man," Jesse said.

Sierra was checking out his clothes, her nose wrinkling with disapproval. "You've got something better than this in your bags, right?" she said, reaching out to finger his wrinkled, travel-stained blue shirt. "I want you all in top form tonight so I can be the rose among the thorns."

"Weed among the thoroughbreds, you mean," Casey said.

"Get your metaphor right, doofus. Thoroughbreds are horses, not plants," Sierra said.

They headed for the house, Sierra walking between the two men.

"Proud, powerful, virile animals," Jesse agreed, exchanging a quick grin with his brother.

"As opposed to stubborn, prolific, homely weeds," Casey said.

"Awesome. Not even five minutes, and you two are ganging up on me already. Can't believe I was actually looking forward to this," Sierra said.

Hard on the heels of her words, she stretched out both arms and smacked each of them on the back of the head with the flat of her hand, a well-calibrated move honed by many a childhood dispute. Then she took off, laughing like a schoolgirl, taking the steps to the house two at a time.

"Welcome home, man," Casey said.

"Yeah, thanks," Jesse said. Then he went after his sister, determined to run her down and teach her a lesson.

IT TOOK NEARLY two hours for all four of them to get showered, changed and organized to head back into town. Sierra made good use of the drive in, poking and prodding Jesse with questions about everything from his diet to his social life.

Jesse lost track of the times he said "none of your business," and even Jed was smiling by the time they found a parking spot in town and walked toward the section of Main Street that had been cordoned off for the parade earlier that afternoon. The space was lined with display tables for the sidewalk sale and food trucks now, all the activity fanning out from the courthouse steps. Many of the shops had decorated their windows with a rodeo theme, and there was a lighthearted, festive feel to the evening.

Sierra called out to a couple of acquaintances as they worked their way along the street, and one of Jesse's old schoolteachers came over to welcome him home and ask which bronc he'd drawn for tomorrow and what he thought his chances were. Jed headed off to catch up with a business acquaintance, and Casey made some excuse about touching base with the other members of the band before disappearing.

"Don't even think of bailing on me," Sierra said, looping her arm through Jesse's.

"Last thing on my mind," he said.

Then he spotted a tall, dark-haired woman ahead of them examining leatherwork on one of the tables set out for the sidewalk sale. It took him a moment to realize it was CJ Cooper—she looked so different with her long hair flowing freely over her shoulders. His gaze drifted down her body, taking in slim-cut denim jeans that made her legs look long and athletic and her ass juicy enough to bite. She was studying the workmanship on a tooled leather belt, her fingers tracing the intricate pattern, and a small smile curved her lips as she said something to the vendor.

It only took him a moment to decide to go talk to her. His conscience had been nagging him ever since the scene at the arena. He'd gone over it a few times in his mind, wishing every time that he'd stepped in and shut Dean down before things had gotten ugly. His only excuse was that it had all happened so fast, but that was poor comfort to CJ Cooper. He could only imagine how she must have felt, arriving at her first rodeo on the pro circuit and being treated like dirt by a bunch of ignorant cowboys.

He turned to Sierra, who was busy tasting samples of jam and chutneys at another table. "There's someone I need to talk to. Won't be a sec."

"I swear to God, Jesse Carmody, if you try to sneak off, I am going to hunt you down and shame you in front of the whole town."

"I'll be right over there, so quit it with the drama, llama, okay?"

Jesse approached CJ with no idea what he was going to say. He figured the words would come when he needed them to.

She appeared to be trying to decide between two belts, and it took her a moment to register his presence when he stopped next to her.

"Afternoon," he said, by way of kicking things off.

She glanced at him casually, perhaps thinking he was simply another customer, then her eyes widened with recognition.

"Oh, God. Not another one," she said.

Chapter Three

"ANOTHER WHAT?" THE cowboy in front of CJ asked, his forehead creased with confusion.

"Look, whatever you've got to say, I'm not interested, okay?" she said, giving him the hand. "Your friend has already pointed out how I'm an interloper, stealing the hopes and dreams of good and decent men everywhere. So consider your message delivered and go back to being an asshole with the rest of your redneck buddies."

The tall, dark-haired man in front of her blinked. Then his mouth curled up ever so slightly at the corners.

"Actually, I wanted to apologize," he said, his deep, low voice rich with amusement.

"Oh."

"I should have jumped in, back at the grounds, and told Dean to pull his head out of his ass. Only reason I didn't was his reaction surprised me as much as it surprised you. But I want you to know I regret it."

His gaze was direct, sincere and steady as it held her own.

She was so surprised it took her a moment to respond.

"Okay. I appreciate it. Thanks." She couldn't remember which of the saddle bronc riders he was—she'd never been good at attaching faces to names, and her run-in with Maynard had wiped everything else from her mind.

"You should know Maynard doesn't speak for all of us, or even most of us," he said. "As long as you can ride, that's all that matters."

"I can ride."

"Then the other riders will respect you as much as any man."

It was nice he thought that, but it hadn't been her experience so far. While she hadn't encountered anywhere near the level of overt hostility she'd experienced today before, it had taken months and several wins before people had started taking her seriously.

"I appreciate the apology," she said, because she did. It had been a pretty shitty day, and it helped that someone had gone out of their way to be nice to her. "Thanks for taking the time to make it."

"Least I can do." He studied her face. "I rode against a guy a few years ago, down in Colorado. His name was Cooper, too. Zach Cooper, I think. Any relation?"

She'd expected him to bow out after he'd said his bit so the question threw her for a moment.

"Um, yeah. One of my brothers. I've got three. They've all done a bit of rodeo in their time. My dad rode a bit, too, back in the day."

"So this is a family dynasty-type situation we've got going on here, then?" he asked, the glint in his eyes letting her know he was teasing her.

It was beginning to really bother her that she didn't know his name.

"I'm really sorry, but I can't remember your name," she said, since she'd always favored the direct approach.

The only giveaway that he was surprised was a quick blink. Then he offered her his hand, a too-charming smile on his lips. "It's Jesse. Jesse Carmody."

She didn't need to be a mind reader to interpret his surprise—she was pretty sure guys as hot as Jesse Carmody weren't forgotten very often, especially by women. With his short, wavy dark hair and lean, hard body, he was pretty much the epitome of rugged masculinity. It was his eyes that most women would probably go weak-kneed over, though—an intense, true green, framed perfectly by dark lashes.

She shook his outstretched hand, noting its strength and warmth and toughness. Like all cowboys, he punished his body, and his hands were no exception.

"Good to meet you properly, Jesse."

She was about to make an excuse to slip away when a woman joined them, sliding into place beside Jesse with a cheeky, mischievous smile on her face. CJ guessed she was mid-twenties, give or take. One glance was enough to reveal she was clearly a close relative—they shared the same distinctive eyes and dark hair—and the way Jesse shot the other woman a fondly exasperated look pretty much sealed the deal.

If this wasn't his sister, CJ would eat her hat.

"Hi, I'm Sierra, Jesse's sister," the woman said, confirming CJ's guess.

"CJ Cooper. Nice to meet you."

"You in town for the rodeo?" Sierra asked, full of friendly interest.

She reminded CJ of a puppy, all big eyes and harmless inquiry.

Before she could respond, Jesse spoke up. "CJ's competing in the saddle bronc."

Sierra's eyebrows rose in surprise. "Really? Against the men?"

"Yep, against the men," CJ said matter-of-factly.

A delighted smile split Sierra's face. "That's freaking fantastic. Imagine if you won. That would be so cool. You could start a revolution."

Jesse gave his sister a nudge. "Hey, how about a little family loyalty?"

"Loyalty schmoyalty. You can win any old time."

"I'm touched. Genuinely moved," he said dryly.

"So, CJ, how do you and Jesse know each other?" The glance Sierra shot back and forth between CJ and Jesse revealed what she was thinking.

"Oh, no," CJ said before she could edit herself.

Sierra's smile got a little brighter. CJ bet she'd given her brother hell when they were kids.

"Oh no, what?"

"Oh no, she can't believe how nosy someone she's just met is being," Jesse said, directing a frown at his sister.

"Excuse me for being interested in my brother's life. For caring about his emotional health and well-being."

Jesse turned to CJ, a rueful expression on his face. "She's got this bee in her bonnet about my social life at the moment. Please ignore her."

Sierra was blushing now. "I didn't mean to be rude. Or nosy. I was just…hoping. You're always on the road. Is it the worst crime in the world that I'd love it if you'd met someone who could be there for you?"

"Okay. I'm going to leave you guys to it," CJ said, taking a step backward. "Hope you have a nice night."

She walked away before she could hear Jesse's response, but she couldn't help wondering why his sister seemed so worried about him. They seemed close, yet Sierra's words hinted at distance between them.

Giving in to temptation, CJ glanced over her shoulder and saw Jesse talking to his sister. As she watched, Sierra gave her brother a friendly shove, and he hooked his arm around her neck and mussed up her hair. CJ had been the recipient of many similar hair mussings from her own brothers, and she couldn't help but smile at the easy affection the gesture revealed. Then she realized she was about to get caught watching Jesse Carmody and whipped her head around.

She moved on to the next stall, where she spent ten minutes trying to decide between a turquoise necklace for her mother or a delicately engraved silver belt buckle. All the while, she was aware of Jesse and his sister nearby, talking to other locals. She heard Jesse's low laugh ring out a few times, and each time she glanced up, turning instinctively toward the sound before she caught herself.

Okay, you are waaay too aware of him, she warned herself.

It was true, and it wasn't just because he was one of the few people who'd been nice to her since her arrival. She had a stern word with herself as she paid for the buckle and determinedly put some distance between herself and the Carmodys.

She was not here to be beguiled by a pair of impossibly green eyes and a devil-may-care grin. She had no time for that kind of nonsense. Better yet, she wasn't interested in it. This weekend was about her dreams, her future.

There was no room in that for a cowboy who was too good-looking for his own good.

JESSE HAD BEEN to more than his fair share of small-town festivals and celebrations. The rodeo arriving in town was usually the signal to break out the barbeque and fire up the local band. He'd eaten more overcooked steak than he cared to think about, drunk gallons of local beer and done his best to be an ambassador for his sport even when he'd been punch-drunk from driving all day.

Marietta was his hometown, though, so this festival felt different. He was surrounded by people he knew—old classmates, neighbors, former teachers, local business owners—not to mention his own family, and even though he'd made a half-hearted attempt to get out of coming into town, he found himself enjoying catching up with everyone and everything.

The streets were strung with fairy lights, and live music played from a stage in the park beside the courthouse. The smell of cooking food wafted from the temporary kitchen that had been set up in front of the courthouse steps. Shops were doing a brisk trade, and the sense of community and prosperity pierced Jesse with a sense of unexpected pride. This was his place, he was with his people, and it was good to be home.

He talked for half an hour with Tara Watkins, his very first girlfriend and now mother to twin boys, then caught up with Reid Dalton, an old school friend who now worked for the Bozeman Police Department. It was nearly six by the time he allowed Sierra to steer him toward the food near the courthouse. Somehow Casey found them in the crush, and they loaded up with hamburgers and hot dogs from the temporary kitchen being manned by local men and women from various community organizations. Jed was nowhere to be seen, a circumstance Sierra shrugged off as they settled on a couple of bales of hay in the park to chow down.

"He's probably talking business with someone. That's all he seems to do these days," she said.

"How've things been, business-wise?" Jesse asked.

He'd noticed a few things at the ranch this afternoon—the barn needed painting, the drive re-gravelling, a few other maintenance issues here and there. All summer jobs, but Jed obviously hadn't gotten to them yet. If he planned to at all.

"Much the same as always, I think. You know Jed—he never really lets on much about anything, just gets on with it," Casey said.

"But calving season was good?"

"Not as good as last year, but good enough." Casey paused in the act of slicing into his steak. "What's with all the questions?"

"I don't know. Jed just seemed…tired, I guess. Thought it might have been something to do with the ranch."

"You know what Jed's problem is? He has no life," Sierra said, stabbing at the air with her fork, a sure sign they were about to be treated to a big dose of opinion. "All he does is work, eat and sleep. I bet he hasn't so much as looked at a woman since he and Mae Berringer broke up."

Casey screwed up his face in disbelief the same way Jesse did.

"What? Don't go trying to turn Jed into some kind of broken-hearted monk," Casey said.

"Exactly," Jesse agreed. "That was years ago."

"Yeah, and he hasn't brought anyone home since then,"

Sierra said, stubbornly holding her ground. "He never talks about another woman, he never even looks at other women, from what I can tell—What? What's so funny?"

Jesse shook his head at his sister. "Like Jed's gonna sweet-talk a woman in front of his little sister. Just because something doesn't happen right in front of you doesn't mean it hasn't happened. I guarantee you that he's getting some from someone, somewhere."

Casey nodded his agreement. "Hell yeah, and amen to that." He lifted his beer and Jesse clinked his own against it.

Sierra rolled her eyes. "Fine. And good. I hope he's happy. That's all I want—for my brothers to be happy."

She looked a little hurt and Casey bumped her shoulder with his. "Sorry to crap all over your big theory, Squirrel."

Sierra pulled a face at the mention of her childhood nickname before going back to her meal, but it hadn't escaped Jesse that this was the second time she'd raised her brothers' romantic lives today.

Stretching out his leg, he nudged his sister's boot. "What's going on, Sierra? Why are you so worried about us being with someone and being happy all of a sudden?"

For a moment he didn't think she was going to answer, but then she set down her plastic knife and fork on her plate and leaned forward a little, her pretty face serious.

"Don't you think it's weird that none of us are married or in a serious relationship yet?" she asked.

Jesse blinked, surprised by the angle of her attack. "No.

Haven't really thought about it, to be honest."

"Such a guy answer." Sierra flicked her hair over her shoulder.

Jesse glanced at Casey, who lifted a shoulder to signal his own lack of thought on the subject.

"Always figured it would happen sometime," his younger brother said.

"Every single girl I went to school with is engaged, married, or living with someone," Sierra said. "Bet it's the same for all the guys you two went to school with, too."

Jesse wrinkled his brow, thinking.

"I'm right, aren't I?" Sierra said. "I think losing Mom and Dad messed us up, made us bad relationship material or something."

"Where do you get that from?" Jesse asked, genuinely perplexed.

"What else can it be? It's not like any of you are hard on the eyes. You could ask any woman here to dance with you, and she'd trip over herself to say yes. Yet Jesse roams around the country risking his life on the back of crazy horses, and the only thing Casey cares about is his guitar, and Jed never does anything but work, work, work."

"What about you? What's your excuse?" Jesse asked.

"I don't know. I keep asking myself that. Am I just too picky? What am I waiting for? Why hasn't it happened for me yet?"

It was tempting to tease her, but Jesse could see this was

something she was genuinely worried about.

"Losing Mom and Dad did not mess us up," he said.

"Yeah, it did. It made Jed kick you out, turned him into our parent instead of our brother. Our whole family hierarchy is screwed."

"Family hierarchy? Have you been watching Dr. Phil again?" Casey asked, looking distinctly unimpressed.

"It's a thing, Casey. You should look it up," Sierra said.

"Nope. I'm going to get another beer, then I'm going to go find the other Shots and get our gear ready for our set. But don't worry, if I see any hot, single babes on my way, I'll do my best to land a wife, okay?"

Sierra gave him dead eyes to let him know she wasn't amused and Jesse was forced to hide a smile.

"I saw that," she said once Casey was gone. "Feel free to mock me along with Casey. Better yet, feel free to prove me wrong by meeting someone awesome and falling in love. Because I would be thrilled to be wrong about this."

As if in response to her words, the crowd behind her split for a moment, giving him a clear view over her shoulder and across the street to where CJ Cooper stood, eating a hot dog with unashamed enthusiasm. As he watched, she finished the last bite and took a moment to lick something off her finger. Then she lobbed the soiled napkin into a nearby trash can, her aim straight and true. She did a muted air punch to celebrate her small victory, and the urge to stand and go talk to her again was so strong his leg muscles actually tensed against the hay bale.

Then the crowd eddied again, and CJ was once again hidden by the sea of people.

"What's wrong? Did you just see someone you know?" Sierra asked.

"Not really."

He couldn't go hunting for CJ in the crowd. After what had happened today, he was one of the last people she'd want to hang out with. Even if he had apologized, and even though she'd seemed to accept it.

"Good. Because I need something sweet. Let's hit the dessert table."

Jesse let his sister pull him to his feet. He cast a final glance over his shoulder, but CJ Cooper was nowhere to be seen.

Probably just as well. She was his competitor, and if she had any idea how interested he was in the way her jeans hugged her backside, he was pretty sure her first reaction would be to kick him where it hurts instead of being flattered or even intrigued.

The thought made him laugh out loud, earning him a curious look from his sister.

"Nothing," he said before she could ask.

"Weirdo," she said.

He just shrugged and let her lead the way through the crowd.

CJ STAYED IN town long enough to see the last act take to the stage, a four-member band called the Whiskey Shots. The lead singer had the sort of raspy, deep voice that gave a person goose bumps, and even though she wanted to get a good night's rest, she was tempted to stay and watch him light up the stage. He didn't appear to be doing anything special, but somehow he effortlessly drew all eyes and CJ wasn't immune to his magic, whatever it was.

Then she realized there was something oddly familiar about the shape of his jaw and general structure of his face, not to mention his build, and it hit her that she was staring at yet another of Jesse Carmody's siblings.

The Carmodys must be prolific. Or she was just unlucky. One or the other. Either way, it was enough to get her walking back to where she'd parked her truck, well away from Main Street. She yawned more than once on the brief drive to the motel. It was going to be good to put her head on her pillow tonight. Between the travel, all the drama and a belly full of food, she was ready for a little oblivion.

She was annoyed to find someone had taken the parking spot in front of her room when she arrived at the motel complex, leaving her to find a spot elsewhere. The moment she was out of her truck she heard loud music and noticed a couple of rooms at the end of the block housing her room were playing host to a shared party. A group of cowboys and a handful of women filled the walkway and lounged against nearby cars, smoking and drinking. Laughter and the occasional high-pitched female squeal rang out into the night.

Awesome. Just what she needed—a loud party to keep her up half the night before her first pro ride.

She wove her way through the parked cars, aiming for her door. She was about to put her key in the lock when some instinct made her look up.

Dean Maynard was standing among the crowd at the party, one shoulder against the wall as he took a pull from what looked like a bottle of whiskey, his gaze intent on CJ as she stood at her door.

Shit. Shit, shit, shit.

She waited for him to head toward her, her hand tight around her key, but he didn't move. After a beat she unlocked the door and stepped inside, shutting it and carefully locking it before pulling the security chain across as well. Not that that was going to stop anyone determined to gain entry.

She kept glancing toward the door as she prepared for bed, her nerves on a knife's edge. Usually she slept in nothing but a tank and a pair of panties, but she pulled on some yoga pants tonight, just in case. After turning out the light, she lay in her bed, stiff as a plank, listening to the sounds of the party, on the alert for heavy boot steps approaching her door.

Slowly she relaxed into the mattress. Probably she was overreacting, worrying about Maynard coming to harass her some more. Although no doubt he would love it if he knew she was lying in her bed fretting over him.

Ugh.

She needed to stop wasting energy on him, put him out of her mind and focus on tomorrow. And she really, really needed to get some sleep.

Easier said than done, of course, with all the noise happening outside. She tossed and turned for what felt like a couple of hours before the music finally died abruptly. She suspected the motel management had intervened. Better late than never.

She was so wired it took her another hour to drift off, but when she did sleep it was deep, heavy and uninterrupted until the alarm on her phone woke her at seven the following morning.

The one benefit of having slept in her yoga gear was that she was half-dressed already for her morning run. After slipping into a sports bra, tying back her hair and putting on her sneakers, she set out to clock an easy two or three miles. Normally she'd try for five, but not when she was riding. This morning, she just needed to work off some adrenaline, find a rhythm and warm up for some yoga back in her room.

By the time she was in the shower it was eight and she felt limber and loose, her mind clear.

Ready to ride, in other words.

She took her time ironing her shirt and jeans, wanting everything to feel crisp and clean. Then she packed her gear bag, ticking off the essentials as she gathered them—rosin for her saddle, her leather chaps, baby powder for her boots, her protective vest, her good hat, gloves, spurs…

She hauled her saddle out to her truck, then came back for her gear bag and locked up. She was officially ready to roll. She was about to start her truck when her phone buzzed in her back pocket—her mom, calling to wish her good luck.

They kept the conversation short, and her mother wished her luck "from both of us," but CJ was very aware that her father hadn't taken the handset to say it in person.

She shook off her disappointment as she drove to the fairgrounds. The lot was already an ocean of cars and pickups, but she managed to find a spot near the contestant entrance. Hefting her saddle onto her shoulder, she made her way past a row of parked horse trailers and cowboy rigs, aware with every step that her belly was fluttering with nerves.

This was a big deal. Her first pro ride. She needed to stay on Hellion Boy for eight seconds, and she needed a good ride with high points to get into the finals—known in rodeo circles as the short round—tomorrow. She wanted to win this thing so much. It would be the ultimate vindication after the crap Dean Maynard had thrown at her, but she would settle for a berth in the short round. There was no way anyone could give her the side-eye when she'd made the finals in her first rodeo.

The women's locker rooms were filled with the scent of

hair spray, perfume and deodorant as she entered, the high whine of hair dryers competing with the chatter and laughter of more than a dozen women, some of them local rodeo princesses and queens, some of them barrel racers. A quick glance revealed an empty spot on one of the benches and she made her way toward it, stopping to check with the woman sitting nearby before dumping her saddle.

"Okay for me to grab this spot?"

"Sure thing. No one else is using it," the woman said.

She was young—barely sixteen was CJ's best guess—and her long blonde hair was styled into glossy curls, her face perfectly made-up. She ran an educated eye over CJ's saddle as CJ dumped it and her gear bag in front of the bench.

"You must be new. I know all the other contestants," she said.

"Exactly what I was about to say," someone else said, and CJ found herself facing an attractive Hispanic woman in her mid-thirties. "Hi, I'm Lena Martinez, one of the barrel racers. I didn't know we were getting new blood this weekend."

"CJ Cooper. And I'm not new blood. Well, I am, but I'm not a barrel racer. I'm competing saddle bronc."

There was a stunned silence in the room, the only sound the continuing whine of the hair dryers as two oblivious princesses primped in front of the mirror.

"Holy shit," Lena said. "When did this happen? How come I haven't heard about it?"

"I only qualified for my pro ticket last month. And I guess cowboys aren't that great at gossiping," CJ said.

"Cowboys are better at gossiping than a church congregation and a knitting circle rolled into one," another woman said, joining them. Like Lena, she was dressed in an elaborate western shirt and neatly pressed jeans. Another barrel racer, most likely.

Her arrival seemed to be a signal for all the other women to gather round, and pretty soon CJ was surrounded by curious females, the questions coming thick and fast. If she had to guess, she'd say that most of them were positive about her gaining pro status, maybe even excited, but there were a few who seemed a little squinty-eyed and passive-aggressive with their questions, too.

Not her problem. And it wasn't like CJ was trying to make some big political statement or force anyone to follow in her footsteps. She just wanted to ride saddle bronc, pure and simple.

She answered their questions and laughed at their jokes and was a little humbled by their well-wishes, but by the time ten minutes had passed she felt in dire need of some fresh air and personal space. Easing her way out of the locker rooms, she exited to the yard and took a couple of deep breaths before checking her watch.

Ten minutes until the rodeo officially kicked off. Just enough time to grab a seat and settle in to watch the rodeo queen and princesses do their thing. She made her way to the bleachers, climbing the same stairs she'd taken yesterday, and showed her contestant pass to the security detail to gain admission to the specially cordoned-off area of the stand dedicated to contestants and their support crew.

Pausing on the steps to get her bearings, she spotted a seat just three rows from the front, right at the end of the first run of seating. Perfect. It wasn't until she'd made her way down the steps and sunk onto the hard seat that she saw Jesse Carmody was sitting across the aisle from her, one row down.

Well, damn.

She tugged the brim of her hat a little lower over her eyes and focused on the arena. With a bit of luck, he wouldn't even know she was there. If only she could say the same about him.

Out of the corner of her eye, she caught sight of him stretching his legs in front of himself, his booted feet encroaching on the aisle space. Unable to resist, she allowed herself a quick glance.

And rolled her eyes at the sight of his muscular thighs, outlined by soft-looking denim.

Of course he had great legs. *Of course.*

She wrenched her gaze back to the arena, but the urge to take a second peek to confirm her earlier findings was like an itch in the back of her brain.

She'd always had a weakness for a man with good legs. She blamed her first boyfriend. He'd been on the football team, and the sight of his muscular thighs in his uniform had sparked a life-long appreciation.

Don't even think about looking again.

She crossed her arms over her chest. The dumbest move she could make this weekend was to become infatuated with one of her fellow contestants. No, strike that, there was a dumber move—she could sleep with one of them. Once word got out that she'd gotten naked with one of the other contestants, no one would ever take her seriously, no matter how competitively she rode. She'd just be a piece of ass, forever and always.

Jaw tight, she kept her gaze front and center. Where it belonged, and where it was going to stay. If it killed her.

Chapter Four

IT WAS A crazy thing, his awareness of Cassidy Jane Cooper. He'd known her less than twenty-four hours, yet the moment she'd taken a seat across the aisle and one row back, all the little hairs on the back of his neck had stood on end.

He turned his head, and there she was, decked out in a deep blue western shirt with white piping and white embroidery on the chest. The color looked good with her dark hair and sun-kissed skin, and the shirt's precise tailoring was a gift to her curves.

He shifted his gaze back to the arena before he got busted staring, but that didn't make the awareness go away. He couldn't remember the last time he'd been so powerfully drawn to a woman. It wasn't just because of the way she filled out her jeans and shirt, either. Although that was definitely part of it—he had a pulse, after all, and the normal amount of testosterone racing around his body. There were plenty of attractive women around, though, and none of them made the small hairs stand up on the back of his neck when they were nearby.

He wasn't sure what it was. He liked her directness. He admired her toughness and determination. He got the feeling she didn't do anything by halves, which was both intriguing and challenging.

He had a sense, also, that she'd be worth knowing.

The crowd stood and he belatedly realized the grand entry was midway and they were playing the "Star Spangled Banner." Pushing to his feet, he placed his hand over his heart and fought the tide of red that was burning its way up his neck and into his face. He'd been so far gone thinking about CJ he'd almost disgraced himself. Time to get his head together, if for no other reason than because he had two events he needed to kick ass in this afternoon.

Soon the music switched to commentary as the queen and her princesses rode out of the arena, flags flying. Bareback was the first event, and he watched as his friends and colleagues did their damnedest to make eight seconds before eating dirt. He stood to cheer when Cody Starr made his eight and landed a great score. He'd always considered Cody a friend even though the guy got a bad rap for his wild behavior at times. This weekend everyone was already talking about him—supposedly there was a story online about some crazy thing he'd done—but Jesse didn't go in for gossip. All he knew was that Cody had just completed a damn fine ride and he deserved a good score.

He got to his feet again when Shane Marvell put in a

mind-blowing eight seconds, cheering for the finesse with which the man landed on his feet. Most days a rider was lucky to land without breaking a bone, but Marvell made it look easy, lifting his hat off and bowing to the crowd in recognition of their cheers and applause. Like Jesse, he was a local, and there was always an extra buzz when you did good in front of your own people.

The smell of food drifting up into the stands had his stomach rumbling by then and he went in search of sustenance, leaving his jacket over the back of his seat to reserve it. He allowed himself a single glance at CJ as he walked past, and she happened to look up at that exact moment. Their eyes locked, and he offered her a friendly nod and a quick smile before walking by, even though it was damn tempting to stop and try to talk to her again.

Still, he walked away feeling pretty happy—maybe it was his imagination, but it seemed to him that there was a flicker of…something in the depths of her dark brown eyes when she looked at him. A slow smile curved his mouth as he made his way out of the stands.

Maybe he wasn't the only one being tortured by an inappropriate and unwelcome awareness.

He bought a bowl of chili and an iced tea to take back into the stands. He'd intended to simply walk past her again on his return journey, but instead he stopped and leaned down for a private word. Startled, she looked up, straight into his face, her full lips slightly parted.

"Hot tip for you—the chili here is some of the best in the state. Do yourself a favor."

She didn't respond, but he didn't really give her a chance, continuing down to his row and lowering himself into his seat.

He ate his chili and managed to follow what was happening out in the arena, where the steer wrestling was now in play. He knew without looking when she left the stand, though, and when she returned ten minutes later. A quick glance confirmed she'd opted for the chili.

It pleased him more than it should, and he gave himself a mental clip over the ear before collecting his jacket and clearing out to go prepare for his events. Saddle bronc was scheduled before the tie-down roping, but he went out to tend to Major first, spending some time brushing him down and taking him for a walk around the practice arena, which was crowded as usual as his fellow contestants prepared for their events. He stayed on the inside, keeping Major to a walk, out of the way of anyone wanting to give their mount a harder workout.

It was a glorious day, the blue sky high and clear overhead, only the occasional fluffy white cloud to mar its perfection.

The sound of the crowd filled the air—the stomp of feet, the shrillness of cheers and whistles. He breathed in the smell of dampness from the nearby Marietta River and turned his mind to the afternoon's events.

No more fooling around, allowing himself to be distracted. It was time to cowboy up and be the professional athlete he was. Like all the guys on the circuit, his spot on the tour depended on his standing and winnings, and if he wanted a chance to win big at the end of the season, he needed to keep placing or winning overall.

Not to mention the prize money would come in handy. He was doing okay this season, but a big win was always welcome. He had other money behind him, but he preferred not to touch it if he could. Jed insisted on forwarding Jesse's share of the ranch profits to him on a regular basis, despite Jesse's repeated instruction that Jed reinvest it in whatever needed doing at the ranch. Because something always needed doing. But his brother was a stubborn bastard, not to mention scrupulously fair, and the deposits kept coming, every quarter without fail.

Once he was satisfied Major was warmed up and ready for the calf roping, he took him back to the corral and put his saddle on. He was third up in the draw for saddle bronc, and he geared up in his protective vest, riding boots and chaps, and made his way to the chutes with his bronc saddle as the mutton busting was coming to a close.

His bronc wouldn't be saddled until it was in the chute, so he set his equipment on the ground alongside the other contestants' saddles and started to stretch. He'd gone for a run around the ranch this morning, as well as completing a rigorous series of stretches and isometrics he'd developed over the years. Now, he took care to stretch out his hamstrings and glutes, and to warm up the muscles of his back, abdomen and shoulders. He'd finished and was applying rosin to the swells on his saddle when he glanced up and saw CJ was doing the same, set off a small distance from most of the men. He frowned, wondering why she'd quarantined herself, then saw that Dean Maynard and the Miller brothers were in the group clustered near the chutes.

It didn't seem fair that she was the one on the outside, given how poor the other man's behavior had been, but her expression was calm and inwardly focused as she tended to her equipment. He was reminded of her poise and self-containment when Maynard had attacked her yesterday.

She was a hard-ass, that was for sure. But she wouldn't be here if she wasn't—being almost stupidly hardheaded was definitely a bronc-riding trait.

Spotting Shane at the rail, he dusted his hands off and went to congratulate him on his score in bareback. They talked for a few minutes before Jesse overheard the tail end of something Maynard was saying to his posse nearby.

"…can't wait till she falls on her ass and we can call this bullshit PC experiment done and dusted."

Jesse's gaze went to CJ, who was now stretching out her hips with an impressive forward lunge. Had she heard what Maynard was saying?

He really hoped not.

"Fifty bucks she doesn't even make it out of the gate,"

Billy Miller said, already reaching for his wallet.

"I'll match that with fifty that says she breaks her neck," Maynard said, his laughter laced with sharp malice.

"Heads-up for you boys that I'm going to be the first one in line to console her," one of the other cowboys said with a leer.

"I've got eight inches of solid consolation for her right here," Maynard said, grabbing his junk.

Jesus.

It was all Jesse could do not to walk over and push the guy's nose out the back of his head.

Shane slid Jesse a dark look. "Maynard's been shooting his mouth off about that CJ Cooper chick all day."

"Has he?" Jesse glared at the rowdy bunch near the chutes again, making no attempt to hide his disapproval. He'd never been close with Maynard, but the guy had just plummeted even further in his estimation—straight from overindulged man-baby to out-and-out dick bag.

"The way I see it, it's the ride that's important," Shane said, one of the many reasons he was someone Jesse was always happy to spend time with on and off the circuit.

"Same." He flicked a look toward CJ, who had finished her prep and was simply standing waiting now, her gaze on the ground. "Figure if she's here, it's because she's had to fight every inch of the way. More than any of us have had to do."

Shane looked surprised by the idea, but after a beat he

nodded. "Yeah, good point."

The music in the arena faded as the PA came to life, announcing the saddle bronc event. The first rider was already hanging off the rail in the chute, double-checking the cinch on his saddle and the length on his rope. Jesse felt the familiar buzz of adrenaline race through his gut.

Not long now.

In step with Shane he moved to the rail, climbing up to get a better view of the arena. He could smell dirt, sawdust and manure, along with the occasional pungent trace of rosin, the pine smell sharp in his nose. In the chute, the first rider was sliding into the saddle. Thirty seconds later, he was out of the gate and hanging on for the ride of his life.

Directly behind the chutes he could see one of the attendants looking around, a clipboard in his hand. He caught Jesse's eye and waved him over.

"You're up. Good luck, man," Shane said, clapping him on the back.

"You, too."

One of the great things about saddle bronc was the sense of camaraderie among the riders. Sure, they were fighting each other to land at the top of the leaderboard, but the real battle was between the rider, the bronc and gravity. Every ride was a test of skill, experience and luck, and every rider knew it. If Buckmaster failed to come out of the chute strong, if the bronc clipped the rails or cornered too fast or one of a million other things that could go wrong, the ride could go south in a split second. If it went badly wrong, he could end up in the hospital, or worse.

It probably made him more than a little bit sick that he got off on the crazy odds, on the risk and unpredictability of this sport. But if it was an illness, he didn't want to be cured, not when adrenaline was spiking every breath and the world was sharpening into intense, detailed focus as he handed his saddle over to the chute crew.

The moment the second rider was out of the gate, Buckmaster was fed in and Jesse's saddle expertly cinched to the bronc's back. Jesse checked the straps on his chaps to ensure they were tight enough before reaching through the rail to double-check the tension on the cinch strap and flank strap. Then he climbed to the top of the rail and threw a leg over, the fringe on his black and tan chaps riffling in the breeze. Lastly, he checked the length on his rope rein.

"Okay, boy, here I come," he said quietly, then he set his boot on the saddle and let a little weight come down onto the bronc's back so the horse knew he was coming.

Buckmaster stirred but didn't overreact, so he braced his arms on the rails on either side of the chute and slid slowly into the saddle. His boots found the stirrups and he pushed down until he felt the familiar pressure as his heel hit the stirrup. He shifted his weight forward to bring his chaps in tight contact with the swells on the saddle, then took up the rope rein in his right hand, running his rosin-coated glove up and down it a few times to activate the gum.

Then he closed his hand around the rope, tucked his chin to his chest, and lifted his left arm in readiness. He could feel his heart beating against his rib cage, feel his lungs expanding as he took a deep, hard breath. He cleared his mind of everything except the need to get out of the chute as fast as possible.

Then he gave the nod, and the gate opened. Buckmaster came out hard and fast, lunging onto his front legs. Jesse kept his toes out and his legs up, ensuring he satisfied the mark-out rule by keeping his feet above the horse's shoulders on the first jump. Anything less meant immediate disqualification. Then Buckmaster kicked out with his rear legs, and Jesse leaned back instinctively to counter the move, his free arm bent at the elbow. He got air beneath him as Buckmaster twisted to the left and kicked out, but somehow Jesse found his center again and a crazy kind of rhythm. Spur, lean, spur, lean, his left arm always in the air, his right clenched around the rope.

His shoulder ached from the sharp yank on the rope rein, his thighs burned from the strain of clinging to the saddle. His head jerked on his neck, and he felt the rush of cool air on his damp hair as his hat fell off.

He heard the shrill sound of the whistle over the noisy tumult of his heartbeat and immediately looked around for the pickup rider. The pickup guys on the tour were second-to-none, and within seconds he was off Buckmaster's back and sitting behind the pickup rider, heading back to the chutes.

He craned his neck, looking toward the scoreboard, and felt a fierce rush of triumph when he saw an eighty-five on the board.

Hell, yeah.

That would land him a spot in the short round tomorrow, almost certainly. He was grinning ear to ear as he climbed back through the rails to collect his gear. Shane and a couple of other riders clapped him on the back in congratulations as he wiped the dirt and sweat off his forehead and accepted his hat from one of the crew.

"Great ride, man," Shane said. "That bronc is rank, I tell you. You're gonna be the score to beat."

Jesse laughed and said something in return, but he never stopped scanning the crowd. It wasn't until he spotted CJ's dark head that he realized who he was looking for. Like a cocky teenager, he was checking to see if the girl he liked had been impressed by his performance.

Moron, he told himself, but then CJ turned her head and met his eyes and offered him a big smile and an enthusiastic thumbs-up. It was a little scary how good her approval made him feel, and for a moment he simply stopped in his tracks, winded by the force of his own feelings.

What *the fuck* was that about?

Then CJ turned away, and he saw they were saddling her bronc, Hellion Boy. Unable to stay away, he pushed his way through the crowd and watched as she checked the cinch strap. She looked like a total bad-ass in her black leather chaps with metallic red fringes and hand-tooled yoke, a black hat on her head.

When she stood, he moved closer and offered some advice.

"Hellion Boy likes to wheel to the left when he leaves the gate. Does it almost every time," he said quietly.

She nodded, a small frown between her eyebrows as she took the information in.

"Make sure you get a good spur out," someone else said, and CJ nodded again.

A couple of other guys chimed in, and Jesse hoped Maynard was noting the support CJ was being offered, much the same as the guys would offer any rookie.

"Thanks, everyone," CJ said with a quick smile, then she turned to the chute. She climbed onto the first rail and was about to throw her leg over when Jesse caught her elbow.

She looked down at him, her face shuttered and serious.

"Have fun," he said, giving her elbow a light squeeze to drive home the point.

For a moment she looked stunned by his words. Then her face lit up, and he saw the wildness and anticipation and recklessness in her, burning hot and strong. The power and primality of it went straight to his groin, a bolt of pure lust.

Damn, he wanted this woman.

Her elbow slipped free from his grasp as she threw her leg over the rail, and he watched as she seated herself in the saddle and took up the rein. The long, dark plait of her hair shifted on her back as she tucked her chin down. Her hand went up, fingers loose and relaxed.

Jesse held his breath, knowing what was probably going through her mind as she steadied herself. Then she nodded, the gate opened, and Hellion Boy exploded out of the chute.

Jesse leapt up onto the rail, eyes glued to CJ as she leaned back in the saddle, performing a textbook-perfect mark out. Her plait whipped in the air as the bronc lunged forward and kicked. Time seemed to slow, to narrow down to the thud of the horse's hooves on the dirt, the sounds of the crowd, the too-fast saw of his breath in his lungs.

It only took a second for him to see that CJ Cooper was the real deal. She seemed glued to the saddle, her body appearing to know which way the horse was going to swerve and jump before the bronc knew himself. She had hot hands and fast feet, and when the whistle sounded he was cheering along with everyone else. He watched as CJ let go of the rein, slipping a leg free and jumping from the saddle. She almost stuck the landing, but overbalanced into a roll. She was back onto her feet straight away, face split into a grin as she kept a wary eye on the bronc to make sure the handlers had him under control. The crowd roared as the announcer's voice became almost painfully loud with excitement, blaring out CJ's achievement at too many decibels.

"Talk about the cowboy who can't be throwed on the horse that can't be rode. Or should I say cow*girl*? Something tells me I better get used to saying that. That was a great ride for CJ Cooper here at her first pro rodeo event, folks. I think we're going to be seeing a lot more of this cowgirl; you mark my words."

Jesse's gaze was on the scoreboard, willing the judges to honor CJ's stellar ride. The screen lit up—eighty-eight. He let out a whoop. Halfway through the event, she'd just landed the highest score so far.

CJ had her hat in her hand as she climbed through the railing, smiling so hard it looked like it hurt. A bunch of other riders came forward to congratulate her, offering high fives and pats on the back. CJ took it all in, nodding along, shrugging modestly, but he hoped she was registering the support of her fellow riders.

Maynard was a minority, and as Jesse had told her at the street dance last night, if she could ride, the men would respect her.

And boy, could she ride.

"Congratulations. That was a wicked ride," he told her when he'd finally muscled his way to her side.

"Thanks. I got lucky."

"You've got great hands," he said, and for the first time since he'd met her CJ Cooper broke eye contact with him.

"Thanks," she said, and it took him a second to realize she was blushing.

He almost laughed. So that was what it took to flatter a woman like CJ—not flowers or poetry or compliments about how pretty she was. This lady was all about bronc riding.

A collective "ooh" from the audience alerted him to the fact someone had taken a bad spill in the arena, and he glanced across to see Dean Maynard picking himself up out of the dirt, a foul expression on his face. Jesse could see the other man's mouth working, four-letter words pouring forth. Then Maynard kicked at the dirt, a piece of bad sportsmanship that didn't win him much sympathy with the crowd.

"What happened?" CJ asked, her view blocked by a tall cowboy.

"Maynard came off hard," Jesse reported.

CJ didn't say anything, but she'd have to be an angel not to feel some sense of satisfaction that the man who had attacked her had taken a fall.

"I've got to get ready for the calf roping, but let me buy you a drink later, to celebrate," Jesse said, more interested in her than Dean Maynard.

CJ's smile dimmed a fraction and Jesse suspected he was about to get his marching orders when he heard Maynard's angry voice nearby.

"This is complete bullshit. Eighty-three. I'm going to miss out on five thousand because they gave the best bronc in the tour to some bitch who's going to wash out in a week or two anyway. Can you fucking believe it?"

It was a twisted piece of logic, but Jesse felt CJ flinch beside him.

Jesse was pushing people out of the way before he could

think twice about it, furious on CJ's behalf. He'd stood by yesterday, but it wasn't happening a second time.

"You need to shut your mouth, Maynard," he said when he was within reaching distance of the other man.

"This has nothing to do with you, Carmody."

"The draw is random. You've been around long enough to know that. Now, apologize to Ms. Cooper."

For a moment Maynard looked stunned, then his mouth curled into a sneer, anger turning his handsome face ugly. "Read my lips, Carmody. Fuck. Off."

"What's your problem, Maynard? Not man enough to handle being beaten by a woman?" Jesse said.

Maynard lunged at him, fists raised. Jesse was more than ready for him, but the Miller brothers caught the other man's shoulders and pulled him back.

"You want to get disqualified?" Billy hissed, using all his body weight to keep Maynard from shaking them off.

Maynard struggled for a few more seconds before giving up the fight. Jesse saw a security guard heading their way, pushing his way through the other contestants. Tempting as it was to stay in Maynard's face, it wasn't worth the risk of disqualification. Not when he was almost certainly in the short round, and not when there would be other opportunities to teach Maynard some manners.

Jesse took a step backward, relaxing his stance, and the Miller brothers ushered Maynard away. The security guard stopped his forward progress, assessing the situation through narrowed eyes. Jesse lifted his chin to let him know the message had been received and understood, and the other man gave him a nod before going back to his station near the access points to the chutes.

Jesse turned away from the drama to see CJ's back as she wove her away from the chutes, her saddle balanced on her hip.

Shit.

He started after her, but he'd only taken a few steps when he slowed to a halt. What was he going to say when he caught her? Ask her out again? The moment of possibility between them had been punctured by Maynard's stupidity. In all likelihood, CJ had probably had enough of dumbass cowboys for the day. And who could blame her?

"That wraps it up for saddle bronc, ladies and gentlemen. Next up we have calf roping. Hope you're ready to see some fancy horsemanship and some flying lassos out there today."

The PA blast cut through Jesse's indecision, reminding him he still had an event to compete in.

Checking his watch, he hustled toward the corral to collect Major.

Chapter Five

CJ WOULD HAVE been lying if she pretended she wasn't upset by Dean Maynard crapping all over her moment of glory. It had felt so damned good, hearing the applause and cheers from the crowd and receiving the congratulations of her peers. It had felt like vindication. She'd gone eight seconds, she'd ridden hard and well, and she was *leading the freaking board.*

It was a dream come true, it really was.

And then Maynard had said what he'd said, and Jesse had felt honor bound to step in and do some macho chest bumping stuff on her behalf.

Most of the time, she loved cowboys, but there were times when the super macho culture and overload of testosterone made her want to kick something—like whatever was dangling between Dean Maynard's scrawny thighs.

The thought was silly and crude enough to cut through her disappointment and she slowed her pace a little. Adjusting the weight of the saddle on her hip, she used her free hand to pull her protective vest away from where it was cutting beneath her armpits.

Letting a mean-spirited jackass like Maynard rain on her parade was foolish in the extreme. She refused to let him get to her.

She'd reached the stands now, the area behind them sardine-can full with rodeo goers keen to buy snacks and drinks. As she picked her way through the crowd, it took her a moment to register the smiles she was getting, along with bright-eyed looks of recognition.

"Great ride, CJ," an older man said, giving her an approving nod.

"You looked great out there," a young woman said, giving her an approving pat on the shoulder. "Way to represent."

By the time she'd reached the locker rooms, she'd been stopped twice to sign the program, and once to take a selfie with a young girl and her mom who told her they'd almost fallen off the bleachers cheering for her.

The goodwill of the rodeo fans went a long way to restoring her joy in her ride—and then she walked into the ladies' locker room and was met with a chorus of whistles, foot stomping and cheers.

"You go, girlfriend," Lena Martinez said. "You were on fire out there. Hope you heard us all screaming for you."

Barrel racing was scheduled after the calf roping and the racers were all on their way out, but their congratulations washed away the last bitterness of Maynard's attack.

Dumping her saddle on the bench in the now-empty locker room, she pulled her phone from her pocket and dialed home, something she'd been wanting to do almost from the second she heard the whistle announcing she'd qualified.

The emotion of it all caught up with her as she waited for someone to pick up and she blinked away the sudden burn of tears. Then her mother's voice sounded down the line, and CJ drew in a shaky breath.

"Mom, it's me. I qualified with an eighty-eight."

Her mother's squeal of delight almost punctured her eardrum. "I know, baby! I was listening to the broadcast over the Internet. I was jumping out of my skin with nerves for you, but it sounds as though you had the ride of your life."

"It was great. Pretty much a dream. He came out of the gate like a hurricane, but I just found my groove and stayed in it," CJ said.

"So now you just have to ace the short round tomorrow," her mother said.

"Oh, yeah. I'll just pull that out of my backside, no problems," CJ said dryly, but she couldn't keep the smile off her face. "Bet you wish you came with me, huh?"

The moment the words were out her mouth, she regretted them. They had never discussed her mother accompanying CJ to Marietta. Given her father's disapproval of his daughter going pro, it would have felt too much as though CJ was asking her mother to take sides, and CJ would never do that.

"Oh, baby, I wish I could have been there, I really do," her mother said, her voice quiet with regret.

"Forget it, I didn't mean it. It was just a joke," CJ said, but her throat felt tight.

"Listen, your father's out at the Hendersons', shoeing that new gelding they bought, but I texted him with the news and I'm sure he'll call once he checks his phone."

"Okay. Thanks, Mom," CJ said. Personally, she wasn't so sure she'd hear from her father. The streak of stubborn in her family ran a mile wide, and her father had remained staunch in his disapproval of the path CJ had chosen for almost a full year. Just because CJ had done well in her first pro rodeo, she wasn't expecting a miracle turnaround.

It would be nice, but she wasn't holding her breath.

She and her mother talked for a few more minutes before ending the call. CJ dropped her head back against the cinder block wall, closing her eyes for a few seconds. She could hear the crowd outside, cheering on the barrel racers. If she was back home, she'd go out with her friends and hit a bar to drink some good bourbon and dance for a few hours. Or she'd kick back at home with her brothers and talk horses and strategy for tomorrow.

She wasn't home, though, and those options weren't on the table, so it seemed to her that the next best thing would be to enjoy the vibe of her first pro rodeo and go out to watch the rest of the events. And then maybe she'd go into town and see if she could hunt down the pendant necklace she'd resisted buying last night.

Last night, treating herself had felt like an indulgence, but today it would be her way of commemorating her first pro ride.

And after that...well, she'd play it by ear. There was a steak dinner in town tonight, and probably more dancing. Maybe she'd put on the red dress she'd packed on a whim, pull on her hand-tooled aqua boots and see if she couldn't find someone to dance with.

Instantly an image of a tall, dark-haired cowboy with arresting green eyes filled her mind. She wondered if Jesse Carmody was a good dancer, or if he danced at all. After a moment's self-indulgence, she banished the thought.

Even if he was as talented as John Travolta in *Saturday Night Fever*, she couldn't dance with him. Not after the way he'd weighed in to defend her today. Talk would be all over the town before five minutes had passed, and she was *done* with being the subject of speculation today. For the rest of her life, really.

Nope. Whatever happened tonight, it would be in a Jesse-Carmody-free zone.

IT TOOK HER half an hour of cruising the shops along Main Street in Marietta before she found the jewelry store she'd seen last night. The pendant she'd lusted after was still available—a silver dollar that had the silhouette of a cowboy on a bucking horse painstakingly cut from the center of the coin.

"Thank you, it's perfect," she said as she handed it to the woman behind the counter.

She did a little more window-shopping, then stopped to have something to eat in the Main Street Diner near the courthouse. The older woman behind the counter sported a genuine beehive, and CJ watched in fascination as the other woman greeted almost every customer by name. She even recognized CJ, insisting on getting her to sign a menu because "for sure, you are going to be famous one day, young lady."

Fame wasn't something CJ hankered for, but the idea of having a career long enough and notable enough for people to know her name was a nice one.

It was nearly five as she pulled into a spot near her room, and she was looking forward to a long soak in the tub before she decided what to do for the evening. She gathered her few shopping bags from the front seat before collecting her gear bag from the truck bed.

It wasn't until she was a few feet from her room that she noticed the door was slightly ajar. There was no visible sign of a break-in, and for a second she thought housekeeping must have accidentally left it open. Then she pushed the door open and was hit with a sour, sharp smell, along with the sight of her clothes strewn across the floor and the bedding pulled from the bed. A dark mark marred the middle of the bare mattress.

For a moment shock held her immobile. Then she set down her bags and stepped closer to the bed. She caught a stronger whiff of the sour smell and this time she recognized it for what it was: urine.

Someone had broken into her room and urinated on her bed and bedding.

A horrible thought hit her then, and she bent to examine her clothes. Sure enough, they were sodden, too, along with her bag. More so even than the bed. She sat back on her heels, her clothes spread before her, all tangled and damp with some asshole's body fluids, and for a moment rage and hurt threatened to become tears.

All she wanted was a chance to compete fairly against the best of the best. Why it mattered whether she was male or female was genuinely the cause of great bewilderment to her. If she was as good as or better than a man, hadn't she earned her place on the tour? Hadn't she earned it just as much as any man?

She tilted her head back and took a deep breath, blinking the dampness from her eyes, willing the tightness from her throat. She didn't have to tax herself to work out who was responsible for this petty piece of vandalism. Dean Maynard had left the arena angry, and he'd become even angrier when Jesse Carmody had challenged his loud-mouthed assertions. It wasn't much of a stretch to imagine him consoling himself with a bottle of whiskey and some sympathetic friends until he'd convinced himself CJ had practically asked for him to break into her room and relieve himself all over her belongings.

The image of him laughing with his buddies was the final push she needed to square her shoulders and clear her head. He would get off on the notion she'd been cowed or wounded by his act. It was exactly why he'd done it.

No way was she giving him the satisfaction.

Leaving the room as it was, she walked across to reception and reported the incident, accompanying the duty manager back to inspect her room. An older, salt-and-pepper-haired man, he was shocked by what had happened, apologizing and insisting the locks on the doors were all state of the art before asking if she was sure it had clicked shut when she left in the morning.

The implication she might be partly to blame for what had happened wasn't lost on her.

"Believe me, it was locked. Someone broke in to do this. This wasn't just someone finding a door open."

"Well, I guess we should call the sheriff," he said, shooting her a doubtful look. "Although technically nothing was actually taken, was it?"

That he was reluctant to involve the law and all that would entail was writ large on his face. CJ simply held his eye. She wanted this on record. She wanted Dean Maynard to pay a price for what he'd done.

"Okay, then," the manager finally said.

She watched as he pulled out his phone and rang a number, quickly relaying the details to whoever answered the phone. He nodded a few times, checked his watch, then nodded some more.

"Okay, I'll pass that on. Thanks, Rose." He ended the call. "So. Apparently they're tied up with a bunch of stuff in town. Big weekend, with the rodeo here and all. Crowd control, drunks and so on. They want you to come in tomorrow to talk to them. Asked me to take some pictures of the room, send them through."

It wasn't ideal, but CJ could appreciate that a vandalized hotel room was probably low priority given the huge influx of people in town for the weekend and the kind of issues the sheriff was probably dealing with.

"All right. Let's do that," she said. "And when you're done, maybe I could have a trash bag and directions to the laundry room?"

His mouth turned down at the corners. "Ma'am, I am real sorry to tell you this, but I'm afraid our laundry is out of order at the moment. There was some kind of issue with the pipes backing up on Thursday, and the plumber couldn't get here till Monday, so it's closed right at the moment."

Well…shit.

CJ took a deep breath. "Okay. I guess I'll need directions to the laundromat in town, then."

JESSE WENT OUT to the ranch to shower and change after washing out in the calf roping. He and Major had done their best, but today it hadn't been enough. He was happy enough with the day's achievements, however—he still had a chance at the prize money in saddle bronc, having placed second behind CJ after today's rides.

His family were nowhere to be seen when he arrived home, and he figured they were either out on the ranch somewhere or in town still. He'd seen Sierra briefly after he'd put Major back in his stall, but they'd barely had a chance to talk before she'd had to hustle or risk losing sight of her friends.

"Have to go, but you're all mine once the short round's over tomorrow," she'd told him before disappearing into the crowd.

He thought about her words as he showered and found something clean to wear, a much easier feat than usual since he'd taken advantage of being home to catch up on all his laundry.

He still hadn't decided if he was hanging around after the rodeo. Technically, he could claim he had work lined up, because he did, after a fashion—a former bronc rider he knew had a spread up near Deer Lodge, and he'd let Jesse know there was a few days' work as a ranch hand on offer if he wanted some extra travel money between rodeos. Since Deer Lodge was more or less on the way to Great Falls where the next circuit event would be held, Jesse had been planning on looking in on his old buddy, but he was pretty sure Sierra wouldn't be thrilled to learn he was bailing on her for a few days' casual labor.

It wasn't as though he hated being home. Just the opposite. But the past always loomed large when he was here. It had taken him nearly four years to come home the first time after Jed told him to shape up or ship out. Sierra had been responsible for that, nagging and cajoling until he'd agreed to be there for Christmas. He'd come home expecting to look his brother in the eye and say what needed to be said to clear the air.

Somehow, it had never happened. He hadn't initiated it, and neither had Jed. At first Jesse had convinced himself that was a good thing, that maybe they should just let it fade into the past, an incident they both regretted. It hadn't faded, though. It was there in the distance between him and Jed, lurking beneath every overly polite question and every wary response, and it had been going on so long now that Jesse almost didn't know how else to be with his brother.

A picture caught his eye as he sat on the end of the bed to pull on his boots, one of several framed family shots someone—most likely Sierra—had arranged on the far wall. The picture had been taken his sophomore year at Marietta High, the year he made the football team. Jed was a senior by then, and had been playing for a few years. The two of them stood side by side, helmets under their arms, both flexing madly for the camera. Jed looked as though he was barely holding it together, and his own eyes held a mischievous glint. Staring at the pic, he tried to remember that day. What had they been joking about? Had he said something to make his brother laugh?

They'd been friends back then. They'd played football together, attended their first rodeos together. They'd laughed at each other's failures, celebrated each other's wins. Sure, there had been moments of rivalry, but they'd had each other's backs. And then Jed had gone off to Montana State to study livestock management, and their parents had been killed in a head-on collision on the state highway heading into Marietta, dying instantly, and Jed had had to give up all his plans to come home and shoulder the burden of keeping the family and the ranch together.

For a moment Jesse sat, stuck in guilt and grief and re-gret. Then he stood, turning away from the picture to grab his coat. One of the first lessons he'd learned after his parents died was that you couldn't turn back time or change the past.

It was what it was, no matter how much you regretted it.

He made the twenty-minute drive back into town and met up with Flynn O'Connell and Shane at Grey's Saloon. They settled down for some beer and a rehash of the day's events before deciding whether to hit the steak dinner or not. After an hour, it became apparent it was going to be a loud and rowdy night at the bar, and Flynn suggested heading over to the Graff instead, where at least they might be able to hear each other talk.

The three of them were making the short walk across town when Jesse happened to glance across and see CJ on the other side of the street, a bulging black trash bag in hand. She was standing in front of the Marietta Laundromat, staring at the Closed sign as though it had done her wrong. As he watched, her shoulders slumped, and he could see the defeat in her from all the way across the street.

His steps slowed, then stopped. Shane threw him a glance over his shoulder.

"What's wrong? Going too fast for you, old man?" Shane asked.

"Just remembered something I need to do. I'll catch up with you boys later, at the dance, maybe."

Shane didn't seem to think much of it, slinging his arm around Flynn's shoulders. "Guess the first round is on you then, hombre."

They kept walking as Jesse crossed the street, just in time to catch CJ before she walked away.

"Hey. CJ," he said, lengthening his stride to cover the last few feet and jump the curb.

She seemed confused for a moment and he realized she'd been deep inside herself when he called out. Contemplating something unhappy, if the expression in her eyes was anything to go by.

"Hey," she said, her tone flat.

"What's going on?" he asked, cutting straight to the

chase.

"I don't suppose you can tell me if there's another laundromat in town?" she asked.

His gaze went to the trash bag she was holding, then the Closed sign behind her. "Pretty sure this is it."

She gave a grim laugh. "Yeah, figures. Listen, I need to go. I'll see you later."

She turned to go, but Jesse moved to block her path.

"Is everything all right?"

"It's nothing you need to worry about."

"Try me."

She stared at him, her jaw working. She was still wearing her rodeo clothes, but they looked tired and wrinkled now. *She* looked tired, and he figured she must be feeling her ride by now, the same way he was.

"Someone broke into my room, pissed all over my stuff, if you must know," she finally said.

For a moment he could only blink, his brain refusing to process what she'd said. "What the hell…?"

"Yeah. Good question," she said.

A surge of adrenaline burned through him, curling his hands into fists. There wasn't a doubt in his mind that this was down to Maynard. The urge to go hunt the bastard down was so strong he actually looked up and down the street, as though by willing it he could make the other man appear. Then it hit him that chasing after Maynard wasn't going to solve CJ's problem or change anything for the better.

He could tear Maynard a new one anytime. Right now, he wanted to erase the tight, strained look from CJ's face.

Reaching out, he took the trash bag from her.

"Come on," he said. "Let's fix this."

JESSE KEPT AN eye on his rearview mirror all the way out to the ranch, making sure CJ was still following him. It had been testament to how beaten down she was by the events of the weekend that she'd barely put up a fight when he suggested she follow him home and take care of her laundry at the ranch.

Now, he watched as her headlights bobbed along the rutted drive behind him. He stopped in front of the barn beside Sierra's truck, waving a hand out the window to tell CJ she should park beside him. They were both silent as they got out of their pickups.

"Nice place," CJ said, looking around. It was twilight, so the full impact of Copper Mountain rising behind the house wasn't quite as spectacular as it could have been, but the house looked warm and welcoming with light spilling out the windows.

"Our parents' place. We all inherited it when they died," he said.

It was always good to get the essentials out of the way early on, he'd learned. Saved people feeling like they'd put their foot in it later on when they asked the inevitable questions about family.

"Oh. I'm so sorry about your parents."

"It was a long time ago now. Twelve years. Let's go take care of those clothes."

"If you or your family have something planned for the evening, don't let me get in the way. I can just take care of my washing and get out of your hair," CJ said as they crossed the yard.

"I haven't got anything important on, and I don't even know who's home," he admitted as they reached the porch. "So you can relax on that score."

She gave a tense smile that went nowhere near her eyes and he felt an overwhelming urge to stop and pull her into his arms, the way he would with Sierra if something like this had happened to her.

God forbid.

Although holding CJ Cooper in his arms would not be the same as hugging his sister. Not by a long shot. Which was why he kept his hands by his sides, where they belonged.

The sound of a guitar being played met his ears as he let himself into the house, and Casey looked up from where he was sitting beside the fireplace, his acoustic guitar in his lap. Sierra lay on the rug in front of him, feet propped on the seat of the nearest couch, a cushion behind her head, her eyes closed as she listened to Casey play.

Casey stopped when he saw Jesse had company, flashing

CJ a quick smile before focusing on the bridge of his guitar. It was baffling to Jesse that he'd watched his brother own the stage last night at the street party, yet Casey still turned quiet when confronted with someone he didn't know.

"Don't stop," Sierra insisted, eyes still closed.

"We clear to use the washing machine? Either of you got anything going on in there?" Jesse asked.

Sierra's eyes popped open then, quickly focusing on the stranger in their midst. "Oh, hi."

Drawing her feet off the couch, she scrambled to stand up.

"It's CJ, right? You had such a good ride today. I nearly made myself hoarse cheering for you," Sierra said brightly. Then she seemed to fully register what Jesse had just asked and she frowned. "Why do you need the washing machine?"

CJ glanced at him, as though looking for guidance as to how much she should say.

"Someone broke into my room at the motel and messed up my stuff."

Sierra's face scrunched up with disbelief and disgust. "You're kidding? Asshats. Did you call the police? Did they steal anything?"

"I don't think anything is missing. And the police are busy. They told me to come in tomorrow to file a report."

Jesse could tell by the way she said it CJ wasn't expecting a big investigation to swing into action once the sheriff heard her tale of woe.

"Man, that sucks. Although I guess it does get pretty loopy in town when the rodeo is on," Sierra said. She gestured over her shoulder toward the kitchen. "Come on, I'll show you where everything is."

Jesse started to move forward, intending to maintain his escort, but CJ shot him a quick look.

"I've got this. I don't want to keep you from anything."

"You sure?" he asked.

"Of course." The smile she gave him this time was small but real.

"Don't let Sierra chew your ear off," he warned her.

"I heard that," Sierra called.

Once CJ had left the room, Jesse dumped his phone and keys on the coffee table and let out a sigh.

"So. Define 'messed up' for me," Casey said quietly, keeping his voice low so CJ wouldn't overhear.

"Someone pissed all over her stuff," Jesse said grimly.

Casey frowned. "You got any idea who it was?"

"One of the saddle bronc riders, a spoiled little dirtbag who can't handle CJ being better than him."

"Happy to go with you if you want to have a quiet word with him."

Jesse shot his brother a grateful look. "Thanks, man. I haven't decided what I'm going to do yet. We get busted fighting on the tour, we can lose our slot. But right now, I'm feeling like it would be worth it just to turn that little shitheel inside out."

"The cops aren't going to do much," Casey said matter-of-factly.

"I know." It stuck in Jesse's craw to think that Maynard might get away with such blatant bullying and harassment, simply because it wouldn't be considered serious enough to warrant real scrutiny from the authorities.

"I saw her ride today. She's damned good," Casey said.

"Yeah, she is," Jesse said, and for some reason he found himself grinning as he remembered the sheer freaking glory of CJ's ride this afternoon. "You see the way she was glued to that bronc's back? She's got amazing instincts."

Casey coughed, covering his hand with his mouth, and Jesse guessed he was hiding a smile.

"What?" he demanded.

"You should see your face."

"What are you talking about?" Jesse scoffed.

"It's okay. I get it. You've got a little crush. She's hot, it's understandable," Casey said.

Jesse rolled his eyes. "A crush. You still in high school?"

"Funny, I was about to ask you that."

The look on his brother's face was so provocative, Jesse could only laugh.

"So is this an unrequited thing? Or are you two...you know?" Casey asked.

"We met yesterday, you clown," Jesse said.

"Ah. So this is all part of your strategy."

Jesse frowned. "This is me trying to show her that not

every guy on the circuit is a jackass. It's fucking disgraceful this happened to her."

Casey's smile faded and Jesse was glad his brother could see he was serious.

"Yeah, good point," Casey said.

"Tell me—when was the last time anyone was out in the trailer?" Jesse asked.

When their parents had first bought the land the ranch was built on, they'd lived in an old Airstream trailer until the house was built, and it had remained behind the barn ever since. When his parents were alive, it had been used as an overflow guest room, but Jesse had no idea what condition it was in these days.

Casey frowned as he tried to puzzle out the intent behind Jesse's question. Then his brow cleared. "You want to offer it to CJ?"

"I'll sleep out there, offer her my bed. Can't send her back to that motel, not when her room's already been broken into once."

"Sierra had some friends from college stay last month, so it should be in good shape," Casey said. "Want me to go check?"

"Thanks, man, but I can do it."

Leaving his brother, Jesse went out into the night.

Chapter Six

"THEN YOU NEED to turn this dial around to regular wash, and just push it in," Sierra said, suiting words to actions. "Looks like you've got a few loads there, so we can dry the first lot while the second load washes."

Sierra reached for the garbage bag lying at CJ's feet, but CJ beat her to it.

"You don't want to open this," CJ said. "In fact, you might want to leave the room."

Sierra frowned. "Why would I want to do that?"

"Because whoever broke into my room took a bathroom break all over my clothes, and it smells pretty bad. I figure only one of us should have to suffer." CJ had been trying to avoid getting into the nitty-gritty of the attack with Jesse's sister, and she could feel her cheeks growing warm now that she'd spilled the beans.

Why she was embarrassed about being the victim of a pathetic misogynist was beyond CJ right now. It wasn't as though she'd done anything to provoke the man or invite his attention, apart from existing and having two X chromosomes.

Sierra's green eyes darkened, her pretty mouth straightening into a tight line. "This wasn't just a random thing, was it?"

CJ sighed. God, she was tired. Her hips ached, her shoulders were sore. She wanted a hot shower and a beer in the worst possible way. More than anything, she wanted for this weekend to have gone a different way, for Dean Maynard to have been a different kind of man.

But he wasn't. And here she was.

"No. It wasn't. One of the other riders doesn't think I should be allowed on the pro circuit. He's been pretty vocal about it."

"Let me guess—that blond pretty boy who spat the dummy today," Sierra said.

"Yep. That's him."

"What a pathetic little man-baby," Sierra said. Then she surprised CJ by stepping forward and throwing her arms around her. "I am so freaking sorry you've had to deal with that. You were like a superhero out there today, and that guy can go screw himself if he thinks he's going to stop you."

It wasn't until she felt the strength of another person's arms around her that CJ understood how lonely she'd felt these past few days. Steeling herself to leave home and drive to her first pro event without the full support of her family had been hard. Arriving in a strange town where she knew she'd be up against it had been hard, too. And then there had been all of the extra bullshit Maynard had rained down on her, topped off with the lovely surprise she'd found waiting in her room this afternoon.

Yeah, it had been a tough few days, and she couldn't stop herself from returning Sierra's hug, wrapping her arms around the other woman and letting her forehead rest for just a few precious seconds on Sierra's shoulder.

She took a couple of deep breaths, trying to keep a lid on the tears that threatened, and Sierra's arms tightened around her, a silent signal that if she needed to cry, there would be no judgment here, only understanding.

After a beat, CJ took a deep breath, and Sierra let her go, taking a step back.

"Thanks," CJ said, her voice still rough with emotion.

"Anytime. You shouldn't have to deal with this. I mean, it's 2018. Have none of these guys read a paper lately? Nobody's going to lie down and take this crap anymore."

"Not sure Dean Maynard *can* read, to be honest," CJ said.

"Excellent point."

CJ glanced down at the trash bag. There was no point delaying this any longer.

"I'm going in," she said.

"Roger that," Sierra said, and they both took a deep breath as CJ undid the knot in the neck of the bag and delved inside for her clothes.

"You need to separate for colors?" Sierra asked, her face

pinched.

The sour smell was even more ripe now, thanks to the magnifying effect of being in the bag.

"Let's just throw it all in together," CJ said.

They filled the machine, knotted the bag over what was left, reserving it for a second load, and then washed their hands thoroughly.

"So. How do we make this chickenshit pay?" Sierra said once she'd put in the detergent and started the machine.

"Good question. I'm not holding my breath on the sheriff jumping into action."

"Even if they did, with something like this, he'd probably just get a slap over the wrist, maybe a fine," Sierra mused.

"So that leaves personal revenge. I've thought about just walking up to him tomorrow and kicking him in the nuts," CJ said. "I kickbox. I could probably do some real damage, turn him into a soprano."

Sierra laughed. "My God, wouldn't that be awesome?"

"He's the kind of guy who'd punch back, though," CJ said. "Anyway, I feel like I'd be stooping to his level if I did that. As satisfying as it would be."

"You should tell the rodeo association. Maybe they'll pull his pro card," Sierra said.

"I thought about that, too, but it just feels like…I don't know, like running to the teacher. Does that make sense? I want to deal with this myself. Somehow. I just haven't worked out how."

"If only we could tell everyone what a pathetic little weasel he is. If people knew what he'd done to you, they wouldn't want to cheer for him or treat him like a hero. They wouldn't even want to spit on his shoes."

"So, what are you suggesting? A raid on the PA system?" CJ joked.

"If only we could make that work. What does Jesse say?"

"I have no idea and I'm not asking him—he nearly got into it with Maynard today already. This isn't his fight."

Sierra looked like she wanted to argue the point and CJ shook her head.

"I'm not his responsibility. I don't want him getting kicked off the circuit on my account. He's been great, stepping up for me today, helping out with all of this, but I don't need a protector."

"I get it. I like to fight my own battles, too," Sierra said. "Which means I usually have to fight off three brothers who want to get in there first."

"I know how that works. I've got three brothers too."

"I knew there was something I liked about you," Sierra said.

CJ laughed, and it felt good. As though she was letting go of a burden she hadn't even been aware she was carrying.

A sixth sense alerted her they were no longer alone, and she turned to find Jesse in the doorway. He'd taken his coat off and he looked impossibly tall and wide in a navy and black plaid shirt and dark denim jeans.

"All good here?" he asked.

"Yep. I was about to invite CJ to stay for dinner. How does grilled chicken, corn bread and salad sound?" Sierra asked.

"You don't have to feed me as well," CJ protested.

She'd already imposed on the Carmodys enough.

"I know I don't," Sierra said, flashing her a smile. "But since I'm going to be cooking anyway, you might as well join us."

CJ wasn't sure if Sierra was just being kind, and she glanced uncertainly at Jesse. His mouth crooked up at the corners.

"Just say yes. It's easier that way," he said.

"Funny," Sierra said. "Just for that you're in charge of the grill."

"Dinner sounds lovely," CJ said, because how could she resist such kindness and generosity? "I'm not the best cook but I can help peel things and cut them up."

"Well, I am *awesome* in the kitchen, but it's Casey's turn to be my reluctant handmaiden, so you relax and enjoy yourself," Sierra said.

Jesse pushed away from the doorframe. "You can come watch me clean the grill if you like. Nothing like watching someone else work to build up an appetite."

He exited to the kitchen and CJ glanced uncertainly at the washing machine.

"You've got another half hour before they'll be done,"

Sierra said.

Which left her with nothing to do but follow Jesse out into the kitchen. He was waiting with two beers in hand, and he passed one to her wordlessly.

"We're out here," he said, indicating the door that led outside from the kitchen.

She followed him onto the wrap-around porch to where a gas grill had been built into a brick retaining wall. Benches ran along the wall on either side, and the profusion of herbs planted in the garden bed behind the retaining wall filled the night air with their scent.

"Take a load off. You must be sore," Jesse said as he lifted the lid on the grill.

"Starting to feel it a bit," CJ admitted as she sank onto the bench to the left of the barbeque.

"Hot shower works wonders."

CJ had a sudden, vivid image of Jesse Carmody standing beneath hot water, gloriously naked and glistening wet.

Okay, definitely not helpful, thank you subconscious.

She took a hasty gulp of her beer, hoping it would flush her brain out, only to be hit with a perfect combination of malty-hoppy goodness and crisp coldness.

"God, that is *good*," she said, closing her eyes for a moment.

When she opened her eyes, Jesse was watching her, an arrested expression on his face.

She wiped her mouth with the back of her hand. "Don't

tell me I've got a beer moustache?"

"Nope. No moustache that I can see," he said, turning his attention to the grill.

He squatted to inspect the gas bottle and twist it on, his thigh muscles bunching beneath his jeans. CJ told herself to look away, but he was one of those men it was simply a pleasure to watch do almost anything—his big, strong body seemed to move effortlessly, confidently, no matter what he was doing, and his hands were sure and dexterous as he manipulated the gas bottle.

But she already knew the man had good hands. She'd seen them in action today during his ride.

She cleared her throat. "So...this is your base, then? When you're not on the circuit?"

"I don't really have one. Tend to follow the circuit round, go from rodeo to rodeo."

"So you pretty much live on the road?" she asked. She should have guessed that, given his standing in the rankings. A rider didn't get that high up the leaderboard without hitting as many rodeos as he could.

"Pretty much. You planning on going all-in now you got your pro card?" he asked, shooting her a searching look.

She kept forgetting how beautiful his eyes were, then he'd look at her directly and she'd be hit all over again by the depth of the green in his irises and the lushness of his thick dark lashes.

"My plan is to play it by ear. I've got enough saved to

survive a while without winnings. So I guess I'll just see what happens."

A lot could change very quickly in pro rodeo. She could get injured. She could fail to place or win and have to rely on her savings to survive. Anything could happen.

"If you're having second thoughts about staying on the circuit because of Maynard, don't. He's not going to bother you again," Jesse said. He was fiddling with the knobs on the grill, but she could see his grim expression.

"Don't go starting anything with him on my behalf," she said quickly. "I don't want you to get into trouble with the law or the association."

"Who said it would be for you?" he said. "He's making us all look like a bunch of ignorant, redneck assholes, the way he's behaving."

She gave him her best 'cut the bull' look. If it wasn't for her, no way would Jesse feel as though he needed to rein Maynard in. If it wasn't for her, none of this would have happened in the first place.

"This is my problem, not yours," she said.

"Consider it professional courtesy," he said.

"If you start something, people will talk," she pointed out.

He frowned. "About what?"

"About us. If you go after him, it'll look like you're doing it for me." She could feel heat rising into her face, but she needed to say this, get it on the table, so they both knew where they stood.

"Right." He used a scraper to clean the grill, the sound loud in the quiet night. Then: "Maybe people should just mind their own business."

"Great in theory, not so much in practice," CJ said. "I don't want rumors flying around about me. I'm here to compete. Nothing else."

He glanced at her, and she knew he'd gotten her message.

"Fair enough." His tone was neutral, almost completely uninflected with emotion.

And why wouldn't it be? There was nothing between them except a certain animal awareness and some kindness on his behalf.

"What sort of cattle do you run here?" she asked.

He smiled slightly at the very deliberate change of topic.

"Mostly Black Angus, but we've got a few hundred head of Red Charolais as well. And Jed's been breeding Appaloosas the last couple of years."

"My first horse was an Appaloosa," she said.

His teeth showed white as he smiled. "Mine, too."

Good Lord, but he was ridiculously handsome when he smiled. Dangerously so.

"What about you? Your family own land?" he asked.

"When I was younger, but they sold it when I was about ten. Nothing like this place, though. My dad's a farrier now, and my mom works in Plentywood at the county office."

"A farrier? That's pretty cool. Does that mean you know your way around a forge?"

"Only enough to get into trouble."

"So what do you do when you're not showing us all how to ride a bronc?"

She pulled a face at his compliment. "I ran a riding school back home, helped out at a local agistment."

He nodded, then reached out to turn down the gas. "I'll just let Sierra know we're ready for her."

"Don't bother. I'm psychic," Sierra said, appearing through the kitchen door with a platter loaded down with *a lot* of chicken. "Don't overcook it, because there is nothing worse than cardboard chicken."

"I'll do my best."

"Don't worry, I'll supervise," CJ said, offering Sierra a wink. Sierra smirked and headed back into the house.

"You're welcome to take over," Jesse said, waving a welcoming hand at the grill.

"No way. I'm even worse with a grill than I am in the kitchen." She grinned at him. "I'm a great armchair cook though, so I'll just yell out when I see you going wrong."

"You do that," Jesse said dryly.

She swallowed the last of her beer and set the empty bottle down with regret.

"Grab another one from the fridge," Jesse said, and she realized he was as attuned to her every action and reaction as she was to his.

She filed the knowledge away for later. When it would be safer to think about what that meant.

"I'd love to, but I can't—gotta drive back into town. I'll grab you another one if you want, though…?" She stood, dusting her hands down her thighs.

"You can't go back to that motel," he said. "I already changed the sheets—you can have my bed, I'll sleep in the old Airstream behind the barn."

"I can't let you do that."

"Sure you can."

"I'm not kicking you out of your own bed."

"You're not, I'm volunteering. And what's the alternative? Because at the risk of repeating myself, you can't go back to that motel."

CJ was tempted to stand her ground, but privately she'd been dreading going back to her accommodation. The room would have been cleaned in her absence—the manager had promised her that—but she was pretty sure she wouldn't be getting a lot of sleep, knowing Maynard had found a way past the lock without leaving so much as a scratch on it.

"How about this—you stay in your bed, I'll sleep in the Airstream?" she offered.

He tilted his head, studying her for a beat. Then he shrugged. "Okay, if that's what it takes. But I want it on the record that I tried to do the gentlemanly thing."

"It's been noted and will go in your permanent file," she said.

That surprised a laugh out of him. "Good to know."

"One other thing—pretty sure that chicken wing in the back corner has passed cardboard and is on its way to cremated."

"Shit." Turning back to the grill, Jesse busied himself with the chicken.

CJ studied his profile. Maybe it was the warmth of the beer spreading through her body, or the smell of rosemary and oregano from the garden behind her, or the clear, bright night sky, but it occurred to her for the first time that this weekend hadn't been all doom and gloom.

Having to confront and deal with Dean Maynard had been pretty damn unpleasant, to say the least—but she'd also met Jesse Carmody. And he was a good man, a kind man. An honorable man. He'd gone out of his way to approach her at the street party and let her know he didn't share Maynard's opinion. He'd offered her advice on everything from good chili to the habits of her bronc, and he'd stepped up when Maynard had started mouthing off in front of the rest of the riders.

And now he'd offered her the comfort of his home and family, no strings, no expectations.

He was one of the good ones, and no matter what else had happened this weekend, she'd lucked out that he'd come into her orbit.

"Jesse?" she said.

He glanced across at her, eyebrows slightly raised in inquiry.

"Thank you," she said quietly. "For everything."

He held her eye for a long beat, then acknowledged her words with a single nod before turning his attention back to the food.

JESSE TRIED TO think of something to say, but CJ's quiet, sincere expression of gratitude had cleared every thought from his brain.

He hadn't done any of the things he'd done because he'd been looking for gratitude—or anything else, for that matter. He'd done them because she'd been unfairly harassed, and because he could empathize with how daunting it was for a rookie to join the pro circuit, where the competition was more intense, the crowds bigger, the pressure more profound than any local rodeo CJ would have competed in before.

The fact he found her attractive was beside the point. He almost wished he wasn't so aware of her in that way, because he was starting to like her a lot and sex almost always got in the way of friendship between men and women. In his experience, anyway. He could count on the fingers of one hand the ex-girlfriends he was still friends with.

He frowned at the chicken, trying to work out how he'd gone from embarrassment over CJ's acknowledgment to thinking about her in terms of a girlfriend. Talk about putting the cart before the horse.

"I might go see if Sierra needs help setting the table," CJ said. "Even I can't mess that up."

"Won't be much longer out here anyway," Jesse said.

He was very aware of the night sounds around him once she was gone—the occasional nicker of a horse in the home paddock, the hoot of an owl, the wind in the old yellow pine behind the house. He could hear Sierra and CJ talking and laughing in the kitchen, too, but not clearly enough to understand what they were saying.

He was glad CJ hadn't been scared off by Maynard's ugliness. He was even happier she'd be competing the next rodeo in Great Falls. He liked being around her, even if she'd made it clear that nothing was going to happen between them.

He could understand why. She was in a difficult position, being the only woman competing in a field of men. Like it or not, the rodeo crowd was a conservative one, and if it got out she'd slept with one of the riders, she'd get a lot of judgment and side-eye from people.

Meanwhile, the male rider would probably get a bunch of high fives and pats on the back. That was how messed up the double standard was.

Aware he was going to take a lot of heat from his sister if the chicken was overdone, he tested a piece and decided it was cooked. Piling a clean platter high with the meat, he turned off the gas and let himself into the kitchen.

"'Bout time, man. I am *starving*," Casey said.

He was loitering in the space between the kitchen island and the scrubbed pine dining table, a beer in hand. Jed was at the sink, washing his hands, and Jesse exchanged a nod with his older brother. Sierra and CJ were nowhere to be seen, but he could hear their voices in the laundry room.

"Chicken's done," he called.

"So I smell. Won't be a minute," Sierra called.

Jesse figured they must be transferring CJ's stuff to the dryer, and made a mental note to thank his sister for stepping up the way she had.

"You met CJ yet?" he asked Jed as he set the platter in the middle of the table.

"Five minutes ago. Gather there was some trouble at her motel?"

Jesse glanced toward the laundry room, unwilling to get into the details yet again when CJ might walk in. She'd had to go over it enough times already today.

"Yeah. I'll fill you in later."

Jed nodded, getting the message, then crossed to the fridge.

"For sure I'll have another one, thanks for asking," Casey said before Jed even had the door open.

"Those arms of yours painted on?" Jed asked, but he pulled out three beers and passed one each to Casey and Jesse.

"These arms have been busy creating amazing music and they require the soothing balm of beer to restore them,"

Casey said.

"Listen to the poet," Jesse said.

"I do, twenty-four seven," Jed said dryly, taking a long pull from his beer. "Apparently I did something real bad in a former life."

Jesse smirked as Casey gave his brother the bird, then they all tried to look innocent as Sierra and CJ joined them.

"What are you three up to?" Sierra asked, looking around suspiciously.

"Just standing here watching our dinner get cold," Casey said.

"Then you should have got the corn bread out of the oven and the salad out of the fridge. Those arms of yours painted on?"

Jesse and Casey both burst into laughter, and even Jed cracked a smile at her echo of his own words.

"Whatever," Sierra said after a beat of bafflement at their reaction. "CJ, I apologize for the idiocy of the Carmody men. It's a weakness that breeds true in our family."

"You have my sympathy. Like I said, I've got three like them at home, and I know what a burden it is," CJ said.

"Ow," Jesse said, placing a hand over his heart. "What happened to 'Jesse, you're my savior'? I liked that much better."

CJ gave him a steady look. "You want to rethink that quote?" she asked, one eyebrow cocked in challenge.

"Careful, Jesse, she's already whipped your ass once today," Casey reminded him.

"The loyalty of this family staggers me sometimes," Jesse said.

"Can it stagger you at the table? Some of us have been fencing all day," Jed said.

Probably the line was meant as a joke, but it felt like a reprimand, and Jesse's smile slipped. No doubt Jed didn't consider competing in two events back-to-back at the rodeo real work. Certainly not the equal of a day on the ranch.

Waving his hand, Jesse invited his brother to take a seat. No one was stopping him, after all. He was aware of CJ shooting him a quick look, trying to understand the shift in the room.

"CJ, sit next to me," Sierra said, indicating the chair to the right of her own.

Jesse took the chair opposite as Casey and Sierra ferried the rest of the food to the table.

"Looks great, everyone," Jed said.

"Hell, yeah," Casey said, already reaching for the potato salad.

"Raised by wolves, I tell you," Sierra said, slapping his hand away. "We have a guest, remember?"

"CJ's got three brothers. She knows the drill—every man for himself," Casey said, reaching for the potato salad again.

CJ beat him to it, whisking the bowl from beneath his hand. "Thanks for reminding me," she said, much to Sierra's delight.

Jesse grinned, too, then let out a bark of laughter at the surprised look on Casey's face.

Her eyes dancing with amusement, CJ offered Sierra the salad first before taking a scoop for herself. Then and only then did she offer it to Casey.

Casey tipped an invisible hat to her. "Respect."

CJ laughed, the sound light and bright, and Jesse felt a distinct tug in his gut as he watched her. Man, she was pretty, with her shiny dark hair and lively brown eyes.

"Heard you had the ride of the day today, CJ," Jed said as bowls and plates were passed around.

"I got lucky," she said modestly.

"Luck had nothing to do with it. She's got natural instinct like you wouldn't believe," Jesse said.

"You still going to say that when she beats you tomorrow?" Casey asked.

Jesse caught CJ's eye across the table. "See what I mean about the loyalty?"

"Jesse's second on the leaderboard. He's got a good draw for tomorrow, too. It's anyone's prize," CJ said.

"Yeah, but if you win it will be so awesome. The best F-you to that dipshit who vandalized your stuff," Sierra said. "You can win next week, Jesse," she added magnanimously.

"Thanks. Appreciate it," he said dryly.

The conversation roamed far and wide then, from Casey's gig at the street party last night to how many mares were in foal, to Sierra's plan to start studying for her commercial helicopter pilot's license.

"You fly?" CJ asked. "That's pretty cool."

"She bugged Jed until he let her start taking lessons when she was eighteen," Casey said.

"You have no idea how long it took to convince him," Sierra said.

"You have no idea how expensive those lessons were," Jed said mildly.

"Think of it as an investment in getting me off your hands," Sierra said. "I've been talking to the Tates's pilot: Jack. He's going to help me get my hours up."

Jesse frowned, then noticed Jed and Casey were wearing the exact same expression. He guessed that like him, they hated the idea that Sierra would be beholden to the Tates for anything. Twelve years ago, Gideon Tate had been driving the SUV that smashed into their parents' car. He'd been the only one to walk away from the accident alive.

No adverse finding had been made in the subsequent accident investigation, but it had always bugged Jesse that Gideon Tate's life had seemingly gone on without a hitch after that night, while their family had been devastated.

The silence stretched a little too long, and Sierra's cheeks turned pink. Jesse guessed that any second now she was going to start defending her decision, and CJ would be playing witness to the Carmody family in full flight.

"Have you—" he said, just as Jed spoke up at the same time.

Jesse gave his older brother a dry look. Apparently they'd both had the brilliant idea of changing the subject at the same time.

"You go," Jesse said.

"Just wondering whether you've got any down time coming up?" Jed asked.

"Not until Christmas. That's if I don't get injured," he replied.

"You given any thought to when you're going to quit?" Jed asked.

"Not really." Why would he, when he was doing what he loved for a living and making decent money while he was at it?

"Can't keep riding bronc forever. Rodeo's a young guy's game," Jed said matter-of-factly.

Jesse felt himself bristle. His brother's casual dismissal of his life's passion—his career—was enough to fire Jesse's temper. He took a long pull from his beer, swallowing the angry words filling his throat.

"You know me—never could get too much of a bad thing," he finally said.

Jed didn't say another word, simply reached out to spear himself another piece of chicken.

Jesse was aware of CJ watching him from across the table and he flashed her a quick smile to try to smooth the moment over.

"Hope you cowboys and girls left room for cherry crisp,"

Sierra said, starting to stack the now-empty bowls and platters.

"I didn't, but it doesn't matter. There is always room for cherry crisp," Casey said.

Standing, he started to collect plates, and CJ quickly joined him.

Jesse could feel his brother watching him, but he deliberately didn't look his way. He couldn't, not right at that moment.

It seemed to him no matter what he did, he'd always get it wrong where Jed was concerned, and it pissed him off to no end that he still gave two shits about his brother's approval.

It had been eleven years. How long were they going to keep this crap up?

The thought propelled him to his feet. "Might take a walk outside before dessert, try to make some room."

He didn't give anyone a chance to respond, simply headed for the door.

Chapter Seven

THERE WAS A profound, heavy silence after Jesse had left the room. CJ fought the need to fill it with pointless chatter. Clearly there was something heavy going on between Jesse and his older brother, Jed, but her rabbiting on with small talk was not going to help anything.

Instead, she concentrated on scraping off plates and stacking them into the dishwasher in the Carmodys' simple country-style kitchen.

After a moment, Sierra started talking about someone CJ guessed must be a neighbor, teasing monosyllabic responses from Jed, who seemed to have retreated inside himself after the exchange with Jesse.

CJ studied him covertly as she worked, wondering about the worry lines around his eyes and mouth. She knew from something Sierra had said that he was only a year older than Jesse, but looking at his lean, weathered face, she would have guessed at the difference being five years, minimum. She'd pieced together enough from what Sierra and Jesse had said to work out he'd essentially stepped into the parental role when their parents were killed.

She wondered what he'd had to give up to do that. He must have had dreams, ambitions, hopes of his own. But instead he'd found himself the only person holding his family together when he'd barely qualified as an adult himself. He'd done a good job, too—this was clearly a family of people who liked each other. And yet all through the meal there had been a buzz of tension, a tautness vibrating beneath the digs and laughs and teasing, as though a whole other conversation was going on beneath the fun and lightness.

None of your business, Cooper.

It so wasn't. Not even close. But her gaze kept straying to the kitchen window, trying to catch sight of Jesse. She'd seen his face when Jed so calmly predicted the end of his rodeo career. He'd looked as though he'd been slapped—but only for a split second. If she'd blinked, she would have missed his wounded reaction. She'd seen the regret in Jed's eyes afterward, too. The way his jaw had gotten tight and his hands had clenched around his knife and fork.

If they were her brothers, she'd knock their heads together and tell them to damn well talk to each other. But they weren't, and she wasn't about to start throwing advice around. It wasn't as though she was an expert on family harmony—look at the way things were between her and her father right now.

Which reminded her—he still hadn't called. She pulled

her phone out and checked to make sure she hadn't missed a message. Nope, nothing.

Which probably meant he wasn't going to call at all. To say she was disappointed was an understatement, but she set her feelings aside for later. Now was not the time or place to get messy over her own complicated home life.

It was another ten minutes before Jesse returned to the house, bringing the scent of the cool night air with him. He met her eyes and smiled slightly, then threw himself into helping serve up dessert. Conversation stayed on safe subjects as everyone spooned up mouthfuls of Sierra's delicious cherry crisp, served with rich vanilla ice cream.

"I got this round," Jesse said when CJ stood to clear the table a second time.

"That first lot of clothes should be close to dry now. I was thinking you might want to grab a shower?" Sierra said, catching CJ's eye across the table.

The thought of hot water and clean clothes was enough to make CJ weep.

"That would be pretty fantastic, actually," she admitted.

"Then let's hook you up," Sierra said.

As Sierra had predicted, her first load of clothes were dry, and the second load ready to transfer. That task completed, CJ selected clean underwear, a T-shirt and jeans, and followed Sierra through the living room to a hallway that branched into the left side of the house.

She hadn't had much of a chance to look around since

she arrived, and she did a quick scan of the living room as they walked through. The room's focus was an enormous stone-clad fireplace boasting a rough-hewn timber mantel scattered with photo frames. Two large sofas and an armchair in worn tobacco-brown leather were arranged in front of the fire, with a coffee table groaning with magazines, books and newspapers positioned between them. Jackets were strewn over the back of the couch, and a couple of empty mugs crowned the stacks on the coffee table.

"Don't look at the mess," Sierra said, waving a hand at the coffee table. "Just pretend it isn't there, like a good guest."

"This isn't messy," CJ said. "My closet is messy. You could perform surgery in here by comparison."

"I know you're just saying that to make me feel better, but I'll take it," Sierra said.

She led CJ down the hallway past a couple of open doorways. The first was clearly Casey's room, easily distinguishable because of the golden-hued acoustic guitar lying on the bed. The next room was neat as a pin, a pair of well-worn cowboy boots lined up side by side next to the bed. The bed was made, and a subtle, familiar scent hung in the air.

Jesse's room, she guessed. It smelled like him.

Then she frowned, not exactly thrilled she was apparently able to identify the man by his scent barely twenty-four hours after meeting him.

"Here we go," Sierra said, pushing open the next door.

"Towels are beneath the sink. Help yourself to shampoo, whatever. And most importantly, take your time. Oh, and there's a hair dryer on a hook beside the vanity."

"Thank you," CJ said. How lucky was she that she'd met this family?

Sierra gave another dismissive wave before disappearing into the hallway.

CJ shut the door and sat on the edge of the tub to pull off her boots. Her socks were dark with dust from the arena, and she rolled them into a ball and put them to one side, along with the rest of her dirty clothes. The water was almost painfully hot when she stepped beneath it, but that was exactly what she needed and wanted. She sighed with relief as she felt the tightness ease out of her shoulders and hips. After a few minutes, she reached for the soap.

She took Sierra at her word and used her fresh-smelling shampoo, then allowed herself another few minutes of simply luxuriating in the warmth before reluctantly turning the water off. Her skin was very pink in the bathroom mirror, but her muscles felt warm and relaxed for the first time since her ride.

Ten minutes later, she stepped into the hall feeling like a new woman. Her hair was clean and almost dry. She smelled like a civilized person, and she'd washed the grit, sweat and emotion of the day from her body.

Sierra looked up from reading a book when CJ entered the lounge, but there was no sign of any of the Carmody men.

"Jesse and Casey are in the barn, checking on one of the pregnant mares, and Jed's in his office," Sierra explained. "Make yourself a coffee if you like, and we can watch TV or a movie if you're up for it?"

"To be honest, I'm probably just going to crash out. It's been a big day."

"You must be ten different types of pooped," Sierra said sympathetically.

The photos on the mantel caught CJ's eye and she stepped closer to check them out. The first was of a good-looking young couple, the man dark and tall and green eyed, the woman smaller, blonde and blue eyed. They stood with their arms around each other, their clothes smudged with dirt and sweat, the timber frame of a house reaching into the sky behind them.

"Is that this place?" CJ asked.

"Yep. You can't tell, but Mom's four months pregnant with Jed in that picture." Sierra came to stand beside her. "And that's Jed on his first horse. And that's Jesse practicing his roping."

CJ homed in on the picture of Jesse, who looked to be about five or six. She smiled at his earnest expression and the tension in his small frame as he gave everything he had to try to lasso a fence post. She'd seen the same look on his face today when he was preparing for his ride—equal parts focus and determination, with a hefty dose of stubbornness thrown in for good measure.

"He was a cute little critter. They all were. Whereas I…" Sierra slid a frame along the mantel toward CJ, her expression chagrined.

It held a photograph of a gangly little girl whose head seemed too big for her body. CJ guessed Sierra must have been at least four or five when the picture was taken, but her head was still covered in soft-looking baby down instead of hair, and her smile revealed two teeth missing front and center of the top row.

"Awww. You're adorable," CJ said.

"Come on. That is a face only a mother could love," Sierra said. "Can you believe I didn't grow a full head of hair until I was *six years old*? Sometimes Mother Nature is a stone-cold bitch."

CJ tried not to laugh but Sierra's richly disgusted tone made it hard not to.

There was a picture of Casey as a child, too, squinting off into the distance, a faraway look in his eye. And one last family portrait, Mrs. Carmody wearing a proud smile as her husband and her tall, summer-brown children overshadowed her. Jed was grinning, while Jesse looked slightly bored and pissed off, as though he had better things to do. Casey had Sierra in a brotherly headlock, but it was clear Sierra loved it.

"That was the last picture of all of us together," Sierra said. "They died about a week later. Head-on collision on the road into town."

She dusted the top of the frame with the flat of her hand, one side of her mouth pulled tight.

"Jesse told me about your parents. It must have been a terrible time," CJ said.

"It was. The weird thing is I can't remember many of the details. Just the feeling, the sense that the world had changed and would never be right again."

CJ didn't know what to say, so she didn't say anything, and after a moment Sierra gave a rueful smile.

"Okay, enough of that. Maybe we should have hot chocolates instead of coffees?"

"Don't s'pose there'd be any bourbon lying around that we could throw in there?" CJ asked hopefully.

"Lady, we have three different types of bourbon. Come take your pick."

They were in the kitchen chatting and finishing their drinks when the dryer beeped to signal its cycle was complete.

"You need a hand with any of that?" Sierra asked.

"Thanks, but I'm good." CJ turned to go, then thought of something. "You wouldn't have a bag I could borrow? I had to throw my duffel away, it was so disgusting. I could get the bag back to you tomorrow once I get a chance to buy something new in town."

"Let me have a look. I'm pretty sure I've got an old duffel bag you can have. I haven't used it for years."

Sierra headed off to search out the bag, and CJ started

pulling the still-warm clothes from the dryer. They smelled fresh and clean, all traces of this afternoon's misadventures washed away.

If only she could wash away the memory as easily. It would be a long time before she forgot the sense of fear, disgust and, yes, hurt that had hit her when she'd opened the door and discovered what Dean Maynard had done to her belongings. Never in her life had she been on the receiving end of so much calculated malice—and all because she'd dared to put her hand up to compete in the same arena as a bunch of men.

She could feel herself getting tense and worked up again, so she concentrated on folding everything neatly, focusing on lining up hems and smoothing folds. The warm, homey smell of freshly dried clothes and the calm, repetitive work went a long way to restoring her calm. She'd just started on a tangle of underwear when she looked up to find Jesse filling the doorway.

"Hey. How's it all going? Find everything you need?" he asked.

"All done, thank you. Your sister has been amazing."

"She's all right," Jesse said, putting on a show of reluctance at being forced to compliment his sibling.

She couldn't hide her smile. "Don't worry, I won't tell her you said that."

"I'd deny it anyway." He moved closer, propping a hip against the washing machine and crossing his arms over his chest. "Sure you don't want to rethink the Airstream? Give me a last chance to be chivalrous?"

"I'm not taking your bed, Jesse," she said firmly.

"In that case, you want me to take you out there, give you the grand tour?"

"Sierra said she'd do all that. But thanks for the offer."

Also, call her crazy, but she was pretty sure it would be a dumb idea to be alone in a small private space with this man. Especially a small, private space with a bed in it.

"Okay, then I guess I'll hit the hay. Unless there's anything else you need?"

His gaze scanned the room as though looking for a task that needed completing, finally coming to rest on the colorful pile of lace and satin that was her yet-to-be-folded underwear. She saw the exact moment he understood what he was looking at, felt the oxygen suddenly suck from the room and heat steal up her chest and into her face.

She had a weakness for pretty underwear. She liked bright colors and lace and flirty styles, liked knowing that while she was all sensible denim and cotton and flannel to the world, underneath she had a sexy, lacy, feminine secret— and now Jesse was in on it.

His gaze lifted to her face, and the heat in her cheeks seemed to rush everywhere at once. She'd seen interest in his eyes before. She'd seen awareness. But the way he was looking at her now, the hunger and desire... Her knees literally went weak and she had to reach out a hand to brace herself on the top of the dryer.

She could feel her pulse beating low in her belly, could feel every breath as it slid in and out of her lungs—and still she couldn't look away from him. She'd told herself to be sensible where this man was concerned so many times this weekend. She'd refused to indulge herself—and yet everything in her still wanted to take the two steps required to close the distance between them.

"Finally found the stupid thing at the back of the—" Sierra came to an abrupt halt in the doorway, her gaze bouncing from CJ to Jesse and back again. "Sorry. Did I interrupt something?"

"No," CJ blurted, too fast and too loud.

"I was just telling CJ good night," Jesse said.

"Okay," Sierra said, her tone skeptical.

"See you tomorrow," Jesse said, and he turned and angled past his sister to exit to the kitchen.

"Sorry. I really didn't mean to walk into the middle of anything," Sierra said, her expression comically dismayed as she passed over the duffel bag she'd dug up.

"You didn't. Jesse was just… He was just saying good night, like he said."

CJ acted on delayed impulse then, grabbing the tangle of lacy panties and stuffing them into the bag. A slow smile curved Sierra's mouth as she followed the action.

"That's some pretty saucy underwear you've got there, Ms. Cooper."

"I *really* don't want to talk about it." CJ could feel her face heating again. She almost never blushed, but she had no idea how to handle this…*situation* with Jesse.

"All right, we won't, then. Let's get you settled into the Airstream instead," Sierra said brightly, her eyes dancing with amusement and curiosity.

CJ finished transferring her clean clothes to the duffel bag Sierra assured her she was welcome to keep, while Sierra grabbed clean sheets from a cupboard beside the dryer. Then the two of them left the house via the kitchen door. They walked across the graveled yard to the barn, skirting the left side on a well-worn path, the way lit by three big gooseneck lights hanging from the sides of the peeling red structure.

"We can leave these lights on for you if you like. There's a bathroom in the trailer, but if you need to come up to the house you don't want to be fumbling around in the dark," Sierra said as they turned the corner.

The Airstream sat on a concrete pad that extended six feet or so in front of the trailer. A set of wooden steps had been built up to the door, and soft light shone from inside.

"Oh. Someone's been out here already," Sierra said.

She climbed the steps and pushed the door open, then gave a small grunt of surprise.

"What?" CJ asked, peering over her shoulder.

The interior of the trailer was neat but original—CJ guessed it had probably been new sometime in the seventies. A galley kitchen lined either wall to her left, culminating in an expanse of bed that looked as though it was easily the equivalent of a queen, maybe even a king. By day, she'd bet it folded into some kind of dining nook configuration, with bench seats and a table. To her right was a closed door that she guessed hid the bathroom and toilet.

"Someone made the bed already," Sierra said, stepping closer to tweak back the duvet and confirm her assessment.

CJ was pretty sure she knew who that someone was. It was getting harder and harder not to be charmed by Jesse Carmody.

"Well, I guess we won't need these," Sierra said, dumping the clean linen on the counter. "So, let me talk you through everything. The bathroom is hooked up to the plumbing in the main house, so feel free to use it at will. Water is all hooked up, too, so go for it there as well. We had an issue with the fuses shorting last month when we had guests, so if that happens, there's a flashlight here—" she opened a cupboard to show CJ "—and spare fuses. The fuse box is just beside the door in that little recess."

"Got it," CJ said.

"There's a shower, but it's coffin-sized and you are welcome to come up to the main house in the morning. What time do you think you'll be up?"

"Um, probably before eight. I need to do my yoga or I'll be a mess when I ride."

"There's a great spot around the back of the house on the porch, gets all the morning sun," Sierra said. "I do yoga there when I'm not being lazy."

"Noted, thanks."

"And there's a pancake breakfast in town tomorrow, in case you didn't know about it. It's usually pretty delicious, so we tend to head in there and pig out rather than bother with breakfast at home when the rodeo is in town."

"I am totally on board for that plan," CJ said.

Sierra smiled. "Is it wrong that I'm a kind of glad your stuff got peed on so I got to meet you properly?"

"A little, but I understand where you're coming from," CJ said. "You've been awesome. Your whole family has."

CJ didn't come from a super-demonstrative family, but it felt right to give Sierra a quick hug then, and she was both gratified and relieved when Sierra hugged her back.

"I'm going to leave you to it now. You've had a huge day, what with striking a blow for womankind and then following that up with two loads of laundry and surviving a Carmody family dinner, complete with unspoken tension and moody walk-out from my ridiculously handsome brother," Sierra said.

"Lots of highs and lows, for sure," CJ said with a grin. "It's been a roller coaster."

Sierra descended the steps to the concrete pad, giving CJ one last wave before disappearing around the corner of the barn. CJ waited until she was gone before shutting the door and letting out a big, gusty sigh.

Sierra was right—it had been a huge day, and now she

had a moment to think about it, she was bone-tired. Her ass, thighs and shoulders had the well-worn feeling she always got after a ride, and she circled her shoulders a little before she remembered she needed to grab her saddle from the bed of her truck. There'd been clouds scudding across the night sky as they walked through the yard, and she didn't want to risk rain.

It only took a minute or two to fetch the remainder of her gear, and she parked it to one side of the galley kitchen on the floor. It only left a narrow pathway, but that was okay, she wasn't planning on doing the tango anytime soon.

Feeling cozy in her shiny aluminum cocoon, she went to brush her teeth, then stripped down to panties and her T-shirt. On closer inspection she discovered the duvet cover featured cowboys on bucking broncos, and she wondered if Jesse had chosen it on purpose or if it was simply the first cover that came to hand.

Whatever, it was cute and welcoming, and she turned off the main light, leaving only the reading light above the bed aglow, and crawled onto the mattress. It was a little firm, but comfortable enough, and she slid beneath the duvet and tested the two pillows, selecting the squishier one and setting the other aside. Then she rolled onto her back and leaned across to flick off the light.

Which was when she spotted the large, eight-legged intruder on the ceiling directly above her pillow.

Well, damn.

Apparently the day's dramas weren't over just yet.

Chapter Eight

JESSE WAS CHECKING the weather on his laptop when Sierra entered the living room, a couple of folded bath towels in hand.

"Forgot to give CJ a towel, in case she wants to shower out in the Airstream," she explained.

Jesse eyed his sister's pajamas and bare feet. "I'll take them out to her. You're ready for bed."

Sierra hesitated briefly before handing the towels over. "All right. Thanks."

He shut down his laptop before heading outside. Gravel crunched underfoot as he made his way past the barn. He was about to turn the corner when he heard a high-pitched yelp of alarm that could only have come from CJ. Speeding up, he caught sight of a shadow lunging across the curtained window in the bedroom area of the trailer.

"Stop being...such...an asshole."

Her words had him yanking open the door and leaping into the trailer, visions of intruders or snakes or some other life-threatening invader at the front of his mind.

He froze in his tracks at the sight that greeted him—CJ, clad in nothing but a pair of black lace panties and a soft white T-shirt, balanced on her knees on the bed, a drinking glass pressed to the wall. Inside the glass, a big brown spider was doing its level best to escape.

CJ glanced over her shoulder. "Thank God. I forgot to get something to lift him off with. There's a magazine on the shelf above the counter there. Would you mind grabbing it for me?"

He turned to the shelf as instructed, fumbling to dump the towels and grab the magazine, his head full of long, muscular legs and firm, supple arms. Trying to keep his eyes on her face, he passed her the magazine.

"Thanks."

He watched as she carefully slid the magazine beneath the glass before walking on her knees to the edge of the bed, tanned thighs flexing with every move. He moved back toward the bathroom zone as she slid off the bed and approached with her captive. He was about to suggest she pass the spider over so he could find it a new home outside but she was already stepping out the door.

Of course CJ wouldn't think twice about going barefoot and barely dressed into the dark. She probably leapt tall buildings in a single bound as a hobby.

She was back half a minute later, empty glass and magazine in hand.

"Okay. Hopefully he's not going to turn this into some

kind of turf war and try to find a way back in," she said, placing both items onto the kitchen counter.

"Yeah. Good call," he said stupidly.

He was pretty sure he could see the dark shadows of her nipples through the fabric of her T-shirt. Not that he'd been looking for them—but he was only human.

She glanced at the towels. "Are those for me?" she asked, one hand tugging at the hem of her T-shirt self-consciously.

His eyes followed the movement. Man, her panties were smokin'. Lace combined with something that looked as though it would be silky to the touch. The way the fabric and lace cupped her ass and hugged her hips was insanely hot…

He realized he hadn't answered her question. And that he was staring at her like a desperate sixteen-year-old from a bad coming-of-age movie.

"Sierra said she forgot to give them to you earlier," he said, wrenching his eyes back to her face. "Sorry for barging in, I thought you were in trouble, which was pretty dumb in hindsight."

Because if the last couple of days had taught him anything, it was that this woman could take care of herself.

He took a step toward the door, heat burning the back of his neck. He needed to go, before she noticed the raging hard-on pressing against the zipper of his jeans.

"Thanks for the towels," she said.

She looked as uncomfortable and off-balance as he felt,

SARAH MAYBERRY

standing there with her dark hair flowing over her shoulders and her body outlined in the soft amber glow of the reading light.

"Pleasure," he said.

And then the world went dark.

For a moment there was nothing but silence as they both absorbed the shock.

"Must be the fuse," CJ said, and he almost smiled at the matter-of-fact acceptance in her tone.

Did anything faze this woman?

"Yeah, Casey mentioned they'd been having problems with the electrics. Should be some fuses in one of the top cupboards," he said.

He took a step forward—and found himself hard up against a warm, firm body as CJ evidently did the same thing. His hands came up instinctively to steady her, one landing on the flare of her hip, the other on her waist.

They both went very still. Beneath his hands, she felt warm and strong. He breathed in the smell of fresh soap and clean hair and felt himself harden into full, painful arousal. The need to kiss her, touch her, taste her was almost undeniable—but if anything was going to happen between them, it had to be CJ's call. She was his guest, she'd had a shitty day, and she had good reasons for keeping her distance. He wasn't going to add himself to her list of problems.

Not unless she wanted him to.

The moment seemed to stretch and stretch. He felt her

inhale, felt the muscles of her torso move subtly beneath his hands. He was so hard it physically hurt, but there was a weird kind of pleasure in the pain and it hit him that he hadn't wanted anyone this badly for years. The realization made his hands curl into her flesh, but somehow he managed to limit himself to the small gesture and cling to his self-control.

A shudder rippled through her, as though she'd just won or lost a fiercely fought battle within herself.

"Fuck it," she said, and then she kissed him.

HE TASTED LIKE heat and coffee and desire, and CJ whimpered with need as he angled his mouth over hers and deepened the kiss she'd initiated. His tongue stroked hers as he laid siege to her mouth, his hands sliding across her back to draw her closer. His body felt amazing against hers, so hard and powerful, the denim of his jeans brushing against her bare legs. Her hands slid over his shoulders and back as she gave as good as she got, fighting for control of the kiss, reveling in the tension she could feel thrumming through his body.

He shifted his hips closer, his hands sliding to her backside as he tucked her against him, and she felt the firm pressure of his erection against her belly. Grabbing his ass in turn, she ground herself against him, driven by the need for more, more, more.

God, she wanted this man, in the best and worst possible way. She wanted him over her, inside her, behind her, wanted to feel his naked skin against her own, his sweat on her skin, his taste on her tongue.

Impatience drove her to break their kiss and reach for the hem of her T-shirt. She pulled it over her head then gasped as Jesse's work-callused hands slid up her sides and onto her bared breasts.

"Oh," she moaned, unable to put into words how good it felt as he stroked her aching nipples with his thumbs.

"Fuck," Jesse said, the single, profane word loaded with awe and lust and intent.

They tumbled together onto the bed, and then she was on her back and he was on top of her, kissing his way down her neck and across her shoulder and finally, finally arriving at her breasts. She clutched handfuls of his dark hair as he teased her with his clever mouth, flicking his tongue over and over first one nipple, then the other.

She'd never been so turned on so fast in her life, desire a greedy, demanding throb between her thighs. When he slid a hand down her belly and beneath the elastic of her panties she lifted her hips to welcome him and sobbed as he stroked two fingers along the seam of her sex.

She felt the shudder that went through him as he discovered how wet she was, heard the rasp as he sucked in air.

"Unbelievable," he muttered, and then he was sliding down her body, tugging her panties down in an impatient, demanding rush as he bared her to him.

She spread her legs wide, unashamedly eager for what he was offering. When he licked between her thighs she gripped his shoulders and let out a low moan, giving herself over utterly to the moment.

The next minutes passed in a blur of sensation and ratcheting desire as he licked and teased her with his mouth until she was quivering and taut, trembling on the brink of climax. She panted, desperate for fulfillment but also not wanting it to ever end because this man was *good* at this. Persistent and inventive and creative in all the best ways. Then he circled her entrance with a single knowing finger and she held her breath, waiting for something…something…

He slid a finger inside her, and she was lost, sobbing his name as her body shuddered into pure, pulsing pleasure. He kept stroking her with finger and mouth until she was limp and breathless. Then she felt the loss of his warmth as he moved away from her.

A belt buckle clinked in the dark and she opened her eyes.

"You'd better be taking your jeans off," she warned him.

"Good, you're still breathing," he said, surprising her into laughter.

"No thanks to you," she said.

"I don't expect thanks," he said. "But I'll take payment in kind."

She laughed again and felt the mattress dip as he landed

beside her. The thought that he was naked chased away the last of her climax-induced lassitude and she rolled toward him.

His chest was leanly muscled and dusted with hair that she bet was as dark as that on his head. She caressed one firm pec and then found the other before lowering her mouth to flick his flat male nipple with her tongue. He tensed minutely, so she did it again and had the satisfaction of hearing his breath rush out in a needy sigh.

She was tempted to keep teasing him, but she was burningly aware that the hot, hard erection that had been pressed against her belly was now all hers to explore and she smoothed a hand down his flat belly, following a silky happy trail to a startlingly hard, hot erection. She wrapped her hand around him, her inner muscles tensing greedily as she registered how thick and long he was.

He shifted his hips as she stroked her hand up and down his shaft, and she knew instinctively that he was wound tight, that he needed and wanted this as badly as she did.

"Tell me you have a condom," she said, stroking her hand down and then up again.

"Back pocket, in my wallet," he said, his voice raspy with desire.

It took her a moment to find his jeans then locate his wallet and finally the condom in the dark. She tore the packet open with her teeth and rolled toward him, sliding a leg over his hips and climbing on board. For a moment she got distracted by the feel of his erection against the soft, wet folds between her legs, but she told herself to stay focused and slid the condom inch by inch down his hard shaft.

"Hold on, cowboy," she said, then she guided him into place and took him inside her—just as the light above the bed sprang back to life.

JESSE THOUGHT HE'D died and gone to heaven as CJ slid down onto his cock—and then the lights came on and he discovered there was something better than heaven, and that was being able to see what she was doing to him as well as feel it.

She laughed in surprise, her face flushed, her hair a dark tangle flowing over her shoulders and breasts. His gaze followed the trail his hands had blazed earlier, taking in her full, rounded breasts and rosy nipples, the flat plane of her belly, and finally the dark curls at the apex of her thighs. His gaze got stuck there as she rose up to the point of almost losing him before sliding back down. The sight of his cock disappearing into her slick warmth was almost enough to undo him, but he grit his teeth and fought back against the pleasure threatening to swamp him.

He wasn't stupid—the likelihood was strong that this would be his one and only night with this amazing woman, and he planned on making it last.

Gripping her hips, he stroked up into her, taking control

of the rhythm. She caught on quickly, her bottom lip caught between her teeth as she rode him. He slid his hands onto her breasts and squeezed her nipples, feeling the telltale increase in pressure on his cock as she responded to his touch.

Of course she liked a little pain with her pleasure—she was a bronc rider, just like him.

He pinched her again, then levered himself up and soothed her with his mouth. Then he bit her, and she laughed and reached out to flick a finger against one of his nipples, hard enough to hurt.

"Behave yourself, Carmody," she said.

She looked so wild and free, her breasts bouncing with each rise and fall of her hips. Capturing one of her hands, he brought it to the neat thatch of curls where he was joined with her. "Show me what you like," he said.

Her eyelids dropped over her eyes for a moment, and her breasts lifted as her breath hitched. Then she started to stroke herself.

It was the hottest thing he'd ever seen in his life—CJ riding his cock, pleasuring herself, her eyes glazed with passion, her chest and face flushed pink. Little strands of hair stuck damply to her temples while the rest of her hair slid back and forth over her shoulders and breasts.

Fucking magnificent. Sexy as hell.

And he was *gone*.

His whole body grew rigid as he came, driving up into

THE COWBOY MEETS HIS MATCH

her, fingers clenched into her hips.

"Cassidy," he said, her name ripped from his chest.

Seconds later she tensed around him and he watched as she closed her eyes, her face contorting as she lost herself for the second time.

She seemed dazed as she came back down to earth. He pulled her down beside him on the mattress, then took care of the condom, wrapping it in a tissue from the box by the bed to dispose of later. Then he pulled the covers up over their bodies and wrapped his arms around her, encouraging her to rest her head on his chest.

Normally, he wasn't big on postcoital cuddling, but it would have felt wrong to lie beside CJ and not hold her. And not because they'd just had mind-blowing sex.

They were both silent for a while, the only sound the distant hoot of an owl somewhere outside and their own slowing breathing.

"Guess it wasn't the fuse, then," CJ finally said.

He huffed out a laugh. "Yeah. Must have been something else." He waited a moment. "Great timing, though."

"For sure. Right on cue."

Because he couldn't help himself, he smoothed a hand down her hair, then down her arm to her hip. He loved the way he could feel the muscles beneath her skin, loved the strength of her hard-trained body.

"How did you start bronc riding?" he asked.

He wanted to know what drove her, what series of events

and circumstances had brought her to this town and this place, into his arms and his bed and his life.

Even if it was only for the weekend.

"My dad used to breed horses when we were kids. Just a few, here and there, and me and my brothers used to help break them. I loved it so much, my father used to say I was part monkey, the knack I had for staying on a horse's back. How about you?"

"Same. I can still remember the first time a horse tried to kick me off. Pure adrenaline."

"Best drug in the world," CJ said, and even though he couldn't see her face he knew she was smiling.

"Take it your father doesn't breed horses anymore?" he asked before he remembered her telling him earlier that they'd sold the family ranch when she was ten.

"He couldn't make it work, and it was really only a hobby. But it was enough to get my brothers and me interested in rodeo."

"Your folks must be pretty proud of you after today," he said.

There was a small, significant pause before she responded.

"Yeah. They are."

He tucked his chin to his chest and angled his head so he could see her face. "Did I just step on a toe?"

She smiled slightly. "Not really. My dad isn't exactly a huge fan of me going pro. I rang to let them know I made it to the short round and spoke to my mom, but he wasn't around and he hasn't called back, so…"

"You know the reception sucks out here? I can barely get a bar on my phone."

"You're sweet, but you don't have to make it okay for me. It is what it is."

"Tell me to butt out, but what's his beef with you riding?"

She sighed, the sound both weary and sad. "He doesn't understand why I'd want to rock the boat. Why I don't just join the WPRA and go in for barrel racing if I want to do rodeo so bad."

"Barrel racing isn't saddle bronc," he said.

"He knows it. He used to ride himself. He knows exactly what it feels like to be in the chute, waiting to give the nod." She levered herself up into a sitting position, one arm holding the duvet across her breasts. "Hell, he's the one who taught me how to break a horse in the first place. If anything, it's his fault I'm like this."

He could feel the tension vibrating through her where her thigh was still pressed alongside his.

"Has he seen you ride?" he asked.

Because he defied anyone to watch CJ ride and not recognize she was born to it.

"He came to the first couple of local rodeos where I competed. But he stopped coming once I started winning."

"His loss," he said simply.

"I keep telling myself that. But it's hard, not having him on my side. He's always been my biggest supporter." She was staring at a spot on the duvet, her thumb rubbing back and forth over the fabric. He caught her hand in his and gave it a squeeze.

"He'll come round. He has to. I refuse to believe that the father who raised you isn't smart enough to be proud of you following your dreams."

She stared at him, a stricken expression on her face. Then she blinked rapidly a few times and shook her head.

"Damn you. You snuck up on me then, nearly made me cry," she said, a rueful half-smile pulling at her mouth.

She looked so sweet and sexy, her eyes still glassy with unshed tears. He felt a powerful impulse to wrap her in his arms and tell her everything was going to be okay. That he'd make it okay for her.

It was so out of left field, so inappropriate, so alien to the way he usually felt in these kinds of situations, for a moment he didn't know what to do or say. So he fell back on something he knew he was good at, reaching out to pull her back down onto his chest, one hand palming the nape of her neck as he drew her into a kiss. She came willingly, her body warm against his, and it only took a few strokes of her tongue for the drumbeat of desire to fire up in his belly again.

He encouraged her to roll on top of him, and for long moments they simply kissed and explored one another with languid caresses. Then he drew one of her nipples into his mouth and she made a small animal sound that went straight to his cock and suddenly he needed to be inside her again.

Which was when it hit him that he'd only had the one condom in his wallet.

"What's wrong?" she asked, her hair a dark waterfall across his chest as she lifted her head so she could see his face.

"We're out of condoms," he said.

"Oh." She looked gratifyingly disappointed. "Guess we'll just have to get creative, then."

She wiggled her eyebrows, her hand slipping between them to wrap around his erection.

"Hold that thought," he said, then he gently disengaged and went on a quick hunt through the drawers closest to the bed.

After all, Sierra's friends had been staying here, and they were in their twenties. There was a chance someone might have—

"Hallelujah," he said, retrieving an almost-full box of condoms from one of the drawers.

"Well played," she said as he rejoined her, a single foil square between his teeth. She plucked it from his lips and tore the packet open, then pushed him onto his back.

He watched as she eased the latex onto his cock, rolling it down with leisurely intent. He waited until she was about to climb on board again before overbalancing her and rolling on top, his hips coming to rest naturally within the cradle of her thighs.

"Hey," she said.

"My turn to be in charge," he said.

Then he took hold of his cock and stroked himself along the seam of her sex. She was slick with need already, and she let out a little hum of pleasure as he found the swollen bead of her sex with the head of his cock. He rocked there, back and forth, back and forth, until her hands found his ass. Then he gave in to his own desire and her urging and slid inside her.

She was so slick and hot and tight he felt his control slip, even though this was the second time and he'd fooled himself into believing he'd have a better grip on his need this time around.

"Oh, God, that feels so good," she breathed.

Her eyes were half closed, her mouth open and pink, her nipples hard with arousal. He stroked into her, deep and steady, watching her face when he was seated deep, loving the way her breath hitched and her knees pressed against his hips. He lowered his mouth to her breast, taking a rosy tip into his mouth. Her hips lifted, urging him deeper, her hands clenching into his ass. He switched to her other breast and slipped a hand between her legs.

"Oh…wow…that's… Don't stop," she moaned as he started to stroke her in time with each thrust. He'd watched carefully when she pleasured herself earlier and he followed her lead, increasing his tempo as her breathing became more urgent and erratic.

"Yes, please. Oh, Jesse… *Jesse.*"

He'd planned to make her come at least twice before he let himself go but the sound of his name on her lips was too much for him. He thrust into her, over and over, as her body gripped his in tight spasms. Then suddenly he was coming so hard he forgot to breathe, his whole body racked with pleasure.

He collapsed on top of her afterward, his breath sawing in and out of his lungs, his body damp with sweat. Her hands were still clawed into his back and he felt her grip loosen as her body softened into the mattress.

After a beat he lifted his head and used one hand to push her hair off her face. She smiled up at him, her eyes soft, her mouth pink and slightly swollen-looking, and he found himself smiling back.

The smile slowly faded from her lips but he didn't look away. Now was usually the time when he made an excuse about having to be on the road early, but he didn't want or need an excuse to leave CJ.

He wanted to be right where he was, and he wanted it with an intensity and a certainty that should have scared the hell out of him.

Except it didn't.

Chapter Nine

CJ STARED INTO Jesse's deep green eyes and understood she was teetering on the brink of doing something even more foolish than sleeping with one of her fellow competitors.

She was a grown-up. She understood what happened between men and women on the road as they followed the rodeo circuit around. What was happening right now in this bed was sex, and only sex. She needed to remember that, despite how good it was, despite how good *he* was, despite the way he was looking at her as though he'd just discovered something new and special and precious in the world.

There wasn't a doubt in her mind that Jesse Carmody had had more than his fair share of casual encounters in his time on the road. The man was sinfully good-looking, he clearly liked women, and he had charm to spare. Plus he was a rising rodeo star who appeared regularly on the leaderboard. In other words, he was a walking, talking invitation for a woman to park her brain at the door and let her libido take over.

She might have taken up that invitation, but that didn't mean she had to compound her recklessness by starting to believe this meant something—because that really would be foolish.

"Think I might need to use the bathroom," she said.

He dropped a kiss onto her lips before rolling to the side. CJ briefly debated trying to find her T-shirt, then gave a mental shrug. He'd already seen everything she had to see. She made the short trip to the bathroom end of the Airstream naked, then shut the sliding door and took care of business.

She spared a glance for her reflection in the small mirror as she washed her hands afterward. She looked exactly like a woman who'd just had several of the best orgasms of her life with a very sexy and charming man—hair tousled, cheeks pink, eyes more than a little shiny with satisfaction and misplaced hope.

"Forget about the hope bit," she muttered to her reflection. "It's never going to happen."

Then she took a deep breath and opened the door. Jesse was lying on his back in the bed at the other end of the trailer, shoulders propped on pillows, arms folded behind his head. The duvet barely covered his crotch, and golden light spilled over his body, showcasing his hard-muscled belly, chest and shoulders.

Against all odds, she felt a fresh surge of need stir her blood. This man floated her boat, big-time.

He watched her openly as she walked to the bed, unashamedly studying her the way she'd just studied him. The admiration in his eyes was both flattering and dangerous. If she let herself, she could get very carried away with Jesse Carmody.

Just as well she had no intention of crossing that line.

He folded back the duvet for her when she climbed onto the bed and she slipped in beside him. He didn't hesitate to pull her close, one arm around her shoulders.

"I guess we should probably try to get a little shut-eye," he said, his reluctance obvious.

"We probably should."

He leaned across to flick off the overhead lamp as she rolled onto her side. She felt him come in behind her, his arm slipping over her hip, his callused hand sliding up to rest possessively over one of her breasts.

His chest was hot and hard against her back, and she could feel his breath on the nape of her neck, warm and slightly moist, and it felt so good and right that she had to swallow an unexpected lump of emotion. Unexpected because she knew she wasn't supposed to feel this way about a man she'd only just met. A man who was going to be her competitor and colleague again come tomorrow morning.

This is not real, she reminded herself. *This is just sex, for one night.*

The thought triggered the realization she'd yet to have a certain difficult conversation with the man wrapped around her body. It was tempting to be a coward and put it off until the morning, when there would be plenty of awkwardness to go around, but she'd never been one to delay unpleasant tasks.

"There's something I need to ask you," she said. Her belly muscles tensed but she tried to keep her voice casual, relaxed. "Tomorrow, when we're at the rodeo... I can't afford for the other guys to know about this."

There was a long pause before he responded, the only sound the gentle tap-tap of rain hitting the trailer's roof.

"You think I'm going to run around bragging about getting you into bed?" He sounded both pissed off and offended.

"I hope not. You don't seem like the type of guy who'd do that. But we barely know each other, so I'm asking you directly to keep this private, just between us." She could hear how stiff and defensive her words sounded, but they were honest words, and she was speaking her truth to him. If he didn't want to hear it, didn't want to understand that she had a whole different set of pressures and standards hanging over her than he did, then he could exit the Airstream pronto and go back to his own bed.

"I don't talk about what's private. With anyone," he said.

She could feel the agitation in him, knew he was lying there behind her, stewing over what she'd said.

"Look, I didn't mean to insult you, but if the other guys find out about this, I'm the one who is going to look bad, not you. You'll get high fives; I'll get slut-shamed and judged. I'd love for that not to be the case, but right here and now that's exactly the way the world is and I want to have a career in rodeo if I can, not a reputation."

She wound up saying a lot more than she'd intended to, and the silence when she finished was profound. Then Jesse's arm tightened around her fractionally, and she felt the warm press of his lips against her shoulder.

"Don't apologize. I get it. It's bullshit, but I get it, and I don't want you having to deal with any of that, either."

Relief washed through her. Falling into bed with a hot cowboy at her first pro rodeo might not have been the brightest, wisest move she'd ever made, but at least she'd chosen a decent guy to do it with.

"Thank you."

He made a frustrated sound, then kissed the back of her neck. "You don't have to thank me. Go to sleep."

She smiled in the darkness, then closed her eyes. Her body was tired, but her mind was busy and she wasn't sure she was going to be able to follow his suggestion. She was very aware of him behind her, of all the places where his skin pressed against hers. She could feel each breath he took, each subtle shift of his body on the bed. What were the odds of her being able to tune all that out and slip into sleep?

After a few minutes, her brain surprised her by slowly slipping into shutdown mode, lulled by the sound of Jesse's even breathing and the soft pitter-patter of rain on the roof.

The last thing she remembered thinking before she fell asleep was that having Jesse Carmody keep her warm was something that would be dangerously easy to get used to.

SHE WOKE TO the awareness she wasn't in her own bed and that she wasn't alone. For a split second she was alarmed, then she felt the faint rasp as one of Jesse Carmody's legs rubbed against hers, and a world of sense memories downloaded into her brain all at once.

Jesse above her, watching her face as he slid inside her inch by inch. Jesse between her thighs, her hands fisted in his thick, dark hair. Jesse shuddering into climax, his big body hard as granite as he held her to him.

Right. That explained that, then.

She blinked a few times, trying to get her brain to move past a salacious blow-by-blow reliving of last night's events and onto today's challenges. Namely, navigating the morning after with Jesse's family playing witness to everything, and then the minor issue of competing in her first final at a pro rodeo.

Small potatoes. Nothing to get too excited about.

"Relax."

His voice came from behind her, sleep-roughened and husky, and just hearing it sent a little thrill through her body, thanks to all those sense memories still percolating through her bloodstream.

"I'm relaxed," she lied. "I just woke up."

"I can hear you thinking from here," he said. A large, warm hand landed in the middle of her back and moved in a soothing circle. "Here's what's going to happen," he said, his hand continuing to circle gently. "It's only five. I'm going to make you come again, then I'm going to go inside and pretend I spent the night in my bed. Then we're both going into town to kick ass in the short round."

She was lying on her stomach, her head turned toward the wall, and she levered herself up onto both elbows so she could look across at him. He was lying on his side, one hand still resting on her back. His jaw was shaded dark with stubble, and his hair stuck up in adorable tufts on top of his head.

"You always wake up this confident?"

"You telling me you don't want to come again?" he asked, a lazy, challenging glint in his eye.

She shrugged a shoulder, affecting a casualness she definitely did not feel. Hidden by the sheets, her nipples were already tightening in anticipation of his touch.

"I guess it'd be okay," she said with studied casualness.

His grin was slow and devastating. "Is that so?"

His gaze stayed on her face as his hand swept down her back, pausing to appreciate the curve of her butt cheek before sliding between her thighs. His eyes darkened as he discovered how ready she was for him already, his fingers sliding into slick heat. She did her damnedest to remain still, to win this game of chicken they were playing, but his fingers were too clever, too knowing. He stroked her folds, circling her entrance, teasing her by almost sliding inside her and then backing away. She wanted him to touch her *there* so badly, she had to hold her breath and grit her teeth to stop from moving.

"Poor baby," he said, laughter in his voice. "Is this what you want?"

His delving finger found the firm little bud hidden between her folds, slicking over it once, twice, three times. CJ abandoned all pretense at distance, clenching her hands into the sheet and widening her thighs to give him greater access.

"You like that?" he asked.

"Shut up and stop messing around," she growled.

He laughed, and she closed her eyes and lifted her hips into his maddening, delicious touch.

"You're so wet, baby. It blows my mind," he said, rolling closer so she could feel his cock against her side. He pressed himself against her in a sensual rhythm as his finger slid inside her.

It was amazing—but it wasn't enough. Opening her eyes, she reached for the box of condoms they'd left lying off to the very side of the bed. Securing a foil packet, she passed it to him.

"Don't make me ask twice."

He laughed, but he ceased his torture and she closed her eyes in gratitude when she heard the sound of the packet opening. There was a short pause, then she felt the weight and heat of Jesse's body pressing down on her own as he rolled on top of her. His hands found her hips to encourage her onto her knees, but she was already rising up, pressing back against his hardened cock.

He murmured something unintelligible before sliding inside her, thick and long, hard and fast.

"Yes," she breathed, and then she forgot everything else as he set a pace that soon had her arching her back and calling his name as she came hard around him. No sooner had she come back down to earth than he slid a hand around her hip and found her with his hand.

"No," she said, trying to bat him away. It was too soon and she was way too sensitive.

"Yes."

He stroked her gently at first, matching time with each deep, powerful thrust, and she groaned as everything coiled tight inside her again. He was with her when she came the second time, mouth pressed to her shoulder, his breath harsh in her ear as he shuddered his way to climax.

She collapsed onto the mattress, boneless, utterly wasted, and he rolled to one side. Her body was still pulsing with tiny residual shock waves as she opened her eyes and turned her head to look at him.

"Okay. You've convinced me on part A of your plan."

His eyes were closed, but a slow smile tugged at his mouth. "No kidding."

He looked pretty amazing, lying stretched across the bed, his body loose and relaxed. The light filtering through the Airstream's windows was tinted gold by the curtains, and he looked gilded, like a decadent statue in a French palace.

After a minute or two he stirred, sitting up to take care of the condom. Then he made the short walk to the other end of the trailer. The moment the door slid shut she scrambled out of bed and went in search of her panties. She found them on top of her saddle and managed to get them untangled and on before she heard the toilet flush. By the time the door opened, she had her T-shirt on and had folded his jeans, boxer briefs and T-shirt on the end of the bed. His gaze went from the neat pile of clothes to her, lingering on her panties.

"If getting dressed was supposed to make me want to leave, you have no idea how hot you look in those panties," he said.

"You need to get back up to the house," she reminded him, recognizing the glint in his eye. This man was insatiable, and, God help her, she was helpless where he was concerned.

"True."

He pulled his boxer briefs on, then his jeans. Next came his T-shirt before he sat to pull on his boots.

"I'll probably shower out here before coming up to the house," she said, feeling suddenly, unaccountably off-balance now that he was about to leave.

Once he walked out the door, everything that had happened between them would be in the past. They would no longer be lovers. This moment in time would be done.

It was a little scary how hollow the thought made her feel. Which was beyond dumb. She'd only met him two days ago. She'd spent a single night in his bed. The feelings tightening her chest and throat were both inappropriate and unjustified.

People didn't fall for each other this quickly. They simply didn't.

He pushed to his feet, and for a beat they just eyed each other, her barefoot in her panties and T-shirt, her hair a tangled mess, him in his boots and jeans, stubble peppering his jaw. His gaze was warm as it traveled her face, mapping her features. Then he reached for her, his thumb sliding along her jaw before he palmed the back of her head. He drew her to him slowly, his gaze never leaving hers, and his mouth was whisper-gentle on hers as he kissed her one last time.

The way he was holding her, the gentleness of his kiss— it was so sweet. But it was also goodbye, and she had to grit her teeth to stop herself from protesting as he took a step backward.

"See you up at the house," he said.

She smiled and nodded because it was beyond her to speak at that moment.

He opened the door. And then he was gone.

THE EARLY MORNING air smelled of damp earth and green things, thanks to last night's rain. Jesse made his way as quietly as he could toward the kitchen door. He eased his boots off when he reached the porch and padded on sock-clad feet to the door. Feeling sixteen again, he turned the handle, fully aware that one of his siblings might have woken in the night and decided to check the house was locked up tight. It turned easily beneath his hand, though, and he slipped into the darkened kitchen. Boots in hand, he made his way into the living room, then up the hallway to his bedroom. Once there, he shut the door and set down his boots before sinking onto the end of the bed.

So far, so good. He glanced at the clock and saw he could probably sneak a couple more hours of sleep before he needed to be up again. Shucking his jeans, he climbed under the covers and closed his eyes.

The idea of more sleep was fine in theory, but his mind was full of CJ. The smell of her, the taste of her, the tiny unconscious sounds she made. The warm silk of her hair sliding over his skin, the tensile strength of her lean, athletic body.

He'd been awake a full twenty minutes before her this morning, but he hadn't been restless or antsy. For the first time in his life, he'd simply been content to lie next to a naked woman and listen to her breathe. Not because he didn't want her again—he was pretty sure he would always want CJ—but because being with her, being near her, filled him with a quiet satisfaction and contentment.

He liked her, more than he could ever remember liking another person. She was straightforward and smart, brave and funny. She had guts and courage to spare, and sleeping with her last night had been one of the hottest experiences of his life.

And now it's over, so go to sleep and get over yourself, Carmody.

The voice in his head was right. He'd known going in they'd only have one night. There was no point wishing it could be otherwise.

He managed to grab another hour's rest, then he got up quietly and showered and dressed for the day ahead. He saw a dark-haired figure out on the porch at the rear of the house as he entered the kitchen, and he realized it was CJ, wearing a pair of black yoga pants and a long-sleeved T-shirt, working her way through a series of yoga poses.

He flicked the coffee machine on and stood at the window watching her move through what was obviously a well-practiced routine, her body fluid and powerful as she lunged, dipped and stretched. She was a pleasure to watch, a true athlete. He bet she'd be good at any sport she chose to turn her hand to.

After a few minutes she seemed to sense his presence, turning her head toward the window. Their eyes met and she smiled faintly, lifting a hand to wave. He waved back, then turned away to empty last night's dishes from the dishwasher. When he looked up again, CJ was gone.

"Ugh. I slept so deeply last night, I was like a log with hair."

Jesse looked over his shoulder as his sister shuffled toward the fridge, yawning widely.

"Coffee's on," he told her.

"Bless you. I take back all the bad things I ever said about you."

He smiled to himself as he dug out three mugs. "That's gonna take you some time, I bet."

"Who's that for?" Sierra asked, indicating the third mug.

"CJ. She was just on the porch, doing some yoga. I'm betting she'll be in soon."

Sierra looked pleased. "I told her the porch caught the morning sun. Plus there's a nice view across to Copper Mountain from there."

He made himself some toast, but he could feel Sierra studying him as he moved between the pantry and the fridge. He knew what she was trying to work out, busybody that she was. Even if he hadn't given his word to CJ, he wouldn't have let on he'd spent the night in the Airstream. Like he'd said to CJ, it was private. Possibly the most private, intimate experience he'd ever had.

Which didn't really bear thinking about right now, with his eagle-eyed little sister watching his every move.

"You coming into town for the pancake breakfast?" he asked.

"As if I'd miss it. Plus I have to be in town to see my brother ace the short round."

"What happened to wanting CJ to strike a blow for the sisterhood?"

"I want that, too. I've got a bet each way," Sierra said.

He poured two cups of coffee and took one to his sister. "I appreciate you looking out for CJ last night, by the way. Making her feel so welcome."

"You don't have to thank me for being kind to her. She's good people."

"Yeah, she is."

Sierra opened her mouth to say something else and he cocked an eyebrow, having a fair idea what she was about to ask. She looked suitably chastened and shut her mouth without saying a word.

Finally he was going to be allowed to have a little privacy, it seemed.

He heard footsteps on the porch, then the door to the kitchen opened and CJ entered, her long hair pulled into a ponytail that sat low on the back of her head, her legs clad in dark denim. She looked fresh and alive and fucking gorgeous and he directed his gaze at his coffee mug before he gave too much away to his too observant sister.

"Look at you. I bet you're a morning person," Sierra said. "You look like you're ready to conquer the world."

"I'll settle for conquering a single bronco," CJ said with a smile.

He got up and poured her coffee, sliding the mug onto the counter in front of her. Standing close to her, he could smell the minty freshness of her toothpaste and the bright scent of her deodorant. Her hair looked like glossy silk, and he had an almost uncontrollable urge to fist his hand around her ponytail and use it to pull her close for a kiss.

"I'm going to go check on that mare," he said.

Both Sierra and CJ looked a little startled by his sudden announcement, but he simply downed the last of his coffee and dumped his mug in the sink.

"Don't mind him. He is definitely *not* a morning person," he heard Sierra say as he left the house.

He crossed to the barn, walking into the smell of hay, warm animal, manure and earth. One of the two pregnant mares was on her side in her stall, her sides swollen with her foal. He made sure she had feed and water, then leaned against the stall door and simply watched her, his thoughts still back in the house.

Turned out it was going to be harder than he'd thought to keep his distance from CJ after last night. Probably because when it came right down to it, he didn't want to.

He wasn't sure where that left him. CJ had made it pretty clear this had been a one-night thing from her point of view. And yet he knew she'd felt it, too. The connection between them, the *something more* that had made last night bigger than just two bodies meeting in the darkness.

"How's she doing?"

He glanced over his shoulder as Jed joined him, taking in the mare's situation with an experienced eye.

"Seems comfortable. I've already taken care of her food and water."

"Thanks for that."

Jed leaned a hip against the stall, then shifted his feet. After a beat he straightened and adjusted the buckle on his belt. It wasn't like Jed to twitch or fidget, and it dawned on Jesse that his brother was nervous.

"What's up?" he asked, because he'd rather have whatever it was on the table than hanging between them. There were enough elephants in the barn already.

"I need to talk to you about the quarterly payment," Jed said. "Not sure how you're situated, but I might be a little late this month and I was hoping a delay wouldn't set you back any."

It took Jesse a moment to get his thoughts together, he was so surprised. Ever since their parents had died, Jed had insisted that even though he was running the day-to-day business of the ranch, he was doing so only as caretaker for all four of them, since they were all equal beneficiaries of their parents' will. Right from day one he'd followed a strict rule of thumb—any profits above wages, the costs of running the ranch and servicing the mortgage were shared equally between the four of them. Some quarters the payments were small, others they were large, but across twelve years Jed had always been scrupulous about meeting his self-imposed deadlines.

"I'm situated fine. You take as long as you need," Jesse said. "Like I said before, if you need to reinvest my share, I'm happy to throw it back into the pot."

Jed shook his head, his standard response to an offer Jesse had made many times over the years. "Appreciate it, but that won't be necessary. Payment should be with you by the middle of next month, if not sooner if I can swing it."

Jesse turned to face his brother fully. "So everything's going okay, then? Casey said the calving season wasn't so great this year."

"It was okay. Not our best, but not our worst, either." Jed's focus was on the mare again, his expression unreadable.

Jesse's gut told him there was more going on here, but there was no point pushing it if Jed didn't want to talk about it. His older brother could be stubborn as a mule when he wanted to be.

"Sierra seems pretty keen on me sticking around for a few more days once the rodeo is done," he said instead. "If there's anything you need a hand with for the next week, I'd be happy to pitch in."

Jed glanced at him, clearly taken off guard by his offer, and for a moment Jesse thought he'd caught a flash of something that almost looked like relief in his brother's eyes.

"There's a run of fencing I've been wanting to upgrade, but Casey and I haven't gotten around to it. Might be good to get it out of the way while you're in town," Jed said.

"Count me in, then," Jesse said.

Jed nodded, then a frown appeared between his eyebrows. "Wages might not be coming your way until next month, same as your quarterly payment. If that's a problem—"

"It isn't," Jesse said quickly. "And you don't need to pay me for a few days' work. Consider it a fair exchange for room and board."

"I'll pay you, like everyone else," Jed said. He was still frowning, but there was color in his cheeks now.

He was embarrassed.

It was such a revelation, Jesse didn't know where to look. For a long time now, his brother had seemed impenetrable, implacable, unreachable. And yet here he was, proving he had emotions after all.

"Better go make a few calls before we head into town," Jed said, pushing away from the stall door.

"You're coming in?" Jesse asked.

"What's the point of competing in your hometown if there's no one to cheer you on?" Jed said, his mouth stretching briefly into one of his rare smiles.

For a heartbeat he looked like the old Jed, the Jed who'd practiced football plays with him in the back paddock when they were both kids.

Then he was walking away, back and shoulders straight as always, and it felt as though Jesse had missed an opportunity.

Chapter Ten

EITHER JESSE'S SISTER was an Academy Award-worthy actress, or she genuinely had no inkling he'd spent the night in CJ's bed. The way Sierra chatted to her over coffee, easy and relaxed, ending any lingering concerns CJ had in that area.

Which just left her with the not-so-easy task of maintaining her game face when Jesse was in the same room. It had been bad enough before, when she'd simply been aware of him, but now it was as though her sensitivity had been supercharged. When he returned to the kitchen not long after Jed put in an appearance, she knew the second he entered the room. She knew when he poured himself a second cup of coffee, even though she didn't dare glance his way. She knew when he checked his phone. She was conscious of every gesture he made and everything he said, and acting as though she wasn't, as though she was just hanging in the kitchen with the Carmodys, nothing to see here, was a major, concerted effort.

It was a huge relief when Jed suggested they get moving

if they wanted pancakes before the rodeo kicked off again. She'd already stripped the bed and put the sheets in the washing machine, and she ducked out to the Airstream to transfer her gear to her truck. By the time she'd finished, the Carmodys were tramping down the front steps, arguing over whose truck to take into town.

"We can all fit in my truck," Jesse was saying, but Sierra pulled a face.

"I don't want to be trapped in town until you want to leave," she said. "I'll take my own truck."

"Suit yourself," Jesse said with an easy shrug.

"I was going to drive in," Jed said, car keys already in hand. "You can come home with me, Sierra."

"Same argument, different brother. How do I know you won't want to catch up with one of your buddies at Grey's?"

Jed fixed her with a look. "How many Sunday afternoons have I spent at Grey's lately?"

"Okay, true, your social life is truly dismal. But I'm still taking my own truck."

"Then I guess it's going to be a Carmody convoy," Jesse said.

"With a Cooper caboose," Sierra added, a cheeky smile on her lips.

"Yeah," Jesse said. His expression was admirably blank, but there was no mistaking the desire in his eyes when CJ's gaze met his.

She looked away almost immediately, but she could feel

heat crawling into her cheeks. Damn, she was going to have to get better at handling eye contact with him really quickly or she'd be spending the whole rodeo avoiding looking his way.

"Before we go, I wanted to thank you all for making me feel so welcome last night. Not really sure what I would have done if you hadn't been so kind," CJ said.

"You're more than welcome," Jed said, offering her a small, sweet smile.

Casey ducked his head in acknowledgment, back to being the quiet guy after last night's slow thaw to friendliness over dinner. She'd quickly worked out that he was the shy one in the family, and it blew her mind more than a little that she'd seen him on stage Friday night, holding the crowd in the palm of his hand.

"You have to come stay with us next time the rodeo is in town, too," Sierra said. "Even though you'll probably be a big star by then."

"I love how much faith you have in me," CJ said, laughing and shaking her head.

"I've got eyes in my head," Sierra said.

They all climbed into their respective trucks, and there was a chorus of engines starting. CJ waited until Jesse pulled out before falling in behind him, Sierra and Jed falling into place behind her. As Jesse said, it was a Carmody convoy.

CJ used the twenty-minute drive into town to try to clear her mind and prepare mentally for her ride. There were too many distractions vying for her attention—Jesse, the situation with Maynard, the nagging disappointment that her father hadn't bothered to make contact. She needed to put all that aside for the next few hours and focus on the short round. Until it was done, nothing else mattered.

Then she hit the outskirts of town and her phone started chirruping with a number of incoming messages and notifications. She risked a glance at the screen while waiting at a red light. There were three calls from home, and three texts from her mom.

Something loosened in her chest. The odds were good those calls were from her father, and the knowledge that he'd tried to make contact with her went a long way toward salving her wounded feelings on that front. She itched to return the call, but managed to hold back on the impulse until she'd pulled into a parking spot at the rodeo grounds. Sierra had explained there was a pedestrian bridge over the river that connected the rodeo and fairgrounds with downtown, and she could see the Carmodys waiting for her. Grabbing her jacket and phone, she slipped out of her car to join them.

"I need to return a phone call," she explained quickly. "Why don't you go ahead and I'll catch up?"

She could tell by the way Jesse hesitated that he wanted to wait for her but she deliberately didn't make eye contact with him. If the two of them arrived at the pancake breakfast together without the escort of his family, talk would be inevitable.

"We'll save a seat for you," Sierra said.

"Thanks. I won't be long."

The Carmodys moved off, Jesse among them. He glanced back at her briefly, and she gave him a small smile that was both acknowledgment and thanks for being discreet. He responded with a barely discernible nod.

CJ transferred her attention to her phone, reading her mother's text messages—three repeats of "please call me the moment you get this"—before listening to her voicemail. The first message was from her father, his gruff, deep voice asking her to call home when she had a chance. The following two voicemail messages were from her mother, each of them variations on "why aren't you picking up?"—her mother's tone becoming more concerned with each one. CJ swore under her breath. Thanks to the terrible coverage out at the Carmody ranch, her mother was probably imagining CJ dead in a ditch somewhere.

She called home and wrapped an arm around herself as she waited for the call to connect. It was stupid, but she felt nervous about finally talking to her father. She might be reconciled to his disapproval on one level, but she knew if he said the wrong thing during this call, it was going to mess with her head. Not to mention her heart.

The phone rang and rang. CJ imagined her father rushing across from the barn or her mother finishing something in the kitchen, but eventually the call simply rang out.

Frowning, she tried again, and again it rang out. She checked the time—nine a.m. on a Sunday morning. She couldn't imagine why her parents wouldn't be home.

Unless something bad had happened.

Calm down, Cooper. No need to be a drama queen.

She called her mom's phone next, growling in the back of her throat with frustration when it cut across to voicemail. She left a brief but hopefully reassuring message: "Mom, it's me. Sorry I didn't get your messages last night. I couldn't get a signal where I was. Everything's fine with me, though. Call me when you can, okay?"

She hovered on the verge of calling one of her brothers for reassurance, just in case something was up, but then common sense reasserted itself. If something really bad had happened with her folks, her brothers or sisters-in-law would have made sure she was in the loop. This was more than likely just a very prosaic case of mutual missed phone calls, and she was allowing her jittery nerves about the day ahead to turn a mountain into a molehill.

She had to pass through the contestants' camping grounds on the way to the footbridge, and she studied the various trailers her fellow competitors used as both accommodation and horse transport as she passed by. Some were large, elaborate and obviously new; others looked as though they were held together with superglue and duct tape. She'd seen inside a few and knew they offered pretty spare accommodation—bed, tiny kitchen, an itty-bitty living space. She also knew having a trailer was the most economical way to live and travel on the circuit—if that was what a person wanted to do.

It was what she wanted to do, very much, but until she'd proven she could hold her own, decisions about trailers would have to wait another day.

She had to dodge the darkened circles of a number of extinguished campfires in the open spots between trailers as she walked and she guessed there'd been a few cowboys partying here last night. She wondered if Dean Maynard had been among them, laughing it up with his cronies over the prank he'd pulled on CJ.

Most likely. He was exactly the type of man who'd brag about his "brave" act. And she bet there'd been a few of her fellow contestants who'd laughed along with him, too.

The thought left a sour taste in her mouth and she made a concerted effort to leave her dark thoughts behind as she stepped onto the footbridge. The Marietta River flowed fast and strong beneath the timber planks, and the smell of cool water and wet stone rose to meet her. The sky was a clear, pale blue with all the hallmarks of turning into a fine day, and a brisk breeze brought the sound of people laughing, along with the smell of hot butter and sugar. Right on cue, her stomach rumbled, letting her know it was ready for more than the cup of coffee she'd had out at the Carmody ranch.

She lengthened her stride as she walked through the park toward the courthouse, only slowing when she reached the area in the park that had been set up for the pancake break-fast. Folding tables and chairs were arranged in long rows, most of them occupied, while a makeshift kitchen was busy with volunteers. Customers formed a snaking queue, patient-ly waiting their turn to be served.

It only took her a moment to spot Jesse's dark head at one of the tables, and almost the moment she did so, he glanced up and their gazes locked. Mindful there were rodeo people everywhere and that Sierra was sitting right next to him, she bit back the smile that wanted to curve her mouth and instead made her way to their table.

"Perfect timing. Casey and Jed are in line. I'll go help them wrangle plates," Sierra said, pushing back her chair and jumping to her feet. "You okay with syrup and whipped butter?"

"Sounds amazing, thank you," CJ said.

"Especially because we don't have to cook any of it or clean up afterward," Sierra joked before heading off to join her brothers in the line.

Leaving CJ alone with Jesse.

After the briefest of hesitations, she slipped into the chair opposite him.

"Was the missed call from your father?" he asked.

"One of them. The rest were from my mom."

"So you spoke to him?"

"I couldn't get ahold of them." She shrugged.

"The signal's fine here in town—they'll call back," he

said.

She nodded, unable to stop herself from looking around to see if anyone had noticed them sitting together.

"Being seen eating pancakes with me won't turn you into a scarlet woman, CJ," he said quietly.

"Being seen eating *breakfast* with you might," she countered. "If Dean Maynard saw us sitting together right now, how long do you think it would be before there was a rumor going round that you'd scored with the new girl?"

She knew the comment hit home because he sat back in his chair a little, his gaze doing a quick, assessing sweep of the surrounding tables. She had no idea if he recognized anyone, but the smile was gone from his eyes when he next looked at her. She felt shitty for making things awkward— then she reminded herself she wasn't the one who'd made the double standard that still governed so many women's lives, all over the world. She wasn't the one who called a man a stud and a woman a slut for doing the exact same thing— she just had to live with the consequences of either abiding by the unspoken rules or defying them.

"Hope you like syrup, because Sierra was beyond heavy-handed," Casey said over her shoulder, and she drew back a few inches as he slid a stack of pancakes in front of her, syrup slopping dangerously close to the rim of the plastic plate.

"The pancakes suck that syrup up like nobody's business," Sierra said, grabbing the seat beside Jesse. "Besides, CJ said she likes it."

"This is true, I do," CJ confirmed.

Jed took the seat beside her, with Casey sliding into place on her other side. There was a minor squabble over whether Jed had collected enough plastic cutlery for them all—he had—before they settled down to feasting on some of the fluffiest, most delicious pancakes CJ had ever had.

"I don't know what they put in these things but they are insanely good," she said as she started on the last of her stack.

"Sugar, butter, and more sugar, is my best guess," Sierra said around a mouthful of food.

"That's beautiful, Squirrel. Show the world what you've got," Casey said.

CJ raised a quizzical eyebrow. "Squirrel. Is that a family nickname?"

Sierra rolled her eyes. "Yes. And yes, it's the worst nickname ever."

"Could be worse. Could have been weasel," Jesse said, deadpan.

"Shut up, *Jessica*," Sierra said meaningfully.

"Jessica?" CJ asked, both eyebrows raised now.

"When he was three, Jesse used to spend half the day walking around in a pair of Mom's shoes. What were they, Jed? Stilettos?"

"All I remember is that they were red, with little bows on the front. And he used to kick up a real stink when Mom took them off him."

"Thanks, guys. Any time I can return the favor, I will,"

Jesse said, giving each of them a pointed look.

They were all too busy laughing to care, CJ noticed.

"What about you, CJ? You got a family nickname?" Sierra asked.

"Sure do." CJ tried to stop herself from smiling as she mopped up the last of her syrup with her final bite of pancake.

"You're not going to share?" Sierra asked, pouting comically.

"Do I look stupid?" CJ asked.

Across the table, Jesse was watching her, his green eyes narrowed speculatively.

"It's Monkey," he said suddenly, sitting back in his chair with a big smile on his face. "I'm right, aren't I?"

CJ gasped. "How did you—"

Then she remembered talking to him about learning to ride last night, telling him how her father had said she must be part monkey, and heat rushed up her chest and into her face.

Swear to God, she'd done more blushing around this man than she had in all previous twenty-seven years of her life.

"He *is* right," Sierra said, clearly delighted by the discovery. Then she frowned. "But how on earth did you guess that?"

Jesse gave a casual shrug. "Just something CJ said yesterday."

His gaze met hers, his green eyes dancing with laughter, and it took every bit of willpower she had not to kick him under the table. Using their pillow talk as ammunition was dirty pool, and he knew it.

"What goes around comes around. Just remember that," she said.

He laughed, and she couldn't stop herself from grinning back at him. Then she realized the rest of the Carmodys were looking either avidly interested—Sierra—or faintly awkward—Casey and Jed.

"I should get back to the grounds. Get my gear sorted," she said, trying to smooth over the moment.

She started collecting everyone's plates, only stopping when Casey cleared his throat.

"Mind if I finish first?" he asked as he tugged his half-finished plate from her hands.

"Of course. Sorry. I'll just, um, get rid of these…" CJ stood and made a beeline for the nearest garbage can, rolling her eyes at herself.

Apparently she sucked at being discreet. Which boded well for the rest of the day. Not.

She took as long as she possibly could getting rid of their plates, and when she got back to the table Jesse's seat was empty.

"He said he had to catch up with someone," Sierra said. "And he'll see you at the arena."

"Great. I should get going, too. Thanks again for everything. You really saved my bacon last night. If any of you are ever in Plentywood, please let me return the favor," CJ said.

"Done," Sierra said, standing and giving CJ a quick hug. "I'll be cheering for you."

"Thank you."

CJ smiled at the remaining Carmody brothers and then turned back toward the river. She made her way back across the bridge, her gaze constantly scanning the crowd ahead, and it wasn't until she was nearly at her car that she admitted to herself she was looking for Jesse.

So dumb. She needed to stay away from him, not just because she had precious little control over her reactions when he was around. He scrambled her brain, sent her thoughts careening back to last night, made her want things that were never going to happen. And she needed to focus. She needed to be clear-headed and sharp, completely on her game. Today was important, something she'd worked toward for months. She'd endured her father's disapproval to be here, not to mention the ugly resentment of Dean Maynard and his ilk.

Don't mess this up because of a hot cowboy with pretty eyes, she warned herself.

It took her two trips to transfer her gear to the locker rooms. The physical labor helped to center her, but she was aware of the background buzz of adrenaline starting to work its way through her body.

Not long now.

Soon, she would be in the chute, and the world would narrow down to her and the bronc she'd drawn and the question of whether she could last eight seconds or not. If the answer to that question was yes, if her bronc put up a good fight, if the judges liked what they saw, she had a chance of winning this thing.

There were a lot of "ifs" in that equation, she couldn't help but notice, and she didn't have control over any of them.

Taking a deep breath, she started working her way through her pre-ride stretches, warming up her arms, legs and torso.

All she could do was be prepared, mentally and physically. The rest was out of her hands.

Chapter Eleven

J ESSE SPENT HALF an hour with Major, taking him for a walk around the grounds, then giving him his head in the practice arena. Afterward, he led the gelding back to his pen and made sure he had enough feed and water before giving him a light brush. All the while, he chewed over what had happened at the pancake breakfast.

CJ's anxiety about being linked to him had been a palpable thing until his family joined them at the table, unwittingly providing a smokescreen for the two of them. He couldn't blame her for being worried—she'd been right about what Maynard would do and say if he'd spotted them together. If he got wind of the fact that Jesse had spent the night in CJ's bed, he'd turn it into something dirty and low and use it to shame CJ. He'd claim it was proof CJ's inclusion in the pro saddle bronc competition would only cause trouble. He'd probably even cite Jesse's inevitable defense as proof that introducing women into the competition was divisive. He'd ensure that every time CJ walked into a room, she'd be subjected to knowing looks and speculation.

There was no upside to Jesse and CJ's involvement becoming public, at all. Especially for CJ.

And yet Jesse had wanted to hold her hand across the table at breakfast. He'd wanted to laugh into her eyes and tease her just so he could watch her rise to the challenge. He'd wanted to hear more about her life and tell her more of his own.

Which left him with a problem, because she had made it very clear she didn't want to get entangled with anyone, let alone a fellow rider.

Major nickered quietly, turning to press his head against Jesse's side, and Jesse smoothed a gentle hand down his shoulder.

"My timing could definitely be better, huh?"

He walked to his trailer afterward to collect his gear, conscious of the roar of the crowd in the arena. He checked his watch and realized the bareback short round was already underway. He let himself into his trailer and piled his vest and chaps on top of his saddle. Sitting on his bed, he pulled off his regular boots and swapped them out for a much-abused pair that were a full size larger than he usually wore. He shook a generous cloud of talcum powder down the shaft before pulling them on. The powder and the larger boot size made it easier to slip his foot free if he happened to get hung up in the stirrups during his ride. It was an old rodeo trick, and it had saved him a broken leg more than once over the years.

His thoughts kept turning to CJ as he fastened his spurs to his boots and strapped on his chaps. She must be nervous. This was her first final and she was bound to be feeling the pressure. He wished he could stand by her, offer his support, but that would only create talk. Feeling more than a little frustrated, he left his trailer, his saddle under one arm and his protective vest under the other.

The steer-wrestling event was announced over the speakers as he made his way behind the bleachers. Foot traffic was thin, with most folks in their seats taking in the action in the arena. The smell of popcorn and hot dogs was heavy in the air as the various food trucks geared up for lunch.

There was still a good half hour before the saddle bronc short event but a number of his fellow riders were already gathered near the chutes when he arrived. Some sat in their saddles on the ground, practicing marking out, while others stretched or prepped their saddles with rosin. His gaze gravitated to where Dean Maynard was holding court with a bunch of his buddies. Most of them looked worse for wear, and Jesse guessed they'd been up half the night, drinking and partying.

A week ago, he'd have called these men friends—not close friends, true, but he'd hung out with them, shared beers with them, partied with them. Now he was hard pressed not to spit in the dirt at the sight of them. What Maynard had done to CJ was petty, low and pathetic, and the man deserved to have his butt kicked from here to

Pasadena.

Jesse was sorely tempted to do just that, rules be damned. The knowledge that it was the last thing CJ wanted was the only thing that stopped him from walking over and feeding Maynard his fist. She was determined to play this her way, to forge her own path, and he had no right to overrule her wishes.

Then Maynard let loose a loud guffaw. Jesse's hands curled into fists and he took a step forward. Never had he wanted to rearrange another man's features so badly in all his life.

He was still hovering on the edge of decision when he caught sight of CJ making her way toward the chute, her stride long and confident as she wove her way through the crowd. She was wearing her black Stetson and carrying her chaps, protective vest and saddle, the latter balanced confidently on her hip. He knew from experience it was no small load, but she made it look easy.

He forced himself to look away and loosen his fists. He wasn't going to get into it with Maynard today. He couldn't.

Not here and now, anyway.

Hunkering down, he pulled out his bar of rosin and began rubbing it along the swells of his saddle. Out of the corner of his eye he saw CJ dump her gear in a clear spot and begin her own ride prep. The sound of loud male laughter drew his gaze back to Maynard's posse. They were watching CJ as she went through her warm-up routine, clearly on the lookout for some sign Maynard's stunt had paid off.

What did they think they'd find? Traces of tears? Some sign she was hurt or cowed or intimidated? CJ was tougher than the lot of them put together. She could take whatever they had to dish out and more—but she shouldn't have to. She had exactly the same right to be here as any other rider, male or female, and it made Jesse's gut hurt that she'd had to take so much crap from a bunch of ignorant assholes.

A shadow fell over him and he looked up to find Shane Marvell at his shoulder, his eyes narrowed as he studied Maynard's group.

"What's going on with them today?" he asked, clearly unimpressed by the frat house vibe.

"You don't want to know," Jesse said darkly.

Shane gave him a sharp look, obviously picking up on Jesse's barely suppressed rage. "You okay?"

Jesse shrugged, not trusting himself to speak without spitting out a bunch of four-letter words. The truth was, his head was all over the place, his belly full of frustration and anger on CJ's behalf.

Shane glanced across at Maynard again. "Whatever it is, don't let it mess up your ride," he said before moving off to where he'd left his own gear.

It was good advice. Jesse had drawn a great bronc— Making Money had a reputation for giving showy, dangerous, high-scoring rides—and he had a good chance of winning or placing if he could make his eight seconds.

He needed to get into the zone and forget about everything else.

Easy in theory, but harder in reality when he couldn't turn off his awareness of CJ. She drew his gaze like a magnet, and he couldn't stop himself from watching as she finished strapping on her chaps, testing the buckles to make sure they were on good and tight around her denim-clad thighs. Satisfied, she reached down to snag her protective vest, shrugging into it and zipping it closed. Finally, she slipped her hat back on, the black brim shading her face.

She looked so tall and strong and composed as she tucked her fingers into the front pockets of her jeans and focused on what was going on over at the chutes. She had to be conscious of Maynard and his gaggle of idiots—how could she not be, the way they were blatantly staring at her, their eyes bright with ugly interest as they looked for some sign of weakness—but she didn't let on for a second she knew they even existed.

Pride swelled in him, along with a tight, hot surge of emotion that constricted his chest. She was amazing, unlike any other woman he'd ever met. He wanted her to go out into the arena and have the ride of her life so she could wipe the smug, knowing, satisfied grin off Maynard's face. In fact, he wanted her to win so soundly it set a new rodeo record. He couldn't think of a better way to prove all the haters wrong and set her on the road to where she wanted to be.

He was moving before he'd consciously made a decision

to do so, driven by the need to right the wrongs done to her. Her gaze met his as he stopped in front of her, her expression carefully blank, not giving anything away.

"I'm withdrawing," he said, quiet enough for only her to hear. He might not be able to punch Maynard's lights out in a civilized society, but he could do this for her.

Her eyes widened with shock. "What? Why? Are you okay?" Her gaze raked his body, looking for an injury.

"Because you can win this thing. I want you to win. I want you to wipe the arena with that asshole."

EVERYTHING IN CJ went still at Jesse's words. He was waiting for her response, his beautiful green eyes alight with purpose, and for a moment, she didn't know what to say.

Because there were so many things to say, so many feelings clamoring for expression. Hurt, surprise, disappointment, anger…

She'd thought he understood she was here to win or lose on her own merit, but one of them had got it wrong—and apparently it was her.

"So, what? You're going to bow out and hand me the win like it's a consolation prize?" she asked.

He frowned, taken aback by her response. Clearly he'd been expecting something else.

Gratitude, probably.

"No. Not a consolation prize."

"But it wouldn't be a real win, would it? Because you would have bowed out, and you're one of the top-ranked riders at this rodeo," she said, waiting for him to get it, to see how insulting his suggestion was when she'd worked so hard to get here.

He shook his head, and she could see he was both baffled and angry at her response. "I'm just trying to do the right thing here."

"The right thing is to *respect* me," she said fiercely, not taking her eyes from his. "The right thing is for you to go out there and do your best, and I'll do the same, and we'll let the damned judges decide who wins."

He blinked at the banked anger behind her words. "If that's what you want." He went to turn away, then decided he had something further to add. "I wanted to help. That's why I offered. No other reason."

Maybe when she was calmer, when she had more time to process, she'd be able to appreciate the misguided generosity behind his offer, but right now all she could see was how patronizing it was.

"How would you feel if one of your buddies made you the same offer?" she asked.

He shook his head in angry confusion. "That would never happen."

"I know, because they know you'd never be interested in a win you didn't truly earn, don't they?"

She didn't wait to see if her point hit home. Turning on

her heel, she walked away, even though she could hear the MC announcing the saddle bronc event. She could feel the rest of the riders watching her—watching *them*—but right at that moment she didn't give a hoot what any of them thought.

She stalked halfway to the practice arena before she stopped and took a half dozen deep breaths. She didn't have time for this. She didn't have time for any of the doubts and worries circling her mind. It didn't matter that she still hadn't heard from her parents. It didn't matter that she'd misjudged Jesse so badly—or, more accurately, projected qualities onto him that he didn't possess.

Lying in his arms last night, she'd started to think—

No. You can't do this right now. Get your shit together, woman.

She closed her eyes and tipped her head back, concentrating on the pure, simple warmth of the sun on her face. She took a deep breath, and when she exhaled, she consciously let all the bullshit go along with the air in her lungs. Then she opened her eyes, turned around and walked back to where she'd left her gear.

A few heads turned, Dean Maynard's among them. CJ ignored them all. She couldn't see Jesse, and for a moment she thought he'd gone through with his crazy idea of withdrawing from the event. Then she remembered he was riding early in the lineup and moved closer to the arena. There was an open spot between two cowboys, and she stepped up onto the rail and looked toward the chute just as the MC's voice blared over the speaker.

"Coming up next is Jesse Carmody, another local boy and one of the leading riders on the circuit this year. Jesse's riding Making Money, a three-year-old stallion with an ornery reputation, so we are sure to see some action here today, folks."

CJ's gaze was locked on the chute where Jesse was easing himself into the saddle. The bronc moved restlessly beneath him, but Jesse simply waited him out before gathering up his rein in his right hand and lifting his left hand away from his body. He tucked his chin into his chest, the brim of his hat hiding his expression from her, and she found herself holding her breath as she waited for him to give the nod.

One second, two, three. Her lungs were starting to hurt, and she sucked in air—just as his head ducked in a brief but firm signal to the gate man.

The gate swung wide in a smooth arc and Jesse spurred his bronc out into the ring, marking the horse out with ease on the first jump. The crowd cheered as Jesse slipped into a teeth-jarring rhythm, shifting to counter every violent kick and twist the bronc threw at him.

The horse spun, then kicked viciously, and Jesse teetered on the brink of losing his balance. CJ was counting the seconds off in her mind, but time seemed to stretch impossibly as she willed him to make it. And then the whistle went and CJ released her death grip on the rail as the pickup riders came alongside Jesse to help him off. He levered his body off the still-bucking bronc and steadied himself one handed on the pickup horse's flank before landing on his feet in the dirt so neatly CJ couldn't help but grin at his skill.

Her gaze went immediately to the scoreboard and the crowd grew quiet as they all waited. The screen lit with two red numbers—eighty-six. Jesse lifted a hand in a triumphant wave, a smile on his lips as he acknowledged the score and the judges. Then he scooped up his hat and walked off the arena, his chaps flaring with every step.

Eighty-six was a good score, maybe even a great score. In all likelihood, it would be the score to beat today.

She wasn't sure how she felt about needing to beat Jesse's score to win. Then she conceded it was something she'd need to get used to pretty damn quickly if she was going to stay on the circuit and try to turn this crazy obsession of hers into a career.

This is why it was a really dumb idea to sleep with him, a little voice whispered in the back of her head. She swatted it away. She had enough crap weighing her down already without generating more of her own.

She was about to drop down off the rail when she glanced across and saw Dean Maynard climbing over the top of the chute. She hadn't realized he was up next, having deliberately blanked any mention of his name. She hesitated, then decided to stay and watch him ride. With a bit of luck she'd get to see him eat dirt. Maybe he'd even get stomped on—preferably in the groin. That ought to stop him from peeing on anyone else's belongings for a while.

"Our next rider is Dean Maynard, out of Texas…"

There was an unusual stir in the stands as the MC continued with his spiel, drawing her attention away from the chute. At first CJ didn't understand what was happening. Lifting her hand to shade her eyes against the bright sunlight, she stared at the bleachers.

People were standing, sometimes two or three at a time, and turning their backs on the arena. Then CJ noticed they were all women, and that their odd behavior was causing a ripple effect across the bleachers, rolling across the crowd in a wave until there was a sea of women standing, two here, three there, a whole row somewhere else, all with their backs turned to the arena.

Refusing to watch Dean Maynard ride.

"What the…?" CJ muttered under her breath.

In the stands, people were talking and looking around, trying to work out what the standing women knew that they didn't.

Something Sierra said last night came back to CJ then. *If people knew what he'd done to you, they wouldn't want to cheer for him or treat him like a hero. They wouldn't even want to spit on his shoes.* And she knew suddenly that Sierra had somehow gotten the word out about what Maynard had done to her, and the women of Marietta had chosen to take a stand—literally.

The realization brought hot tears to CJ's eyes. She'd decided to take the high road after her conversation with Sierra last night, and she'd convinced herself that would be okay, that she could live with her decision. But this…this was so much better than quiet dignity. This was exactly what a coward like Dean Maynard deserved for his foul deed—a public shunning.

"My goodness, not sure what's going on here," the MC said. "Someone want to let the rest of us in on the joke? No? Then we'd better let this rider out of the gate."

CJ blinked and sniffed away tears, turning her focus back to the chute where Dean Maynard still sat, one leg on either side of the top rail as he stared out at the stands. He looked confused—and more than a little angry.

CJ's mouth curved into the smallest of smiles.

Karma is a bitch, dirtbag.

One of the officials leaned in to say something to Maynard, who shook his head impatiently and gestured the man away. Then he climbed fully into the chute, sliding into the saddle with more haste than finesse.

CJ glanced across at the stands where hundreds of backs were still turned and felt a wash of chest-expanding gratitude. Sierra Carmody didn't know it, but she was getting the biggest damned hug in the world once this event was over. And maybe some emotional tears, the kind women only shed with each other.

The gate was swinging open when she looked back at the

chute.

The bronc spun out into the arena with a wild kick, and Maynard managed to mark it out, although it was a close-run thing, his boots barely clearing the horse's shoulders. Things went downhill quickly from there, the bronc's unpredictable spins and kicks throwing Maynard off-center in the saddle. There was barely four seconds on the clock when he got so much air under him there was no way he could recover.

He hit the ground belly first, eating a face full of dirt. For a long beat he just lay there, not moving. Then he shoved himself to his feet with jerky, angry motions and stalked to the railing, leaving his hat in the arena for the pickup riders to collect.

CJ let go of the rail and dropped to the ground. There was only one more rider before it was her turn, but she lingered by the rail as long as she could, giving Maynard time to clear the chute area. When she could wait no longer, she went to collect her saddle and hand it over to the rough stock team so they could prepare her bronc.

Nerves jumped in her belly as she hovered near the chute, watching Shane Marvell check the cinch on his saddle alongside the flank man before climbing over the rail. A familiar dark-headed cowboy clung to the side rail, offering Shane last-minute advice. The two men bumped fists, then Jesse dropped to the ground and took a step backward, giving his friend room to gather himself before dropping into the saddle.

CJ allowed herself a single quick glance at Jesse's face. He looked grim, his jaw set, and she guessed he was still pissed off after their fight.

Regret bit her. Maybe she hadn't handled his offer too well. Maybe she could have explained herself better. But maybe he could have stopped to think about what his offer to pull out said about his respect for her ability, too.

It doesn't matter. He's just a guy you slept with when you shouldn't have. In other words, a mistake.

Even though it hadn't felt like a mistake last night, or even this morning.

She jerked her eyes and her thoughts back to the arena as the clang of the gate opening sounded, releasing Shane and his bronc into the arena.

Which meant she was up next.

Adrenaline washed through her in a wave, stealing her breath and making her fingers tingle. She shook her hands out, then reached up and tugged nervously on her ponytail, checking the elastic was still holding it tight. Her pulse pounded hard and fast in her neck, and she could feel cold sweat beneath her arms.

Shit was getting real. And it was about to get even more real, because her bronc was being fed into the chute, her saddle on its back. Jumpin' Jack was a four-year-old stallion, a circuit veteran known for his power and unpredictability. At the previous rodeo he'd spun out of the gate and smashed his rider into the rail, breaking the rider's leg. The rodeo before that, he'd taken his rider to the top of the leaderboard and sent him home with a pocket full of prize money.

In other words, this bronc did not do half measures.

The flank man caught her eye and gestured her over. She moved closer and leaned over the lower rail to check the cinch on her saddle. When she straightened, she gripped the lower edge of her vest, pulling it down firmly. Then she climbed up to straddle the top rail.

This was the moment when Jesse had grabbed her elbow yesterday and told her to enjoy herself.

That was yesterday. This is today. Let's do this.

She lifted her leg over the rail and leaned across the bronc's back to grip the rail on the other side, taking some of her body weight through her arms. Only then did she rest a boot on the horse's rump to let him know she was coming. Jumpin' Jack lifted his head and tried to kick out, but the chute constrained him and he quickly settled. It was enough of an invitation for CJ. She eased her leg over the saddle, then slid down, making sure she felt the hard clink of the stirrups hitting her boot heels. Then and only then did she shift forward so her thighs were tucked in nice and tight behind the swells of the saddle. Someone handed her the rein, and she measured the length she'd worked out based on the horse's size and her own reach before positioning the plaited rope across her palm and locking her fist around it.

She lifted her free hand high, out of the way, and tucked

her chin to her chest. Then she took a moment to simply breathe.

She'd trained for months, eaten the right food, punished her body with workout after workout. She'd studied endless footage of other riders and practiced on countless mechanical bulls and bronc simulators. She'd ridden her way to qualifying for a pro ticket, defying expectations as well as her father.

And now she was here, under the sun, in front of the crowd at the Copper Mountain Rodeo.

She wet her lips. Took a deep breath.

Then she nodded.

Chapter Twelve

THE GATE SWUNG open and she made sure she got her boots good and high on Jumpin' Jack's shoulders as he lunged into the arena. There was no time to think after that. The stallion bucked and kicked, twisting in the air, doing his damnedest to shake her off. She twisted and bent, ducked and wove with him, countering move for move, thighs pressed tight against the saddle as her body whipped back and forth.

The world shrank down to just the two of them, her and the bronc, locked in battle. Her thigh muscles burned; her shoulder felt as though it was going to pop from its socket. But still she held on.

Then she got too much air, and she felt herself lose her center.

Shit.

The shrill sound of the whistle cut through the roar of the crowd and a surge of elation filled CJ as she tumbled off the bronc and onto the back of the pickup horse that appeared at the exact right moment to save her.

"Well done, cowgirl," the rider yelled over his shoulder, his smile a mile wide.

CJ grinned, relief and triumph a heady brew in her bloodstream. The pickup rider wheeled in a circle, taking her back to the chute, and she dropped to the ground. Another pickup rider handed over her hat, and she thanked them both before turning to the scoreboard.

She didn't have long to wait, but it felt long enough. She closed her eyes when she saw the numbers flash up. Eighty-nine.

Eighty-freaking-nine.

She'd bettered yesterday's score. And she'd beaten Jesse.

Now hers was the score to beat. And if neither of the remaining two riders could do so… Then she'd won her first event at her first pro rodeo.

As vindications went, it didn't get much better than that.

Feeling more than a little dazed, she waved to acknowledge the cheering from the stands, then climbed out of the arena. Cowboys she didn't know or recognize thumped her on the back, congratulating her on her score. CJ thanked them, unable to hide her relief and happiness, even as she reminded herself she hadn't won, not yet.

Her score could be beaten in the next few minutes. Nothing was ever certain in rodeo.

Standing a few feet from the chute, she lifted shaking hands to tug the zipper open on her vest. Her thighs were trembling, too, and her neck and shoulders burned. She didn't care—she was too buzzed on adrenaline and hope.

Was it possible she could really win this thing?

"Great ride, Cooper," Shane said as he passed by, thumping her on the shoulder approvingly. "Looks like you got this thing in the bag."

"Don't go jinxing me," she said with a laugh.

"No one's gonna top that score," he said over his shoulder, lifting a hand in farewell as he disappeared in the crowd.

God, she hoped not. She turned back toward the arena, waiting to hear the next competitor's score—and all the while, she scanned the crowd, on the lookout for a certain dark-haired, green-eyed cowboy.

Even though they'd fought, she'd half expected Jesse to be there when she'd exited the arena. Which was pretty foolish, when she stopped to think about it. Not to mention revealing.

Probably time to remember that no promises were asked for or given last night, Cooper. Not to mention that most men don't like being beaten by a woman.

It was sadly true and she was frowning as the PA system crackled to life.

"And the judges are awarding eighty-two points for that ride by Owen Prentice. Not enough to knock CJ Cooper from the top of the leaderboard. Only one ride left before we find out who's taking home the prize money today, and I don't know about you, but I'm starting to feel like this might be a historic occasion for the Copper Mountain Rodeo."

CJ's heart skipped a beat and she pressed a hand against her belly. Waiting to find out if someone could top her score was almost as bad as waiting to ride. She found herself scanning the crowd nearby again—and this time she spotted Jesse, talking to a security guard near the entrance to the competitor-only area.

He nodded, shook the man's hand, then turned and spoke to a couple standing behind him, their faces obscured by baseball caps. When he turned back, his gaze searched the crowd near the chute, looking for someone.

She told herself to turn away, that it would be too revealing if she was caught staring at him, but then their gazes locked and Jesse started moving forward. Toward her.

Suddenly she didn't know what to do with her hands, first clasping them in front of her, then sliding them into the front pockets of her jeans. Then she got a good look at the middle-aged couple following the path Jesse was cutting through the crowd, and disbelief momentarily froze her in place.

Her father was frowning—he'd never been a fan of crowds—while her mother was looking both anxious and excited, one hand clutching at her handbag strap where it lay over her shoulder.

How on earth…?

She started forward, angling past people, slipping through gaps, until she and Jesse met halfway, her parents a few steps behind him.

"How…?" she asked, still not quite able to comprehend that her parents were really here.

They must have driven all night, a journey of many hundreds of miles.

"No idea, I just overheard them trying to talk their way past the guard," Jesse said, stepping aside to let her parents move closer.

"Such a ride. You were so good out there, baby girl," her mother said, her eyes bright with unshed tears.

"Thanks, Mom," she said, but her gaze was already shifting to her father.

He looked very serious, his cheeks unusually pink. CJ's smile faltered. Was he unhappy to be here? Had her mother dragged him across the state against his will?

"Perfect form," he said, the serious expression falling from his face to be replaced with a brilliant smile. "The way you marked that horse out… Never seen anything like it."

Then his eyes got bright with emotion, and CJ understood the color she could see in his face was simply excitement on her behalf.

She was about to respond when a roar went up in the stands.

"What happened?" her mother asked, looking around like a startled bird.

"And it's official, folks," the PA boomed. "A score of eighty-five is not enough for Hardy Brooks to top the leaderboard today, which means CJ Cooper wins the saddle bronc event with a score of eighty-nine on Jumpin' Jack. A reminder that this is CJ's first pro rodeo, and I can't think of a more fitting way to welcome her to the circuit. Let's hear it for CJ."

Another roar went up, and CJ found herself in her mother's arms, the older woman all but squealing with joy.

"Congratulations. Oh, I knew you could do it. I knew it. I'm so glad we came, baby."

It was her father's turn next, and his arms were warm and strong as they closed around her.

"Well done, Monkey," he said near her ear, and the familiar scent of his aftershave and the affection beneath his words almost undid her.

"Thanks, Dad."

His arms tightened around her briefly. "I need to apologize to you properly later, but know that I'm sorry for being such a stupid old man about all of this. You did right to ignore me. I'm so damned proud of you."

It was too much. CJ squeezed her eyes tight, her chin wobbling as she buried her face against her father's shoulder.

How long had she waited to hear those words from him? How many months had she dealt with his quiet disapproval and refusal to acknowledge her pursuit of her dream?

"Oh, don't cry, sweetheart," she heard her mother say, then they were in a three-way hug, her mother's arms coming around them both.

When she pulled back, the first thing she saw was Jesse

standing to one side, a small smile playing around his mouth. Feeling more than a little exposed, she lifted a hand to wipe the tears from her cheeks.

"Congratulations, CJ. Was a hell of a ride," he said.

There was no doubting his sincerity.

"You, too," she said, because Jesse would also pocket a fair chunk of prize money for coming in second.

"Hope you brought a big wallet to take home that big check," he said, making her laugh.

Her parents laughed, too, and CJ remembered she hadn't introduced them.

"Mom, Dad, this is Jesse Carmody. He competes in saddle bronc, too—"

"We saw him ride. Fantastic effort, Jesse," her father said, pumping Jesse's hand enthusiastically. He was even more pink than before, CJ noticed, his smile so wide it looked like it almost hurt.

She hadn't seen him so happy in years, and it made her throat close up when it hit her all over again that he was happy for *her*. Because of *her*.

Finally.

"Thank you, sir. Pleasure to meet you both," Jesse said, making eye contact with both her parents, his manners impeccable.

"Are you allowed to come sit with us now?" her mother asked CJ. "Or do they need you for something else?"

CJ looked to Jesse, eyebrows raised. Things were much

more informal at the smaller local rodeos where she'd earned the prize money that qualified her for a pro ticket. She was aware there would be an award ceremony at the close of the rodeo, but otherwise she was in the dark.

"They'll want you at the announcer's booth fifteen minutes before the award ceremony, to get you up to speed." He checked his watch. "But that means you've got half an hour with your folks before you have to be anywhere."

"Perfect," her mother announced. "We can catch up on each other's adventures." Her gaze shifted to Jesse. "Can we buy you a coffee, too, Jesse?"

"Thank you, Mrs. Cooper, but I'll leave you all to catch up. It was nice meeting you though."

Jesse's gaze found hers briefly as he offered her a quick smile.

"Before you go… If you see Sierra, tell her thanks from me," CJ said, aware the words didn't even come close to expressing her gratitude. "She'll know what I'm talking about." She'd make a point of talking to Sierra personally before she left Marietta, but it felt wrong to let him go without acknowledging his sister's actions.

"I'll pass that on to her," he said.

Then he nodded to her father and turned and walked away.

CJ stared after him, unable to stop herself from contrasting this afternoon's distance to the passionate heat and connection of last night.

This is the way you wanted it, she reminded herself. *The way it has to be.*

"Let's go find that coffee," her mother said, and CJ brought her thoughts back to the here and now.

"Great idea," she said.

JESSE CARRIED HIS gear to his trailer and changed into his everyday boots before going in search of his family. A text to Sierra elicited their location in the stands, and he climbed the steps to where they took up the last three seats in a row.

"Hey, congratulations. Second place is awesome," Sierra said, jumping up to give him a kiss and a hug.

"Yeah, great ride, man. Thought the judges were a bit light on the points, though," Casey said.

"Nah, they were pretty much on the money," Jesse said.

He'd had a good ride, but CJ's had been outstanding and he didn't begrudge her the win in any way.

"Did us proud," Jed said, leaning across Casey to shake his hand.

His quiet words and the way he held Jesse's eye hit Jesse like a thump in the chest and it took him a moment to find a response.

"Thanks, man," he said.

"Have you seen CJ? She must be over the moon," Sierra said.

"She's with her folks. They made the drive from

Plentywood to see her ride," Jesse explained. "She didn't say much, but I think it's safe to say she's pretty happy with the result."

Sierra snorted inelegantly. "I bet she is."

His legs were aching from his ride and he sank onto the concrete step in the aisle beside his sister and rested his elbows on his knees.

"She asked me to pass on her thanks, by the way," he said.

Sierra affected an innocent look. "For what?"

"You telling me you weren't behind everyone turning their backs on Dean Maynard?" he asked. Because he'd guessed who'd come up with the scheme the moment he'd seen women standing to turn their backs.

Sierra lifted a shoulder in a modest shrug. "All I did was send a few text messages and make a few phone calls."

Jesse suspected she'd done a lot more than that in order to recruit so many women to her cause.

"Whatever you did, you're an evil genius," he said. "I owe you one."

"I just couldn't stomach that bottom feeder getting away with what he did."

"People are going to be talking about this for weeks," Jesse said with no little satisfaction. "Won't be long before most everyone knows what he did to CJ."

"That's what I figured. Living in a small town drives me insane sometimes, but there are times when the local gossip network is worth its weight in gold."

"Amen to that," Jesse agreed.

"With a bit of luck, Maynard will wimp out and bail on the tour rather than deal with the fallout."

Jesse wasn't so certain about that, being more familiar with the other man's ego and sense of entitlement.

"So, where's the party at?" Sierra said after a moment, rubbing her hands together in anticipation. "We've got some celebrating to do."

Jesse smiled at her enthusiasm, even though partying was the last thing on his mind. Truth was, he felt...flat. And it wasn't because he'd come second in saddle bronc.

He'd messed up with CJ, big-time.

He'd climbed into the chute feeling angry and more than a little defensive about the things she'd said. Thankfully, years of experience and muscle memory had kicked in once he was on his bronc's back, and he'd managed to put in a creditable ride.

It wasn't until afterward that he'd let himself think about what she'd said to him before walking away. *How would you feel if one of your buddies made you the same offer?*

He'd fobbed her off at the time, but the truth was he'd be majorly pissed off if one of his buddies offered to step aside so Jesse could have a clear shot at winning an event. To do so would imply Jesse couldn't get there on his own, something that wouldn't sit well with any competitive athlete.

He'd never want a win he hadn't earned—but that was exactly what he'd offered CJ.

He'd wanted to kick something when it finally sank in what he'd done. He'd been so intent on helping her, he hadn't stopped to think about the message his offer would send. He'd just…waded in, intent on fixing things, because for some reason he'd felt like it was his place to right the wrongs in her world.

No one had asked that of him, especially not CJ. In fact, she'd explicitly asked him to butt out.

Even now, a good hour after their fight, the memory of his dumbass, blundering offer made him want to squirm. Was it any wonder CJ had ripped him a new one?

"Hey. You okay?" Sierra asked, and he realized he hadn't responded to her question.

"Yeah, of course."

"You're not upset about not winning, are you?" Sierra asked, lowering her voice a little.

He gave her a hard look, genuinely offended. "To CJ, with that ride? She earned that prize ten times over and I'm glad she won."

Sierra held up a hand to ward off his anger. "Geez, sorry. You just seem…not yourself."

"Didn't get much sleep last night," he said without thinking.

His sister raised a too-innocent eyebrow. "Didn't you? Why not?"

He huffed out a reluctant laugh. "Do you ever stop?"

"Hey, you dangled the bait, I just took it."

The stand filled with the sound of applause and cheering and he focused on the arena and saw the bull riding was done, which meant they were just minutes away from the award ceremony. Around them, people started to gather their coats and hats, which was pretty typical for a rodeo crowd. They already knew who'd won, they'd done their cheering, and now the race was on to get out of the parking lot with as little pain as possible.

There were plenty of people staying put, however, and he was glad. He wanted CJ to hear the crowd cheering for her as she accepted her prize. He imagined how buzzed she must be as she waited for her name to be called, the moment made extra-special because her folks had made the long trip to witness her achievement.

He was that fucking happy for her, he really was. On all counts. He just wished he had a right to celebrate her win with her, instead of being the guy who'd given her a big vote of no confidence minutes before her ride.

Down on the arena, volunteers ran out with sponsor flags and took up position. Moments later, the MC interrupted the Garth Brooks's song blaring over the PA to announce Travis McMahon, one of the people who'd pulled the Copper Mountain Rodeo together this year. Tall, lean and gray haired, Travis strode to the center of the arena accompanied by one of the rodeo princesses, the poor girl struggling to manage an armful of oversized checks for most of the short walk.

Travis made a mercifully short speech praising the work of the people who'd helped fundraise to rebuild the arena, then quickly moved on to announcing the winners. Jesse clapped along with everyone else as cowboys came out one by one to collect their oversized checks and trophy buckles. Some of them were friends and he cheered for them, but when CJ's name was announced he surged to his feet and gave an ear-piercing whistle, adding to the clamor the crowd was making.

Down on the arena, CJ laughed and shook hands with Travis before accepting her buckle and check. Then she turned toward the stand and held her buckle hand high, silently thanking them for their support. For the second time that day Jesse's chest got tight as he watched her stand tall and proud, totally owning the moment.

"God, she's like a freaking superhero," Sierra said, and he realized she'd stood to cheer for CJ, too.

"Yeah," he said, because he didn't trust himself to say any more.

He was thinking about the way she'd talked about learning to break horses when they were tangled in bed last night, and the wild, untamed look in her eye when he'd told her to remember to have fun before her ride yesterday.

Cassidy Jane Cooper was a one-off, and he knew in his gut she was going to do great things in rodeo. Watching her walk across to join the rest of the event winners, he made a decision: he needed to square things with her, to apologize for his inept attempt to support her. Not for a second did he think doing so would get her back into his bed—it wasn't about that. He simply wanted the right to call her his friend, and friends apologized when they'd fucked up.

"Hey, cool," Sierra said, her phone in hand. "CJ texted me earlier—she says her and her folks are going to be at Grey's celebrating this afternoon, and she wants to buy us all drinks."

She gave Jesse a pleased nudge in the ribs before starting to tap out her response. Jesse returned his gaze to the tall, dark-haired woman on the arena below.

Looked like he'd be getting a chance to extract his foot from his mouth sooner rather than later.

"MY GOODNESS, I think we'd better order some food," CJ's mother said, lifting a hand to her forehead. "I'm feeling a little woozy."

CJ didn't bother to hide her smile. She was *definitely* feeling a little woozy, her mother's euphemism for drunk.

They'd been at Grey's for nearly an hour now, and neither she nor her parents had had to buy a single drink the entire time.

The first round had been on the house, to celebrate her win. After that, a bunch of local women had insisted on buying them a round after raving about how awesome it had been watching CJ hold her own in the arena. Then a group of cowboys had claimed it was their turn, and so on.

Hence CJ's definitely woozy status.

"I'll get us something," she said, already sliding out of the booth.

"See if they have buffalo wings," her father chimed in, earning himself an exasperated look from her mother, who fought a daily losing battle with his fondness for deep-fried food.

CJ gave him a wink to let him know she was on it, then made her way to the bar, frowning at all the aches and pains that sprang to life the moment she moved. Tomorrow was not going to be pretty.

And yet she didn't regret a single bump, bruise or ache.

She bellied up to the bar and ordered food for their table, as well as a round of Cokes. When she was done, she caught herself checking the entrance for the twentieth time that hour and gave herself a mental kick.

Keeping watch for Jesse Carmody's arrival was both pathetic and pointless. Either he'd come or he wouldn't—and if he did come, it wouldn't change anything, because they'd had their one night together and it wasn't going to happen again.

Also—and this was important—she was still hurt and disappointed about what had happened before her ride. She'd already acknowledged she hadn't handled his offer well—but she really, really wished he hadn't made it in the first place.

But maybe it made it easier, knowing that despite what he'd said previously and the way he'd supported her up until that moment, deep down inside Jesse didn't think she was his equal.

It wasn't a thought or a memory she wanted to dwell on, and she pushed it from her mind as she returned to the booth. She was sliding in beside her mother when she registered movement in her peripheral vision and turned to see the Carmodys arrive, Sierra in the lead.

The younger woman spotted CJ immediately. "There she is, the woman of the hour," Sierra hollered.

CJ could feel herself going red as all heads turned their way. Trust Sierra to turn a few quiet drinks into an Event.

"Shut up and come over here," CJ said, waving the Carmodys over.

"You must be so proud," Sierra told her parents as they arrived at the booth. "Wasn't she amazing out there?"

"She was. And we are," her father said, and CJ shook her head because it was either that or get choked up all over again.

Everyone was looking at CJ expectantly. "Oh, right. Introductions."

She reeled off names as the Carmodys slid into the booth, Sierra beside her, Jed, Jesse and Casey on the other side of the table. It was cozy, but bearable—except for the fact that someone's knees were pressed against hers, and she was pretty sure they were Jesse's.

Either that, or she was ridiculously attuned to anyone with Carmody genes, and she was pretty sure that wasn't the case because she was rubbing shoulders with Sierra and it wasn't doing a thing for her.

Glancing across the table, she met Jesse's green eyes and knew without a doubt that it was him and that he was as aware of her as she was of him.

"We need champagne," Sierra said, twisting to face the bar. "Hey, Reese, we need bubbles. The real French stuff."

The bartender raised a hand in acknowledgment, and Sierra turned back to the table looking pleased with herself.

"As you can see, Sierra's the quiet one in the family," Jesse said dryly.

"Who wants to be quiet when CJ just won her first pro rodeo?" Sierra said.

"You going to wear your buckle or mount it in a frame?" Jed asked.

"I don't know. I kind of want to do both." Her gaze found Jesse's across the table. "Is it dorky to wear it?"

He rose from his seat, enough so she could see his belt buckle, an engraved silver nickel square with black enameled writing on it.

"Is that your first buckle?" she asked.

"First pro one," he said, sinking back into his seat.

"Where's it from?" she asked.

"Flint Hills Rodeo, 2011," Jed said.

Jesse frowned, patently surprised. He turned to look at his brother.

"How do you know that?" he asked, the words almost an accusation.

"It was your first win. Sierra and Casey were crowing about it for weeks."

Jesse studied his brother for a long beat before looking away, but CJ could see Jed's comment had thrown him.

"You should wear the belt," her father said suddenly, his fist hitting the table like a king delivering an edict. "Let everyone know how good you are."

"Listen to your father—he's speaking good sense," Jesse said, a teasing light in his eyes.

The food arrived then, along with the champagne, and their booth got rowdy as people started proposing toasts.

"To CJ, for being a superwoman."

"To Jesse, for taking defeat like a man."

There were more, many of which made CJ blush as well as laugh, but finally she was able to get a word in edgewise.

"I want to propose a toast—to Sierra, for making sure that justice was done. Thank you for being my avenging angel."

The moment the words were out her mouth she realized her parents would want to know what they meant, which meant she'd have to tell them about Dean Maynard's harassment, something she hadn't intended to do. Sure enough, her mother piped up straight away.

"Why would you need to be avenged?"

CJ pressed her lips together, annoyed at herself, then happened to catch Jesse's eye across the table. He lifted a shoulder, the movement barely noticeable, but she understood what he was saying: *Tell them. It happened. They deserve to know.*

"I had a little trouble with one of the other riders," CJ said.

It took ten minutes for her to fill them in and another ten to talk her father out of hunting Dean Maynard down and "beating the living snot out of him." Sierra finally convinced him to stand down when she described in vivid detail how his infamy would follow him from rodeo to rodeo.

"He's going to be the gross urine bully for the rest of his rodeo career," she said, taking a self-satisfied sip from her champagne flute. "We don't need to do anything else, just let his reputation drag him down."

"From your mouth to God's ears," CJ's mom said.

"So, CJ, you going home now, or heading off to the next rodeo?" Casey asked, and CJ wanted to kiss him for the deft change of subject.

"Next rodeo's in the wrong direction to make it worth going home, but I've always wanted to check out Glacier National Park, so I figured I'd sightsee a bit, then double back to Great Falls."

"So you're going to be a rodeo bum like Jesse and follow the circuit around?" Sierra asked.

"If I can make it work," CJ said.

"Should look into getting a trailer, make it cheaper to live on the road in the long run," her father said thoughtfully, a change of tune so profound CJ nearly choked on her beer. Just last week he'd greeted every mention of the rodeo with stubborn silence, and now he was thinking about the most economical way for her to follow the circuit?

"What?" her father said, but CJ simply smiled and shook her head.

The conversation shifted to her father's work as a farrier then, and Sierra started talking to her mom about flying. CJ glanced over her shoulder, looking for the sign for the restroom.

"Need me to let you out?" Sierra asked, picking up on the action.

"You're a true gentleman," CJ said, and Sierra wrinkled her nose at her as she slid out of the booth.

"I think there's enough testosterone in the Carmody family already, don't you?"

"Good point," CJ said.

CJ followed the signs to the ladies' room and took care of business. It was only afterward that she caught sight of herself in the restroom mirror.

"Good Lord."

Her cheeks were pink from all the champagne, her hair a kinked, rumpled mess after being in a ponytail half the day.

There was dust from the arena on her boots and jeans. Her shirt was a wrinkled rag…

Not exactly her best look.

She started to finger-comb her hair into some kind of order, then paused. Exactly who was she trying to impress right now? Jesse?

She turned away from her own stupid face, unhappy with the answer she saw in her eyes.

Was she really such a slave to her hormones, even after his vote of no confidence?

It's probably just the champagne.

It was as good an excuse as any, and she decided to believe it. For now, anyway.

Then she pushed open the door to the ladies' room and came to an abrupt halt when she saw Jesse was hovering in the dimly lit corridor.

Waiting for her, unless she was wildly mistaken.

"Hi," she said.

"Got a minute?"

"Sure." She crossed her arms over her chest, then realized she probably looked defensive or nervous and immediately uncrossed them.

Jesse cleared his throat. "I should never have made that dumbass offer to withdraw, and I want you to know that even though it came across as though I didn't think you could do it on your own, that wasn't the way I meant it. I just…I wanted to make things right for you and…" He shrugged, apparently out of words. "I fucked up," he said

215

simply.

She stared at him for a long moment, a little shaken by how relieved she was that he'd apologized and that he understood where she'd been coming from.

When had this man's opinion come to count for so much in her world?

"Apology accepted," she said. "For the record, while I appreciate the noble impulse, I don't need to be rescued."

"Fuck, no," he said.

He sounded so vehement she couldn't help but smile.

"Then let's just call it water under the bridge and move on." She offered him her hand to shake on it.

He hesitated a moment before sliding his hand into hers, the strength and roughness of his big hand triggering a hundred sense memories of his touch in the darkness. Memories that were strong enough to send a pleasurable shiver down her spine.

Just as well it was going to be a week before she saw him again. She needed the time and distance to get her head straight where he was concerned.

Belatedly she realized she was still holding his hand.

"I'd better get back to the table," she said, slipping her hand free.

"Sure thing."

Taking a step to one side, he let her pass. Somehow she stopped herself from looking back over her shoulder as she walked away.

Chapter Thirteen

S HE'D ACCEPTED HIS apology. The knowledge left Jesse feeling many pounds lighter as he made use of the facilities before following her back to the booth.

He'd been worried she'd be so pissed off with him that she wouldn't want to hear it, but she'd listened, her gaze never leaving his, and she'd taken only a moment to gather her thoughts before letting him know he was forgiven.

He should have guessed she wouldn't be a grudge keeper, or the kind of person who liked to stretch out misunderstandings to wring the maximum angst from them. CJ said what had to be said as honestly as possible, then put it behind her and moved on.

As Sierra had said, CJ was good people.

If she wasn't his competitor, if she didn't have so much to prove and so much to lose by being involved with him, it hit him that he'd be moving heaven and earth to make sure this weekend was not the end of them.

But she was, so he was going to have to cowboy up and accept it like a man.

It wasn't going to be easy. Sitting in the booth, watching the light play on her pretty face and dark hair, listening to her laugh, he knew with absolute certainty that he was going to be nursing a crush on her for months to come. How could it be otherwise when every new thing he learned about her only made him like and admire her more?

Like the way she interacted with her parents. It was obvious she had huge respect for both of them as well as a lot of love. But that didn't mean she was above teasing both of them, particularly her father.

Watching her rib him, he understood why she'd been so wounded by his failure to support her rodeo ambitions. They were clearly close, and he suspected she'd been a regular daddy's girl growing up.

"What's your vote, Jesse?" Sierra asked.

Everyone was looking at him, waiting for his response.

His sister sighed heavily and rolled her eyes, correctly interpreting his blank look to mean he hadn't been paying attention.

"Let me recap for you. Should we move this party to Rosita's for some real food and margaritas?" Sierra said. "Casey and Jed are arguing for steak at the Graff. CJ and I want margaritas. Roy and Susie are split. So you've got the deciding vote."

"It's CJ's night," he said.

Sierra did a little air punch. "Yesss. Totally called it. What CJ wants, CJ gets."

"Tonight, anyway," CJ said, her brown eyes bright with laughter.

She was so stinkin' pretty, it made his chest ache. Along with other parts of his anatomy that hadn't forgotten the way she'd climbed on top last night and taken charge.

He made a point of falling back to walk with Roy and Susie Cooper as they made the short journey to Rosita's, and when they got to the restaurant he made sure he was sitting at the other end of the table from CJ. It was that or make a fool of himself.

They ordered enough food for two armies and jugs of margaritas, and when they were stuffed and happy, Sierra suggested looking in at the Graff to see if there was any dancing to be had. The Coopers tapped out at that point, explaining they had a long drive tomorrow, and CJ said goodbye to them outside Rosita's.

They discovered a local band playing covers at the Graff, and Sierra immediately threw her coat at Casey and dragged CJ onto the dance floor. Jesse stood with his brothers watching the action from the sidelines. He tried not to stare at CJ's swaying hips and perfect ass and failed miserably.

After ten minutes, Casey leaned across and spoke in his ear.

"I'll leave you to your self-flagellation," he said, clapping a hand on Jesse's shoulder before heading off to join a bunch of local cowboys.

Jesse shoved his hands into his back pockets, unimpressed with his brother's words and the knowing smirk Casey had been wearing when he walked away. This was the curse of having smart-asses in the family.

Jed stuck it out another five minutes before making some excuse about having an early night.

"You all right to get home?" he asked, car keys already in hand.

"I'm good," Jesse assured him. He'd cut himself off and stuck to soda after a couple of margaritas. He figured by the time Sierra and CJ were done dancing, he'd be more than fine to drive them home.

"Then I'll see you tomorrow." Jed turned away, then almost immediately turned back. "Ask her to dance. Worst thing she can say is no."

Jesse shook his head as his brother headed for the exit. Apparently he was doing a truly dismal job of hiding his feelings for CJ. He was going to have to get a grip on that before next weekend.

Casey had left Sierra's jacket over the back of a nearby chair, and he collected it and went to the bar to see if he could get a coffee. He could, and he nursed it at the bar while Sierra and CJ continued to whoop it up on the dance floor, laughing and bumping hips and generally having a good time.

Once or twice he caught himself smiling in response to a move or a face CJ pulled and had to have a stern word with himself. Was it any wonder his whole family knew he was into CJ, when he was watching her like a lovesick teenager?

He was on his second cup of coffee, his back firmly to the dance floor, when Sierra appeared out of nowhere and grabbed his arm.

She was slightly out of breath, her cheeks flushed, and clearly in the middle of having a damned good time.

"I need the bathroom. Go dance with CJ, keep her company."

"I don't do dancing."

"Yeah, you do. Come on. For CJ. She's celebrating, remember?" Sierra's tone was cajoling as she tugged on his arm.

"You're a pain in the ass," he said as he set his coffee cup down.

"It's part of the job description."

CJ was sitting in a seat by the dance floor when Sierra towed Jesse back to her.

"Here. Jesse's subbing for me."

Neither of them had a chance to say anything before she disappeared.

Jesse offered CJ a wry smile. "You want to keep dancing? I don't have Sierra's moves but I can keep you company."

A small frown appeared between her eyebrows before she shrugged. "Sure, why not?"

Together they moved onto the dance floor, quickly finding a few square feet to call their own. Jesse started shuffling his feet from side to side, hoping his hands weren't doing anything too dumb. CJ lifted her hands in the air, her hips moving sinuously.

"I actually really love this song," she shouted over the music.

She certainly knew how to move to it. Meanwhile, he felt like someone had swapped his own feet for two tree stumps as he clomped back and forth.

And he had only himself to blame for letting Sierra drag him into this.

Like an answer to a prayer, the song ended, and he scanned the room, looking for his sister. How long did it take for a woman to go to the bathroom, anyway? There was no sign of her, however, and the next song started up almost immediately. From the opening bars it was clear it was going to be a ballad, and everyone around them either stepped closer to slow dance or abandoned the floor altogether.

CJ paused, a question in her eyes, and he figured he'd be a fool if he gave up the opportunity to hold her, even if it was in public. He'd probably never get the chance again.

He gestured for her to step closer, and after a heartbeat she did so, her left hand sliding into his right, the other coming to rest on his bicep just below his shoulder. He positioned his hand high on her back, then led her into the simple two-step his mother had drummed into him before his high school prom so many years ago.

CJ went with him easily, effortlessly, and he bit back a smile.

"What's so funny?" she asked.

"Don't take this the wrong way, but I was half expecting you to want to lead."

"Careful, or you won't escape this dance floor with your toes intact," she warned him.

"I should probably warn you, Carmodys don't scare easily."

"And I should probably warn *you*, Coopers are complete animals when we're bent on revenge."

"Yeah? What kind of animal?" he asked, not bothering to hide his smile now.

"The kind that eats Carmodys for breakfast."

"I seem to remember enjoying that, to be honest," he said.

CJ's head tilted back as she let out a loud, earthy laugh at his shameless flirting.

Which was when he registered they'd drawn close enough to be almost hip to hip, with barely an inch between her chest and his.

Close enough that if he lowered his head, their mouths would meet.

He could feel himself getting hard just thinking about it.

CJ seemed to realize what they'd unconsciously done at the same time he did and the smile slipped from her lips. For a long moment they simply danced, the electric promise of mutual awareness crackling between them, their gazes and bodies locked together.

The need to kiss her, taste her, get closer to her was like a drumbeat in his chest and groin, but he wasn't so far gone he'd forgotten where they were—on the dance floor in one of Marietta's most popular venues.

So even though it killed him, he eased a couple of inches away. Enough to make them look like friends enjoying a dance instead of lovers indulging in publicly acceptable foreplay.

CJ's hand tightened around his, almost as though she was protesting the move, and he saw a flicker of something that looked a lot like disappointment in her eyes before she dropped her gaze to the collar of his shirt.

"Thank you," she said, her voice subdued.

"Wish I could say it was my pleasure," he muttered.

She huffed out a little laugh, her gaze meeting his again, and there was so much warmth and light there, so much of her spirit and wildness and courage, he couldn't stop himself from asking what he shouldn't.

"Stay," he said. "Don't go sightseeing this week. Stay with me out at the ranch."

Her mouth opened on a sudden intake of breath.

But she didn't look away.

"People would talk," she finally said, and he felt a surge of hope, because she hadn't said no.

"Jed needs help repairing some fencing. We'll say you just stayed on to help. You know how to wire a fence, right?"

"Could do it in my sleep."

He gave her his best slow smile. "Darlin', I've got other plans for bedtime."

She laughed, but she looked troubled and her gaze fell away from his. "Can I sleep on it?"

He tried not to let his disappointment show. "Of course."

The song ended, and they released each other and moved apart by mutual unspoken accord. Jesse saw Sierra lurking on the edge of the dance floor, a cheeky smile on her lips.

So much for keeping what was happening between him and CJ on the down low. Although his family would work it out pretty quickly if she took him up on his offer.

A pretty big "if" when all was said and done.

"You two ready to call it quits?" he asked, fully expecting Sierra to give him grief for being a wuss before dragging CJ back onto the dance floor.

To his surprise, she checked her watch and pulled a face. "Hate to say it, but we've got an early start tomorrow."

"And I'm doing breakfast with my folks before they leave," CJ said.

"Then let's hit the road, ladies."

He drove CJ back to the rodeo grounds to collect her gear from her truck, then to the B&B on Bramble Lane where she'd managed to score a room for the night. It was within easy walking distance of downtown, which meant she'd be able to use the pedestrian bridge to cross to the rodeo grounds in the morning to collect her truck.

He stayed behind the wheel when she climbed out of his pickup, but Sierra got out and gave her a big hug.

"You stay in touch, okay? I don't want to be a liar when I brag about my big rodeo star friend, CJ Cooper," Sierra said.

"You'll hear from me, I promise," CJ said.

She hefted her duffel bag and met his gaze through the side window.

"Thanks for the ride, Jesse. I'll see you in Great Falls."

There was a finality to her words that made him think she'd already made a decision about his offer and he did his best not to let his disappointment show.

"You will. Drive safe."

She smiled and waved, then turned away. Sierra got back into the pickup, but he remained idling at the curb until CJ was safely inside.

"Such a gentleman," Sierra said.

"Shut it, Squirrel," he growled, then he pulled into the road and headed for home.

CJ GAVE HERSELF a stern lecture as she showered and got ready for bed.

It would be madness to take Jesse up on his offer. As good as it had been between them, it would only make future rodeos that much more difficult if she indulged herself by letting their one night of passion slide into a week. First thing tomorrow, she needed to text him and tell him thanks but no thanks and draw a firm, black, indelible line under the craziness of this weekend.

It was the smart, sensible thing to do.

Decision made, she finished brushing her teeth, rinsed out her mouth and climbed into the antique oak four-poster bed that was the centerpiece of her room. As she'd learned when she checked in, each of Bramble House's guest rooms was themed after a color—she'd been assigned the White Room. The decor could have been stark and cold, but instead it was both calm and comforting, with delicate *broderie anglaise* curtains at the window and an intricately quilted, snowy-white duvet cover on the bed.

The comfort was more than just an illusion, too—the mattress was firm but soft in all the right ways, the duvet light and fluffy, the linen fine as silk on her skin. Turning off the light, she settled onto her pillow with a small, weary sigh and closed her eyes.

It had been a fun night, and an amazing, challenging, emotional, exciting day, and she fully expected to drop off in seconds.

Memories floated up as she drifted toward sleep. The joyful moment when she'd spotted her parents in the crowd. The rush of euphoria when the whistle sounded and she knew she'd covered her bronc. The moment when Jesse had looked her in the eye and congratulated her on her win.

Which somehow seemed to lead inevitably to the loaded, heated moment on the dance floor when she'd almost forgotten everything that was at stake thanks to the proximity of Jesse's big body to her own.

She'd been so close to kissing him. To saying to hell with it all. But Jesse had stepped back. Then he'd asked her to spend the week with him at his family's ranch instead of sightseeing before the rodeo in Great Falls next weekend.

Lying in the luxurious softness of her bed in Bramble House, CJ could still feel an echo of the shock that had raced through her at his words—shock that had been followed by a rush of heat that had licked through her like wildfire. Being in his arms, having him moving inside her, his mouth on her breasts, his hands coaxing pleasure after pleasure from her tightly wound body...

There was no denying that those few hours they'd spent together had been some of the most decadent, erotic and sensual of her life.

Her eyes popped open. Why had rejecting Jesse seemed so much more clear-cut when she'd been brushing her teeth in the bright light of the bathroom ten minutes ago?

In the darkness, it was so much easier to remember the brush of his fingers across her skin and so much harder to hang on to all the reasons why she needed to be sensible. And she needed to be sensible.

Didn't she?

No one need ever know, a little devil whispered in her mind. As Jesse had said, they could put it around that she'd picked up some casual work out at his family's ranch. If she was one of his male competitors, no one would blink an eye at the arrangement; rodeo cowboys signed on for casual work all the time to subsidize their incomes.

But she wasn't a man, and the likelihood was that she'd get some side-eye from people if word got out.

But how likely was that, really? Most of her fellow competitors had left town already, hitting the road so they could be back at their nine-to-five jobs or their own ranches come tomorrow morning. And it wasn't as though she and Jesse were going to be roaming around town putting on a show for the locals. Most likely they'd simply be busy working out at the ranch, keeping their heads down. Keeping to themselves.

It'd be a way to pay back the Carmodys' kindness and generosity, too, helping them out with their fencing.

Aren't you the Good Samaritan, her little devil mocked.

Because if she opted to stay with Jesse, it wouldn't be because she wanted to repay the Carmodys' kindness.

Once she started to genuinely entertain the possibility of giving in to her own desires, every trace of weariness left her body. All she could think about was Jesse. The smell of him. The feel of his skin against her own. The silky-rough hair on his legs and chest. His big, talented hands. The way he'd trembled with the force of his climax as he lost himself. The violent pleasure of her own climax when he'd tortured her with his mouth.

Muttering a four-letter curse, she rolled onto her belly

and pushed her pillow into a different shape. And still the fantasies and memories kept coming. Liquid and hot, they turned her body molten and moist with desire, to the point where she was seriously considering jumping out of bed and stepping into a cold shower.

It would only be a temporary reprieve, she knew. The moment she'd met Jesse, she'd been aware of him, and that awareness had only intensified since. It wasn't going to go away just because she willed it to, because if that was the case, she wouldn't be lying here, horny and wet and frustrated as hell.

The only way she was going to kill this awareness was to satisfy it.

She sat up, blinking in the darkness, a little shocked at her own audaciousness. Was she really going to get out of her luxurious, welcoming bed to travel out to the Carmody ranch in the dead of night so she could crawl into Jesse Carmody's bed for a booty call?

Was she seriously that far gone?

Her answer was the tight, needy clench within her as she pictured herself sliding into bed beside a rumpled, sleep-warm Jesse.

"You're crazy," she whispered to herself, but she was already throwing back the covers and reaching out to flick on the bedside lamp.

Moving quietly, she dressed in jeans and a sweater. Grabbing her boots, wallet, phone and car keys, she made her way quietly, carefully out of her room, downstairs and out of the house.

No need to tell the whole of Bramble House she was about to go climb in a man's window at one in the morning.

She sat on the edge of the porch to pull on her boots, then she pulled up a map of Marietta on her phone and got her bearings. It only took her fifteen minutes to walk through the quiet streets to the park and across the footbridge to the rodeo grounds. Her car was cold and covered with mist, and she let it idle for a few minutes before pulling out onto the highway.

Doubts started to tickle at about the halfway point—then she remembered the way Jesse had looked at her on the dance floor, his body rigid with barely suppressed desire. There wasn't a doubt in her mind he would be happy to see her.

The trick was going to be sneaking into the house without alerting the rest of his family.

She took it slowly up the driveway, turning off the engine to coast the final few feet. It made her feel both foolish and giggly as she pulled up behind Jesse's truck, like a teenager sneaking her father's car back into the garage after an illicit joyride.

The Carmody house was in darkness, the only light coming from the quarter moon hanging overhead in the pitch-black sky. Sliding out of her truck, she eased the door shut and made her way as quietly as possible to the front porch.

One hand on the balustrade for balance, she pulled off her boots and padded barefoot around the porch to the rear of the house.

She had a good map of the interior in her mind, and she quickly identified the bathroom window by virtue of the fact it was set higher in the wall. Walking quietly, she followed the line of the hallway, counting off rooms. The first was Casey's.

The second was Jesse's.

Setting her boots down, CJ took her courage in both hands and tapped lightly on the glass.

AT FIRST JESSE thought the tapping was part of his dream. Then his conscious brain kicked in and he came fully awake. It took him a second to orient himself and locate the source of the noise: the window.

Instantly he knew who it was.

Throwing back the covers, he went to let CJ in, too sleep-befuddled to think about pulling on a pair of boxer briefs or his jeans. Instead, he flicked the lock open and slid the window up.

"Hi," CJ said, and he could hear both nervousness and excitement in her hushed voice.

"Hi." His brain was catching up with events. He couldn't believe she was here. Couldn't believe how freaking lucky he was that she'd decided to take him up on his offer.

"Were you asleep?" she whispered.

He smiled. What did she think he was going to do, tell her to come back after he'd gotten a solid eight hours?

"Get in here," he said, popping the screen out and resting it against the outside wall of the house.

CJ climbed over the sill, her long legs making short work of the task. He pushed the window shut behind her, letting the curtains fall back into place.

"Maybe I should have called but I—"

He kissed her, stemming the flow of her words, both hands sliding through her hair to cup her head. God, she tasted so good, better than he remembered. Toothpaste and heat and an indefinable *something* he associated only with her.

She made a small needy sound, then her arms slipped around his torso as she shifted closer. His hands found her backside, hauling her closer still, the pressure amazing against his already-hard cock.

Desperate for more, he walked her two steps backward until they'd reached the bed. She scrambled onto it, hands fumbling at the stud on her jeans. He helped her undress, both of them panting with anticipation as he pulled her jeans and underwear off in a tangled rush. Then he was on top of her, his hands sliding beneath her sweater to find her breasts as they kissed with greedy urgency.

She wrapped her legs around his hips, holding him to her as she moved against him. For long, hot minutes they ground against one another, until the urge to be inside her became overwhelming. Rolling to the side, he yanked open the drawer on his bedside table and reached for a condom. His hands were shaking as he tore the foil open, only steadying when he rolled the latex down over himself. CJ's eyes glinted in the darkness as he rolled back into place, her hands clutching at his ass.

"Hurry," she urged, and he obliged her by thrusting inside her with one powerful stroke.

Her thighs pressed against his hips and he felt the pull of tight muscles deep inside her as she welcomed his invasion. She felt so good, so wet and warm around him, he pressed his face into the soft skin of her neck and groaned.

"You feel fucking amazing," he told her.

"You, too. So good."

He started to move, pulling out to the point of almost withdrawal, then thrusting back inside her. Quickly they found a demanding rhythm as he pumped into her, abandoning all hope of finesse as urgency took over. She felt too good, and he couldn't keep a leash on his own desire.

Then she tensed, her back arching off the bed, and he felt the telltale flutter as she came. The tremors shaking her body kicked him over the edge and he came in a long, hot burst of pleasure that seemed to last forever.

They were both panting afterward, their bodies slick with sweat. He could smell the musky saltiness of sex, could feel the small aftershocks still working their way through her body. He rolled to one side, pulling the covers over them both.

"Fuck…me…" CJ said after a moment, her voice husky with satisfaction.

"Give me a minute," he said.

Her belly and chest shook with silent laughter, and he lifted his head and pressed a kiss to her mouth.

"Promise me this isn't a dream," he said.

"Pretty sure I wouldn't be lying in the wet spot if this was a dream," she said.

It was his turn to laugh then, and he reached for her, rolling her away from the sex-damp sheet so that she was tucked against his side.

Her hand snaked around his waist, her palm flattening against his back, and they were both silent.

"What made you change your mind?" he asked after a beat or two.

"Who said I needed to change it?"

"You telling me you weren't planning on leaving town first thing when I dropped you off earlier?"

There was a small pause before she responded.

"It would have been the smartest thing to do." She sounded rueful.

"Fuck smart," he said.

He'd sacrifice smart for the feel of her body against his any day.

"Give me a minute," she said, and he smiled at her echo

of his earlier words.

He ran a hand down her body—shoulder to arm to hip to thigh.

"You won't regret staying," he said quietly. "I'll make sure you don't."

He felt the press of her mouth against his skin as she kissed his collarbone.

"Not sure that's in your power to promise."

"Yeah, it is. I'll show you," he said. Then he started kissing his way down her body, heading south. "Going to make you feel so good, baby."

Then he lowered his head and showed her exactly what he meant.

Chapter Fourteen

CJ WOKE WITH a start, her internal body clock telling her she needed to be somewhere or do something important today. She immediately registered the hard male body half sprawled across her own, and a stupid smile curved her lips.

Last night had been incredible. Even better than the first time, which she hadn't thought was possible. The combination of pent-up need and growing familiarity with each other's bodies had been incendiary.

The things he'd done to her…the way he'd made her feel…the things she'd done to him…

She could feel herself growing warm with the heat of her memories, and she lifted her head to check the time. It was still early, barely five thirty. If she woke him now, they'd have plenty of time for a rematch before she needed to meet her parents in town for breakfast.

Shit. That was why she'd woken up—she needed to get into town for an early breakfast with her folks.

"Why'd you just turn into an ironing board?" Jesse

mumbled, lifting his head.

"I'm meeting my parents for breakfast. I need to get back into town."

"It's only twenty minutes from here. No rush."

"I've got no clothes, nothing. I can't turn up like this. I need to go back to the B&B, make myself presentable."

She wriggled out from under his arm, sliding to the edge of the bed. His arm snaked back around her hips, holding her back when she tried to stand.

"Wait. You're going now?"

"Yep."

"But you're coming back, right?"

There was an endearing note of uncertainty in his voice, and she looked over her shoulder at him. His hair was sleep mussed, his green eyes drowsy. He had a crease on his cheek from the pillow, and more than his fair share of sexy-looking beard scruff.

"I'll be back. But maybe I should stay out in the Airstream, for appearance's sake."

"I was going to suggest that, anyway. For different reasons."

"What's your reason?" she asked, narrowing her eyes.

She was getting more proficient at reading him now, and she could tell he was about to say something outrageous.

"Don't take this the wrong way, but no one would ever call you the quiet type, if you get my drift. We'd be doing my family a favor, staying out there."

THE COWBOY MEETS HIS MATCH

She could feel her cheeks warming. "Are you saying I'm too loud?" she demanded, casting her mind back to last night.

It was hard to remember specifics, but she had the mortifying suspicion she might have been more than a little vocal when he made her come the second time.

"There's no such thing. Not in my book. I like hearing you scream my name."

He gave her a cocky grin and she dug her elbow into his chest and pulled free of his encircling arm.

"I didn't scream your name," she said. She was pretty sure she'd have remembered that.

"Not last night. But I'm confident I can get you there again."

He was so audaciously confident lying there in all his naked glory, a teasing light in his eyes, she found herself laughing.

"You're such a troublemaker."

"I'm not the one who came knocking on my bedroom window in the middle of the night," he reminded her.

She spotted her panties and bent to scoop them up. "True. That was pretty badass."

That made him laugh, a smile lingering on his mouth as she finished dressing. She did one quick scan of the room, then picked up her boots. "I don't know how long I'll be with my folks. Will that be a problem? When did Jed want to get started with the fencing?"

"Pretty sure he needs to go into town to get supplies, so you're good," he said.

"All right. Then I guess I'll see you later." She stepped closer to the bed and dropped a quick kiss onto his lips.

"Hold your horses. I'll walk you out."

"You don't have to."

"I want to."

She watched with unashamed admiration as he stood and reached for the jeans he'd left on the chair in the corner last night. He had a beautiful body, the muscles honed by years of riding and hard work. She was pretty sure the memory of him pulling his worn, faded jeans over his hips was going to torture her all day.

And then some.

Boots in hand, she followed him to the front door, reflecting that this was her third clandestine entry or exit in less than twenty-four hours.

He opened the door and stepped onto the porch with her. It was still not light yet, and the night air was bitterly cold, biting at her face and hands as she pushed her feet into her boots. Then she realized he was standing there in nothing but his jeans. The big, sexy idiot.

"Go back inside, it's freezing out here," she said, pushing him toward the house.

"Stop fussing and come here," he said, hooking a finger into her belt and pulling her toward him.

His goodbye kiss was long and thorough, and when he

finally let her go she wasn't one hundred percent certain her knees were going to hold.

"Okay. I'll see you later," she said.

"You will."

She took a step backward, then another one, then turned on her heel and went down the steps to the yard. Her truck was even colder than last night and she had to wait until the windshield had defrosted before she could reverse out.

Jesse stayed on the porch the whole time, only raising a hand and going inside when she started down the driveway.

"Idiot," she said, but she was smiling as she pulled onto the highway into town.

HER PARENTS WERE waiting for her when she arrived at the Main Street Diner just before eight. She wasn't surprised— they were notorious for being early to everything—and she gave them both a kiss on the cheek before taking a seat opposite them.

"Did you guys sleep okay? What looks good?" she said.

"Someone's perky this morning," her mother said.

"Of course she's perky—she's a saddle bronc champion," her father said.

"Thank you, darling, I hadn't forgotten," her mother said dryly, rolling her eyes a little.

CJ lifted the menu and gave it a quick glance. "French toast for me," she said.

"Wouldn't that be nice?" her mother sighed, pushing the menu away. "I'll probably just have the oatmeal."

She'd gained a little weight in the last few years and was in a perpetual struggle to drop five pounds.

"You will not. We're on vacation. And we're still celebrating CJ's win. Have whatever you want," her father said, nudging the menu back toward her.

CJ couldn't help being amused. Her mother spent half her life trying to curb her father's hedonistic tendencies, while he spent half of his trying to encourage hers.

The waitress came over, the same older woman with the beehive hairdo CJ had noted on her last visit. Her mother was talked into having the French toast, coffee was poured, CJ was congratulated on her win, then the waitress bustled off again.

The next hour slipped by easily as she chatted with her parents, checking in on their proposed route home, discussing options for rest breaks, then speculating about her chances at the next rodeo.

Every now and then it hit her all over again that they were here, that the dark cloud that had hovered over her life for the past twelve months was gone. She'd had similar moments last night as they talked and laughed together at Grey's, and then later at Rosita's. Her mother no longer had to feel guilty for supporting her, and CJ didn't have to bear the weight of her father's disapproval anymore. It was no small thing, and it was going to take her a while to get used to it.

Amazing what a person could become resigned to. Because she *had* been resigned to dealing with her father's opposition. She hadn't let it stop her, but the awareness of it had weighed on her on a daily basis.

When they were done with their meal, her father paid and CJ walked her parents to where they'd parked their car on Main Street.

"You know what? I just realized I never got a chance to look in the cute shop I noticed last night. I'm just going to duck off and take a peek at it. CJ can keep you company while I'm gone," her mother suddenly announced.

CJ blinked with surprise as her mother took off, her step brisk, almost as though she was worried they were going to try to stop her.

"What was that about?" CJ asked.

Her father had a half-amused, half-annoyed expression on his face. "I made the mistake of saying I hadn't had a chance to talk to you properly yet, and I think this is your mother's way of making it happen."

"Ah." Good old Mom, subtle as a sledgehammer.

Her father gave her a quick glance before shifting his focus to his car keys. "Want to walk for a bit?"

"Sure." CJ's stomach got tight as they turned and started walking slowly uptown. She had no idea what her father was about to say, but it felt important.

For a moment the only sound was the traffic around

them and the scuff of their boots on the sidewalk. Then her father took a deep breath.

"You probably don't remember, but you almost drowned when you were four."

It wasn't what CJ had been expecting and it took her a second to respond.

"I didn't know that."

"We were over at Jenny and Mack Tyler's place. It was summer; we were having a barbeque and a swim in their pool. Your mom wanted to make sure you all had sunscreen on, so we were in the kitchen, coating you kids in lotion, when you and Tommy decided you couldn't wait to jump in the pool."

Tommy was Jenny and Mack's son, about the same age as her. They'd been firm childhood friends until he'd hit ten and decided she had cooties.

"You remember that big doggy door the Tylers had? You and Tommy slipped through that thing while no one was looking. I looked up from rubbing lotion into Zach's back and saw you go straight to the deep end. You just…stepped off the edge of the pool, and you sunk like a rock. No splashing, not a squeak out of you. Of course, I freaked. Tried to get out the door, but my hands were covered in sunscreen. The handle wouldn't turn. Your mother was screaming; Jenny and Mack were panicking. I finally got the door open, dove straight in and scooped you out. And you were okay. You said you'd been holding your breath."

"Wow. What a naughty little shit I was," she said, imagining how shaken her parents must have been. "No wonder you and Mom were always so careful around water when we were kids."

"You were never naughty. Your problem has always been that you're fearless. You throw yourself into things. The first time you rode a horse, you just got up there, didn't hesitate. Even Tyson had to be talked into letting me put him in the saddle the first time, and it took him a couple of shots at it to love it. But you took to it straight away."

CJ smiled, knowing how much her tough older brother would hate hearing that.

"I was actually relieved when you started to get interested in makeup and boys," her father continued. "Not a lot of fathers that'd say the same, I'm sure, but it kept you out of the kind of trouble that can break a person's neck. Then last year you came to me and told me you wanted to go for your pro ticket so you could compete in saddle bronc, and honestly, CJ, it was that freaking swimming pool all over again. All I could think about was you getting hurt. Getting your head kicked in, or your back broken. So I reacted badly. I thought if maybe I didn't encourage you, you'd go off the idea." He gave a grunt of frustrated amusement. "Should have known better, huh?"

CJ frowned, reading between the lines of what he was saying. All the talk of her not rocking the boat, of pursuing barrel racing instead of saddle bronc—that had been about keeping her safe, not being worried about what his conservative friends and neighbors might say?

"I thought you were embarrassed because I was pushing my way into a sport where I wasn't welcome. Being one of those women who wants to break into the boys' club whether they want me there or not."

"I know. I let you think that, because I figured if I told you the thought of you climbing onto the back of a nine-hundred-pound animal that has been bred and trained to buck scared the living daylights out of me you wouldn't listen."

"I'd have listened," she said. "But I'd also have reminded you that all the boys competed in rodeo. Tyson broke his arm twice. You never tried to stop him from going back on the circuit."

"I told him he was a fool a few times, but you're right, I never gave him the kind of grief I've given you."

They'd both stopped walking and were facing each other on the sidewalk, blind and deaf to everything except their conversation. Her father looked away, trying to gather his thoughts, and his eyes were watery with emotion when they met hers again.

"The thing is, you're my baby girl, CJ. From the moment you were born, it's been my job to protect you. I know you're tough and smart. I know you can ride. But the thought of you getting hurt… It undoes me. It really does. And I know that's not politically correct to admit, because girls are supposed to be the same as boys these days, but it's the way I feel."

CJ could feel her own eyes getting hot with unshed tears. Her father almost never talked about his feelings. He told her he loved her on special occasions, and he showed her his love in ways small and large every day, but he didn't often open up and share himself the way he was right now. And even though she was frustrated by the way he'd handled his fear, she understood it, too.

She wished he hadn't allowed it to come between them, but she understood it.

"I get it," she said when she could trust herself to talk. "I really wish you'd just talked to me about it, but I get it."

"Like I said yesterday, I've been an old fool. But I want you to know, I did try to get over it. Made myself watch those first rides you did when you were trying to earn your pro ticket. First time I had to go lose my lunch behind the outhouse. Second time I thought I was going to have a heart attack."

"Dad…" CJ didn't know what to say. She'd had no idea he was so affected by her riding. She'd thought he'd stopped coming to watch her because he didn't approve.

"Watching you drive away on Friday, knowing you were heading off to your first pro event without the support you deserved…that was almost as bad. Along with knowing that your mother has felt so torn between us."

CJ nodded in acknowledgment. Her mother had been so

unhappy, being caught between them. She'd always listened on the rare occasions when CJ railed against her father's apparently conservative response to her desire to ride saddle bronc, but she'd never given any hint that there was more to the situation than CJ understood. Her silence made perfect sense now—she would consider anything else a betrayal of CJ's father's confidence.

"So what made you change your mind?" CJ asked, because she still didn't understand what had shifted.

"After you spoke to your mother yesterday, she drove out to where I was working. When she told me how well you'd done, I didn't know what to do with myself, I was that proud. And then your mother floored me by saying it was time for me to make a decision between being afraid for you and proud of you. She told me we'd raised you to be brave, and that meant we had to be brave, too. And I knew she was right. So we got in the car and we drove half the night to get here."

CJ sniffed back a rush of tears. "I'm glad you came," she said, then she threw her arms around her father and held on with everything she had.

"I'm sorry for making you afraid for me," she said. There was a part of her—the dutiful daughter, the good girl—who wanted to offer to bow out, to back away from the ambition that was causing her father so much angst. But she knew if she did that, she'd be betraying herself, and that she'd eventually come to resent him for hobbling her dream.

Riding pro rodeo was dangerous. It might even be reckless and foolish—but she loved it. The challenge of it was unmatched by anything else in her life, and she wasn't ready to give it up.

"I don't want you to change who you are," her father said, his voice thick with emotion. "You're a wonder to me, and I'm that proud of you."

They stood locked together for long moments, then finally CJ sniffed and lifted her head, and her father let his arms drop to his sides. The sight of her father's tear-streaked face nearly set CJ off again, but she blinked hard and after a second she held out her hand.

"Hand over your handkerchief. I know you've got one," she said.

He huffed out a laugh and handed over the folded cotton square, and she blotted his face dry, then mopped up her own cheeks.

"Well. This has turned into quite the breakfast meeting," she said.

"Your mother will be feeling pretty proud of herself, I'm guessing," he said.

CJ laughed. "Oh yeah, she is going to be smug."

They turned around and started walking back to the car and this time the silence between them was warm and expansive, filled with a new understanding.

Sure enough, her mother was waiting at the car. Her sharp gaze took in their tear-blotched faces for a moment before she smiled.

"Thank God, and about time."

JESSE STARTED COFFEE and had breakfast after CJ left. He was washing his cereal bowl when Jed entered, already dressed for work.

"Good timing, just about to pour coffee," Jesse said.

"Make it a large one, thanks," Jed said.

Jesse poured them both a cup and propped his hip against the sink while he took his first mouthful.

Jed grabbed the bread from the pantry and fed two slices into the toaster. "I'm heading into town for the fencing supplies now, if you want to come along for the ride?"

"Sure thing," Jesse said. Then he cleared his throat. "I asked CJ to stay on for the week in the Airstream. Hope that won't be a problem for anyone."

Jed's hands stilled momentarily on the peanut butter jar, the only sign he was surprised by Jesse's announcement. "Don't see why it would be."

"Figured she could help with the fencing, too. Always good to have another pair of hands, get things done faster."

Jed frowned, his face suddenly looking tight and hard. Then he nodded, and turned away to open the fridge. "Sounds good."

Jesse stared at his brother's back. "If that's a problem, just say so."

"Not a problem. Like you said, extra pair of hands is always welcome. Hope she's happy to take ranch hand wages."

Jesse let out a small, frustrated sigh. "I'm sure she will be."

Something had just happened with Jed, but getting anything out of his taciturn brother was like pulling teeth. What more could he do, though, other than ask directly if something was up?

"Is there time for me to shower before we head into town?"

"Go for it. I've got some paperwork I need to get on top of in the office, anyway," Jed said.

Jesse had a quick shower and shave, then dressed in work clothes. He was pulling on his steel-toed work boots when his sister stuck her head in the door.

"What's this I hear about CJ staying for the week?"

Jesse stood and adjusted his belt. "Yep. I invited her to stay, and she said yes. She's going to help with the fencing."

Sierra frowned. "Please tell me that's not how you asked her." She lowered her voice and put a dopey look on her face. "'Come and help us do some fencing, it'll be awesome.'"

"If that was supposed to be an impression of me, it needs some work," he said. "I would never say awesome."

"At least you have good taste in women. I'll give you that. Bit worried about CJ's taste, though."

He grabbed his wet towel off the bed and threw it at her,

but she dodged into the hallway.

"Missed," she called.

"Meant to," he yelled back.

Her derisive laughter echoed down the hallway.

He went looking for Jed then, and found his brother in his office, frowning intently at what looked like a spreadsheet.

"Ready when you are," Jesse said, noticing that his brother was quick to hit the button to minimize the screen.

The furtiveness was so unlike Jed that Jesse stepped further into the room.

Originally their father's office, the room had been Jed's space for many years now, yet still remained essentially the same: old wooden desk on one wall, battered bookcase against the opposite wall, and an office chair with cracked leather upholstery.

He could remember his father sitting in that chair, bitching about having to do paperwork. From the looks of things, Jed didn't love doing it, either.

"What you up to?" he asked.

"Just going over projections for the next six months."

His brother wasn't a liar, so Jesse figured that was probably the truth. So why the haste to minimize the screen?

"Better get going or we'll lose half the day," Jed said, pushing to his feet.

Jesse had no choice but to step back and follow him out of the room.

The trip into town was uneventful enough. Jesse trailed his brother around Big Z's Hardware, acting like a pack mule when required. To say his brother was pumped when he discovered fencing wire was on special was an understatement—Jed talked about it for most of the drive back out to the ranch.

Jesse's spine straightened when he saw CJ's truck parked behind his as they arrived home. He craned his head, looking for her, and was rewarded when Sierra came out of the barn with CJ in tow.

"Hey," he said as he climbed from the truck.

She was wearing a pair of faded jeans, a green and black plaid work shirt and well-worn boots. She even had a pair of leather work gloves tucked into her front pocket.

Ready to dive right in. No surprises there.

"We already fueled the four-wheeler and hitched the trailer up," Sierra said. "Casey's saddling up Pedro, Meteor, Gem and Major."

"Great. Good to see you, CJ," Jed said, tipping his hat to her.

She ducked her head in acknowledgment. "You, too. Thanks for allowing me to stay again. Hopefully I won't slow you down too much."

Jed laughed. "From what I've seen, I bet we'll be struggling to keep up with you."

Jesse's hands twitched at his sides, eager to touch her again. If she was his girlfriend, he wouldn't hesitate to kiss her hello, but what they had between them was far less defined than that. They were lovers, but there'd been no talk of tomorrow. And CJ had been up-front about her desire to keep their situation under the radar.

So what did that make them? A fling? An affair?

Something like that, he figured, even though none of those words felt exactly right.

"I'll go make some sandwiches for lunch," Sierra said. "Give me ten and we can hit the road."

CJ pitched in to help unload the pickup, transferring the supplies to the trailer on the four-wheeler. Then Jed started loading up the rest of the equipment they'd need—a robust cordless drill with a wicked-looking oversized drill bit, pliers, tensioners, a couple of sledgehammers. Jesse watched the pile grow with a frown.

"Thought we were just redoing some fence?" he said.

"Upgrading it," Jed corrected. "Deer and elk numbers have been through the roof last couple of years. We've lost so much feed to them it isn't funny, not to mention the risk of brucellosis transmission. The current fences are next to useless at stopping them, but it'd cost more than we can afford to replace 'em all with deer-proof fencing. So we're modifying it, bit by bit. Using the rebar to add height to the existing posts, running the mesh in between."

"Huh," Jesse said. "Smart plan."

Jed flashed him a quick grin. "Carmodys are good improvisers."

Jesse recognized the saying as one of his father's and felt a bittersweet pang, followed by the usual lash of guilt. If fate hadn't intervened, his father would be here right now, loading up the trailer alongside them.

Casey led his and Jed's horses out of the barn then, both of them Appaloosas bred from their own stock.

"You want to grab Major and Gem?" he asked.

"On it," Jesse said.

CJ followed him inside to help with the second horse.

"What were you thinking about back then, when you were talking to your brother?" she asked as she led Gem from her stall. "You looked so sad."

"Did I?"

"Yeah. Sad and angry at the same time."

"That was Dad's saying, the thing about Carmodys being good improvisers."

CJ nodded, then ran a gentle hand down Gem's nose.

"How'd things go with your folks this morning?" he asked.

Partly to change the subject, but also because he genuinely wanted to know.

She smiled, her eyes lighting up. "Really well, actually. Dad and I talked."

"Take it it was a good talk?"

"Yeah. It was. I'll bore you with the details later if you're interested."

"I'm interested."

She looked so happy, as though a weight had been lifted. He stepped closer, claiming her pretty pink mouth in an impulsive kiss. She opened to him straight away, and he felt the instant rush of heat and want he always experienced when he touched her.

"We ready to rock and roll?" Sierra called from the front of the barn, and CJ broke their kiss.

"Probably just as well," she said quietly, and he laughed.

She was right—five more seconds and he would have forgotten the obligations of the day.

"Come on, then, Ms. Cooper. Let's go mend some fences."

Chapter Fifteen

CASEY TOOK THE wheel of the four-wheeler, which left CJ to ride his gelding, Meteor, with Jed on Pedro, Sierra on Gem and Jesse mounted on Major. It took them half an hour to reach the section of fence Jed wanted to tackle, and once they'd unloaded the trailer they set to work.

It had been a while since Jesse had pitched in with his siblings, but he was surprised how easy it felt, how natural. There was some mandatory swearing and shit-giving when things went wrong, but lots of laughter, too. And it was hard to overstate the pleasure of looking up from his work and seeing CJ hard at it nearby, more than holding her own.

By lunchtime they had a good stretch of newly extended fence behind them, and they sat down among the tools and supplies to eat the sandwiches Sierra had made, feeling as though they'd well and truly earned their meal break.

"Rate we're going, we're going to need another trip into town for supplies again tomorrow," Jed said, and Jesse could see the satisfaction in his eyes.

"Exactly how much feed did we lose to deer and elk this

year anyway?" he asked.

The invoice for the fencing materials they'd bought to-day had been several hundred dollars, and they had miles of fencing to upgrade, which meant Jed hadn't undertaken this project lightly.

"Enough," Jed said grimly. "Too much."

"Sometimes we've had to do two or three times the feed drops we would normally," Casey said. "Not sure why deer and elk numbers are so high the past few seasons, but they've been causing problems all over. Couple of ranches down south had to cull and quarantine after their herds tested positive for brucellosis."

"How much of the fencing have you managed to up-grade?" Jesse asked.

"Maybe forty percent. Got to fit it in when we have time. And even though it's less expensive than replacing the fencing entirely, it's still not cheap," Jed said.

"Yeah, I noticed that," Jesse said.

CJ stood, dusting off the seat of her jeans. "I'm going to go see what's over that hill," she said. "Stretch my legs a bit."

"Good idea. I'll come with you," Jesse said, because working alongside her all morning and not touching her had been its own special form of torture.

As they started up the hill, CJ shot him an amused look. "You know going for a walk was code for 'I need to pee,' right?"

He laughed. He'd been too busy plotting to get her alone

to read an ulterior motive into her words. "Guess we'd better hope there's some good brush over the other side of this hill, then."

Sure enough, there was a small stand of trees and brush halfway down the slope on the other side. Jesse turned his back and whistled to himself while CJ disappeared.

"Better?" he asked when she rejoined him.

"Definitely."

He studied her face, noting her nose was a little pink from the sun.

"Better put some lotion on that nose when we get back."

"Yes, Mom," she said.

"You coping okay with the workload? Just shout out if you can't keep up," he said.

Because she wasn't the only one who could be provocative.

She shot him a scornful look. "What do I look like, some kind of wimp?"

He gave her a slow head-to-toe, lingering in all the good places. "Not even close. Tell me—that bit of black lace I keep seeing when you bend over—that your bra?"

She tilted her head, a challenging glint in her eye. "You been checking me out, Carmody?"

"Every chance I get." He stepped closer, and she held her ground as he reached out and hooked a finger into the neckline of her shirt, tugging it out so he could get a good look down her top. He was rewarded by the sight of her full

259

breasts clad in black lace and nearly transparent mesh, the pink of her nipples visible through the fine fabric.

"Jesus," he said. "You have any idea how hot that is?"

"Some idea, yeah," she said, laughter in her voice.

He dipped his hand inside her shirt, tracing the edge of the bra along the curve of her breast. "Were you thinking of me when you put this on this morning?"

Her eyelids dropped down over her eyes for a moment. "Maybe."

He glided his finger down over her nipple, flicking it lightly until it beaded into hardness. "Only maybe?"

Her mouth parted on the smallest of gasps. "Yes. Yes I was thinking of you."

He closed the distance between them, kissing her, his hand fully inside her shirt now, her breast heavy in his hand. He was contemplating urging her into the trees when he heard Casey's laughter from the other side of the hill and remembered where they were.

CJ looked flatteringly dazed when he pulled back. He huffed out a laugh and reached out to straighten her shirt. "Who knew I could ever forget my family was around?"

She gave a rueful shake of her head, then double-checked she was decent before following him back over the hill to rejoin the others.

They worked until midafternoon, when the second battery for the cordless drill ran flat. Jed was philosophical as they reloaded the trailer.

"Got more done that I thought we would," he said.

"Thanks to me and CJ," Sierra said.

"You're right, CJ being here made all the difference," Jed said.

"Funny," Sierra said, reaching out to try to shove him off-balance. Jed was ready for her, resisting the move and then using her momentum to try to trip her.

Jesse watched the small scuffle with a smile. Some things never changed.

"Take him to the ground, Sierra," CJ encouraged. "Go for the eyes."

"So bloodthirsty," Jesse said. "Remind me not to get on the wrong side of you."

"I will, don't worry. Whenever you need it," CJ said.

He was still smiling when Casey fired up the four-wheeler and the low throb of the motor filled the air. Casey started off, the trailer rattling over the uneven ground, the rest of them following a few minutes later.

Casey and Sierra disappeared when they got back to the ranch, off to deal with regular chores, while Jed headed into the office.

Which left Jesse and CJ to their own devices.

"Want a shower before dinner?" he asked.

"Wouldn't mind washing the dust off."

"I'll hook you up with a towel," he said, leading her through the living room to the bathroom.

Once there, he dug out a couple of towels from beneath

the vanity, then leaned past her to push the door shut.

CJ cocked an eyebrow at him.

"What?" he said. "You don't want me to wash your back?"

"Just my back, huh?"

"I might be prepared to help in other areas if you ask nicely."

He kissed her, pressing her against the door. She met him kiss for kiss, her hands going straight for the buckle of his jeans. Then her hand was inside his underwear and she was stroking him, her grip firm and sure. He returned the favor by unbuttoning her shirt and pushing her bra up, filling his hands with the warm smoothness of her breasts.

She was so fucking hot, the way she felt, the way she looked at him, the way she smelled. There wasn't a single thing about her that didn't turn him on.

He took as much torture as he could stand before bumping her hand away.

"Enough," he said, then he pushed her jeans and panties down and helped her step out of them.

It only took a moment for him to roll on a condom, then he lifted one of her legs to his hip. She made a small, greedy sound, tilting her hips forward, and he slid inside her.

The world became urgent and breathless as he worked himself inside her, smothering her gasps and moans with kisses, his fingers curled into her gorgeous ass and hips. She came quickly, her body grasping his, and he finally let himself go, pumping into her wildly until he came so hard his knees went weak.

"You all right there, cowboy?" she laughed.

"Am now," he said, pressing a last kiss to her lips.

He disposed of the condom, then turned the shower on. Once he'd got the temperature right, he drew her beneath the spray with him. He spent the next ten minutes sliding soapy hands over her supple muscles and curves while she returned the favor.

Afterward, he dressed and went out to her car to collect her bag and bring it inside so she had clean clothes to change into.

The door to the office was closed when they entered the living room, the low murmur of Jed's voice just audible as he talked to someone on the phone. Otherwise the house was empty, and Jesse headed into the kitchen to find something to snack on.

"We should make a start on dinner. Any idea what's on the menu?" CJ asked.

Her suggestion gave him pause. He'd only been thinking of himself and his currently empty stomach, but CJ was always thinking ahead, anticipating what might need to be done, how she could pitch in.

It was just one of many things about her that he liked a lot.

"Let me check the fridge, see what we've got to work with," he said.

She came to stand behind him, resting her chin on his shoulder as he inspected the contents of the fridge.

"Ground beef. Onions. There are bound to be some beans in the pantry. We could make chili?" she suggested. "It's one of the few things I can do reasonably well."

"Sounds good," he said, even though he was mostly just appreciating the press of her body against his and the fresh smell of her skin, along with the easy familiarity of the gesture.

Together they worked to prepare the meal, CJ making up some corn bread from a mix they found in the cupboard while he chopped onions and tomatoes for the chili. He was browning the beef when Sierra entered the kitchen, stopping in her tracks with an astonished look on her face.

"Someone pinch me. Am I hallucinating or is someone else actually cooking dinner?" she asked.

"Jesse insisted," CJ said, shooting him a cheeky look.

"Had to talk CJ into it, though. She wanted to shop for shoes online, but I finally convinced her to pitch in," he said.

CJ laughed, while Sierra followed their banter back and forth like a spectator at a tennis match.

"You kids are adorable, you know that?"

"Just for that you can set the table," Jesse said.

Forty minutes later, they were all sitting down to a meal of chili, corn bread and salad. Casey headed off to town afterward, claiming band practice, while Sierra had a scheduled book club meeting at a nearby ranch. Jed disappeared into his office, which left CJ and Jesse free to fire up the TV and collapse on the couch.

It felt good to relax after a hard day's labor, especially when the person at the other end of the couch was CJ. They quickly settled on a rerun of an old Tom Cruise movie, and after a few minutes CJ toed her boots off and curled her legs under her.

"Give 'em here," he said, patting his lap, and she stretched out so that her feet were resting on his thigh.

Gripping her foot in his hand, he ran his thumb firmly along the arch, eliciting a small moan from CJ.

"Good?" he asked.

"Oh yeah."

He applied himself to the task of pleasing her, his attention divided between the action on the screen and CJ's occasional murmurs of approval. The knowledge they would be sharing a bed that night was the only thing that stopped him from jumping on her again, the small shifts of her body and inarticulate pleasure sounds driving him more than a little crazy. He thought she was oblivious to the effect she had on him, then she slid one of her heels higher on his thigh and rubbed it along the hard length of his erection.

He turned his head to look at her, only to find her watching him with heavy-lidded eyes, a secretive smile on her lips. He reached out to flick off the TV.

"Bedtime," he said, pushing her feet off his lap with an abruptness that made her squawk comically.

Then he hauled her to her feet and led her out to the Airstream, where there'd be no chance of his family interrupting what he planned to do to her.

THE NEXT MORNING, the sense that the bed next to her was empty dragged CJ out of sleep. Stretching her hand out, she found nothing but cold sheets.

Jesse was gone.

Blinking herself to full wakefulness, she propped herself up on her elbows just as the door to the bathroom slid open. She watched with blatant admiration as Jesse traveled the short distance to the bed.

"You're up," he said. "Good."

He climbed back onto the bed, lifting the duvet to slide in beside her before pulling her into his arms. She went willingly, slipping a leg over his hip, sliding her palms onto his chest as his mouth found hers.

Last night had been crazy good. Maybe it was her imagination, but it seemed to her that every time it got better between them. Which probably explained why she was becoming a bit of a glutton where his lovemaking was concerned. All day yesterday she'd had to consciously concentrate to stop her thoughts from drifting to what would happen once the day was over and they could retire to the Airstream. She'd been so worked up by the time they were alone in the bathroom yesterday afternoon, she'd almost sobbed when he pushed her against the door and slid inside her.

Now, she pressed herself against him and luxuriated in the feel of his body against hers and the knowledge that soon she would be clawing at his back and moaning his name as he made her come.

True to form, he made her body sing, but instead of letting her go or rolling away the way he usually did afterward, he wrapped his arms more tightly around her, one hand cradling the side of her face. She felt the same need to stay close, to hang on to the intensity of their connection, and she wrapped her legs around his hips and pressed her cheek into the palm of his hand.

They lay locked together for long moments, his body still joined to hers, neither of them saying a word. Then the distant sound of a door slamming prompted Jesse to stir, and finally they drew apart.

CJ avoided meeting his gaze for a few seconds afterward, uncertain exactly what the moment meant—for her, or for him.

She liked him a lot. She was wild about his body and couldn't get enough of his lovemaking. But she was aware of a small, cautious part of herself that was holding back whenever she was with him.

Getting serious about someone was not what she wanted or needed in her life right now, and she was pretty sure Jesse wasn't looking for anything more, either. Not that they'd ever talked about the future, or what they were doing—which pretty much said it all, really.

This was a fun-while-it-lasted type deal. She needed to remember that, no matter how tempting it was to let herself get swept up in how it felt when she was in Jesse's arms.

"You want to shower out here or up at the house?" he asked.

"Might be easier out here, if everyone else is in line," she said, hoping she didn't sound as stiff and uncertain as she felt.

If he picked up on her tension he gave no sign of it, teasing her throughout their shower, and slowly she let go of the sudden caution that had gripped her.

No need to panic, she told herself. *As long as we both know what this is, nothing can go wrong.*

They all ate breakfast together, then Jed decided to hit town again to get more fencing supplies, since they'd burned through the first lot so quickly the first day. CJ and Jesse went along for the ride, soaking up the morning sunshine, warm air flowing into the truck as they raced down the highway. Outside the car window, the sky seemed to stretch on forever, framed by the snowy peak of Copper Mountain, and CJ couldn't seem to stop smiling.

Right at that moment, there wasn't anywhere she'd rather be in the world.

She left Jesse and Jed to round up the fencing supplies, and wandered the aisles with a lazy lack of purpose. Jesse found her in the lumber section and took the opportunity to steal a kiss, leaving her more than a little flustered when they rejoined Jed at the front counter.

Which was why it took her a few beats to realize Jed seemed off-balance himself, his movements unusually jerky as he shoved his wallet back into his pocket.

"Okay, let's go," he said, not looking at either of them before heading outside.

The supplies they'd collected were stacked beside the truck, but Jed only loaded a couple of rolls of mesh and one bundle of rebar into the truck bed. When Jesse went to heft the remainder, Jed gave a terse shake of his head.

"Don't worry about the rest of that. Probably overkill to get so much at once."

Jesse frowned. "The way we tore through it yesterday, we'll need all of this."

"Let's see how it plays out," Jed said.

Jesse studied his brother's face, clearly trying to work out why he'd changed his mind. "Save us another visit into town if we take this now. And it's not like you won't use it at some point."

"I've made the call. Let's just go," Jed said, his tone clipped.

He cut off further discussion by heading around to the driver's side and climbing into the truck. A muscle flickered in Jesse's jaw as he absorbed the dismissal and for a moment something dark and dangerous seemed to hang in the air.

Acting on instinct, CJ reached out to rest a calming hand on Jesse's hip. He seemed startled by her touch, and it took a moment for his gaze to come back into focus when he looked at her. Then he forced a small smile.

"Guess we'd better get moving," he said.

No one talked as Jed pointed the truck out of town. Then he reached out and punched the radio on and the sound of Kenny Chesney's latest hit filled the cab.

It wasn't the most comfortable twenty minutes of CJ's life, but by the time they'd reached the ranch both Carmody men seemed to have regained their equilibrium. They worked in tandem to load up the trailer for another day of fencing, and soon the four of them were heading out on horseback again, Casey bringing up the rear with the four-wheeler.

It didn't take long for them to fall into the rhythm and roles they'd established yesterday and the hours flew by. Every now and then CJ found herself taking the temperature between Jesse and Jed, looking for signs of their earlier conflict, but neither man seemed to be hanging on to what had happened. If anything, Jed seemed to be going out of his way to interact with Jesse, laughing at his jokes, offering praise for a well-drilled hole or well-tensioned length of mesh. Almost as though he was subconsciously trying to make it up to his brother.

They ran out of rebar partway through the afternoon, but Jesse didn't say a word. Still, Jed's expression was shuttered as they packed up for the day, and he rode ahead of the pack on the way back to the house, claiming he wanted to get back in time to make some phone calls before close of business.

Once again Casey and Sierra peeled off to deal with other chores once they'd unloaded the equipment and dealt with the horses, and Jesse and CJ were left to their own devices.

"Should have the draw for Great Falls by now," Jesse said as they climbed the steps to the porch. "We can check how we did on my laptop."

"Sounds good," she said. With luck, they'd both get great broncs.

They entered the house and she watched as Jesse's gaze went to the closed door to his brother's office.

"You should go talk to him," she prompted.

He shot her a look. "Who?"

She simply cocked an eyebrow. He knew exactly who she was talking about.

"He's busy," he said, turning away with a frown. "You want something to drink?"

He headed into the kitchen, and CJ followed him, hands tucked into the back pockets of her jeans.

"Look, it's none of my business, but has it occurred to you that maybe Jed didn't take the rest of the fencing supplies this morning because he couldn't afford them right now?" she asked, lowering her voice so that there would be absolutely no chance of Jed overhearing her. "Maybe that was why he was so snappy when we were heading home."

Jesse didn't say anything as he opened the fridge and pulled out a jug of water. Finally CJ got sick of waiting for a response.

"So…no comment?" she said, head tilted to one side.

He glanced at her. "You're right—it's none of your business. So maybe we should leave it at that."

There was no heat in his words, but the flat firmness of his tone was almost worse. CJ told herself she had no right to feel rebuked—she'd known the moment she opened her mouth she was wading into deep, unknown waters, so his response was hardly a surprise.

And yet her chest and belly muscles still felt tight and she had trouble making eye contact with him. "Fair enough."

He slid a glass of water across the counter toward her, and she swallowed it in a couple of long gulps.

"I might try to get a run in," she said. "That okay with you?"

Jesse's green gaze scanned her face. "Of course."

"Then I'll see you in an hour or so."

She offered him a small smile before heading for the door, fully aware that it was absurd to feel so burned by his stonewalling.

The man had a right to his privacy. Just because she was sharing his bed didn't mean she had an all-access pass to his life.

If she was smart, she'd consider what had just happened a timely reminder: this was just about fun, nothing else.

Chapter Sixteen

J ESSE CLOSED HIS eyes briefly as CJ let herself out the back door. He was such an asshole. She'd been trying to help, and he'd slapped her down and hurt her feelings.

He hadn't meant to, but he'd been trying to convince himself all day that his suspicions regarding the incident at Big Z's were wrong—and then she'd validated his fears and it had freaked him out so much he'd simply shut her down.

Like an asshole.

He sighed and ran a hand through his hair. He needed to apologize to her. And he also needed to decide what to do about the situation with Jed, because it was becoming increasingly obvious that the ranch was in some kind of financial trouble.

The puzzle pieces were all there if a person was looking for them—the peeling paint on the barn, the worried look in his brother's eyes, the delayed quarterly payment, his reaction when Jesse told him he'd asked CJ to help out with fencing, the incident at the hardware store.

If it was anyone else, he'd simply ask what the problem

was and offer to help in any way he could. But it wasn't anyone, it was Jed, and there was no way Jesse could get into that conversation with his brother. There was too much sitting between them, too much history. And that wasn't about to change anytime soon.

Which left Jesse clueless as to what to do. Walking away wasn't an option. He knew that. Which left him…nowhere.

He sighed and ran a hand through his hair. He might not know how to handle Jed, but he knew what he owed CJ—an apology, and sooner, rather than later.

Dumping their water glasses in the sink, he headed for the back door. He took the steps from the porch in one big leap and started across the yard, his strides long, only to stop in his tracks when he caught sight of CJ disappearing down the driveway, her ponytail bobbing as she jogged.

Damn.

He turned back to the house to go wait for her there, then realized he actually felt more comfortable in the Airstream these days.

Which said a lot, really.

The truth was, if CJ hadn't agreed to stay the week with him, he'd probably have come up with an excuse to be out of here by now. There were too many memories here, good and bad, and the weight of the past and the part he'd played in it messed with his head.

He made his way to the trailer and sank onto the top step to wait. He'd had plenty of time to formulate an apology and get the words straight in his head before he heard the crunch of gravel underfoot and CJ appeared around the corner of the barn.

"Hey," she said, plucking a pair of earbuds out of her ears. She seemed…wary, and he hated that he'd made her that way.

"Hey. How was your run?"

"Good. Except I didn't realize how much of a slope there was on your driveway until I tried to run up it."

"I'm sorry about before," he said, not wanting another moment to pass before he put things right between them. "It's a messed-up situation, but it's not your fault, and I was an asshole speaking to you like that."

Her face softened. "I think asshole is a little harsh."

"I don't. Come here," he said, holding out a hand.

She took it, and he used it to draw her onto his lap. To his relief, she came willingly, slipping her arms around his neck.

"I'm all sweaty," she warned him.

"Exactly the way I like you," he murmured before kissing her.

She deepened the kiss, making a small approving sound, and the tension across his shoulders eased as he understood they were going to be okay.

Even though he could hold her like this all day and all night, he broke the kiss to execute stage two of his apology.

"You got anything other than jeans in that bag of yours?"

he asked.

"One dress—why?"

"Go put it on. I'm taking you somewhere nice for dinner," he said. "Don't know if I told you, but I won second prize at a rodeo recently and the money's burning a hole in my pocket."

"Is that so?"

"How long will it take you to get ready?"

"Not long. Probably less than you, pretty boy," she said with a smile.

"Care to put a wager on it?"

She slipped off his lap and stuck out her hand. "First one waiting at the truck gets to be on top."

He laughed and shook on their deal. "That's what I call a win-win."

"Thought you'd like it."

She seemed to hesitate then, her gaze scanning his face as though she was looking for something.

"What?" he asked, catching her hand again.

"Nothing," she said, shaking her head quickly. "Better get your skates on, cowboy, because you're going to need to move fast to beat me."

Slipping past him, she disappeared into the trailer, and seconds later he heard the door to the bathroom sliding shut.

He remained where he was for a moment, the smile slowly fading from his mouth as his thoughts shifted back to the more difficult problem of how to help his stubborn, proud brother.

But CJ was going to win their wager hands down if he didn't hustle, so he pushed himself to his feet and headed back to the house.

He had three more days before he had to leave for Great Falls. Hopefully something would come to him before then.

CJ'S SKIRT SWISHED around her calves as she rounded the barn and headed for Jesse's truck. There was no sign of Jesse himself, and a small smile curved her lips when she realized she'd been on the money when she'd predicted it would take him longer to get ready than her.

She leaned against the side of the truck, arms crossed, and waited for him to emerge from the house and register his loss. Twenty-seven years' experience with three brothers had taught her to take her wins where she could find them, and she was going to enjoy this one.

She deliberately kept her thoughts light as she waited, not allowing herself to dwell on the one thing missing from Jesse's otherwise perfect apology: an explanation. Sure, he'd referenced the situation being "messed up," but he hadn't explained why, and even though she'd waited for more, she'd quickly understood she wasn't going to get it.

Which was *fine*. They were lovers, they were becoming friends, but they didn't owe each other anything. It was what she'd spent the entire five miles of her run telling herself.

And just because it didn't feel that way didn't mean it wasn't true.

Realizing she'd fallen into the trap of thinking about the exact thing she didn't want to think about, CJ straightened the skirt on her red dress and smoothed a hand over her hair.

You're here to have fun. Hang on to that.

Jesse was a grown, adult man. He would sort his own life out. He'd been doing it for years before he met her, and no doubt he'd be doing it for years after she'd gone, too.

The sound of the front door opening drew her gaze to the porch and she smiled her cockiest, most challenging smile as Jesse descended the steps.

"Well lookee here, if it ain't slowpoke Carmody," she said in her best old-timer accent.

"Before you gloat too much, Casey was in the shower," he said, his gaze tracking over her body. "You look beautiful."

"So do you." He did, too, his dark blue shirt and slim-cut black pants showcasing his lean body to perfection. He'd shaved away this morning's beard scruff and tamed his dark wavy hair and she was pretty sure she was going to be the envy of every woman in Marietta tonight.

Another reason to concentrate on the here and now, because soon Jesse wouldn't be hers to claim.

The thought made her smile falter, and she quickly pushed it away.

"Shall we do this, then?" she said.

"Wait a second," he said, stepping forward to beat her to the door handle.

She gave him an amused look as he opened the car door for her.

"Nice manners, Mr. Carmody."

"I like to dust them off occasionally, keep them in working order."

They joked around all the way into town, where Jesse parked his pickup on First Street and led her into Rocco's Italian, a cute, cozy place with Tuscan landscapes painted on the walls and red and white checked tablecloths. There were even candles in Chianti bottles on the tables, along with crisp white linen napkins.

"Hope you like Italian," Jesse said. "Sierra said the food here is good."

"If this place has Sierra's seal of approval, I am all in," CJ said.

He reached across the table and took her hand as they both turned their attention to the menu and CJ felt an odd little pang somewhere in the region of her heart. He'd laid hands on every intimate part of her, but there was something very sweet about the old-fashioned courtliness of the gesture.

"What looks good?" he asked after a beat, and she realized she hadn't taken in a single word of the menu.

Jesse Carmody in full romance mode was that charming.

"Ummm…I'm aways a sucker for a good spaghetti carbonara," she said.

"Lasagna for me. How do we feel about garlic bread?" he asked, one eyebrow cocked.

"I am strongly pro, but only if we both eat it."

"It's official, you're the perfect woman." His eyes were steady on hers and his thumb brushed across her knuckles.

"You're good at this cozy-dinner-for-two business," she said.

"Wait till we get to dessert."

"Really? What's for dessert?"

"You," he said, his grin nothing short of wicked.

Her laugh came out too loud and she pressed her fingers to her lips.

"Don't. I love your laugh," he said.

"That's because you've never watched *Talladega Nights: The Ballad of Ricky Bobby* with me," she said. "My brother Tyson tells me I sound like an elephant seal when I get going."

"I love that movie," he said, looking genuinely delighted they'd found yet another thing in common.

They talked movies and books and high school disasters for the rest of the meal. Jesse made her laugh so many times her stomach ached by the time she'd spooned up the last mouthful of a decadent tiramisu, although that could have been down to all the food she ate, too.

"I'm so full. You're going to have to roll me out to the car," she groaned.

"You want to skip coffees and walk a while, see if we

can't work some of that off?"

"Please. I'm actually scared my stomach might explode. Everything was so delicious."

Jesse settled the bill, then held the door for her to exit.

"There are those manners again," she said as she brushed past him and out into the street.

"Putting them through their paces tonight, that's for sure," he said with a small smile.

He reached for her hand and they walked half a block or so in companionable silence. CJ caught sight of herself in a shop window and realized she was wearing a goofy-looking smile. She tried to school her features, but the smile kept creeping back.

He'd made her feel special tonight, and even though there had been moments when he'd looked at her and she'd known he was thinking about what was going to happen when they got back to the privacy of the Airstream, the sense he was enjoying her, enjoying being with her, had left her feeling more than a little giddy.

As she'd said, he was good at this.

They walked all the way down to Fourth Street before cutting across a block and going back the other way, sometimes talking, sometimes just enjoying the crisp night and the clear sky overhead and the pretty western storefronts.

When they arrived back at Jesse's pickup he slipped an arm around her waist and pulled her body against his.

"How do you feel about going parking?" he asked after

pressing a brief kiss to her lips.

She laughed. "Seriously?"

"Hell, yeah. It's a long drive back out to the ranch, and you look great in that dress."

"It's only twenty minutes."

"Like I said, a long drive."

"Okay, I'll go parking with you, Jesse Carmody. But you should know that I'm the type of girl who only goes all the way."

His smile was slow and appreciative. "Cassidy Jane, you are my kind of woman, head to toe."

He drove them to a secluded stretch of parkland down near the river and switched off the engine. Then he pushed back his car seat and patted his lap.

"Get your sweet ass over here so I can get my hands on it," he said.

"I'm guessing the well-behaved part of the evening is over," she said as she followed orders and scrambled over the center console.

"Don't worry, it's still going to be ladies first."

He cranked the seat back, then pulled her into his lap, her bent legs straddling his. She leaned forward to kiss him, a sensual shiver racing down her spine as his big, rough hands slipped beneath her skirt to glide up the outside of her thighs and curve over her ass.

They fooled around for a long time, teasing each other through their clothes, stretching it out as long as they could.

When he finally pushed the bodice of her dress out of the way and pulled one of her nipples into his mouth she almost came, she was so turned on. Then he started to stroke her through her panties and she did come, her head falling back as she gave herself over to pleasure.

"Baby, you are the hottest thing I have ever seen," Jesse whispered.

He pushed her panties to one side then, quickly rolling on a condom, and she slid down onto him with a grateful, greedy sigh.

"Yes. That feels amazing," she said.

The world shrank to the slide of his body inside hers, the beautiful friction stroking her closer and closer to a second climax.

"I love being inside you," he said, his voice rough and low.

"I love having you inside me."

And then she couldn't speak, because the pleasure was too intense, and he held her close as they came together, bodies shuddering with release.

She rested her cheek on his shoulder afterward, her eyes closed, savoring the afterglow. His hand landed on the back of her head, warm and steady, and she felt the press of his lips against her temple.

"I don't want Friday to be the end of us," he said quietly, his words rumbling through his chest to hers. "I know that wasn't the deal, that this was only supposed to be fun, but this isn't just about sex for me, CJ. Not anymore."

"Me, either," she said, even though she'd barely even admitted it to herself yet.

She lifted her head and they looked into each other's eyes. Then he smiled and reached up to tuck a strand of her hair behind her ear.

"Guess that means I can stop freaking out about losing you at the end of the week."

She cocked her head slightly. "You were not freaking out."

"Practically wetting my pants," he said.

"I thought that was my job," she said.

His laugh was loud in the small space, and he pulled her down to kiss her. "It's my job to make you wet," he growled against her mouth.

The distant sound of a train horn made her start then and he laughed again.

"Panic much?" he said as she dismounted inelegantly, almost falling back into the passenger seat.

"I don't want to be booked for indecent exposure, or whatever they book you for when you get caught having public sex."

"If getting lucky is a crime, I am happy to do the time," he said.

Which made her laugh, and she was still laughing when he started the car and pulled back onto the road.

She wasn't stupid enough to think that trying to make a

go of it with Jesse would be a walk in the park, but no one had ever set her on fire the way he did, or understood her so easily. And it hadn't been lost on her that he was that rare thing, a man who wasn't threatened by a successful woman.

Not that he was perfect—the man clearly had issues with opening up—but she wanted more of what they had together. Much more.

Glancing at his profile, she experienced another heart-region pang, an ache that only intensified when he reached across to capture her hand.

It might not have been a great day, but it had been a perfect night.

And with luck there would be many more to come.

JESSE HAD THE worst night's sleep on record. After the discussion he'd had with CJ, he should have slept like a baby, but instead he'd been unable to stop his brain fixating on the issue of Jed and the ranch.

By six thirty he'd been staring at the ceiling for half the night, CJ sleeping beside him. He'd been going over and over the idea that had come to him in the small hours. It wasn't perfect, but it was something.

Moving carefully so as not to disturb CJ, he shifted to the edge of the bed. He pulled on last night's clothes as quietly as he could, then padded outside in his bare feet before stuffing his feet into his boots.

It was cold enough to turn his breath to mist and he rubbed his arms as he crossed to the house to grab his coat. Traffic was light on the way into Marietta and he had no trouble getting a parking spot at Big Z's. The guys on the front desk were all busy when he arrived so he decided to collect the fencing supplies he needed before trying again. When he returned, the tall, skinny guy who'd served his brother yesterday was free. Jesse checked his name tag before stepping up to the counter.

"Hey, Ken, I'm Jesse Carmody, Jed's brother," he said, offering the other man his hand.

"Jesse. Pleased to meet you. How can I help you?" Ken said, his tone professionally welcoming.

"I'll grab some more fencing mesh and rebar, but Jed also sent me in to pay off the ranch credit account. You able to help me out with that?"

Ken looked surprised. "He wants to pay it all off?"

"Figured we might as well knock it on the head," Jesse said easily.

"Not a problem. Give me a sec to print off the latest statement so you can check it out first," Ken said.

The other man's surprise that he'd be paying off the entire balance gave Jesse an inkling of what to expect when he looked at the statement, but he still blinked with shock when he saw the total. Jed owed nearly ten thousand, most of it in feed costs. He searched for the interest rate and felt his eyebrows rise at the far from competitive figure. Jed was crazy paying these prices when he could have gotten much cheaper money by refinancing the mortgage. That was the way their father had always paid for winter feed, paying the mortgage back down again when the cattle went to market.

Jesse stared at the account, trying to understand. Then it occurred to him that maybe Jed hadn't had the option of borrowing more money from the bank.

Jesus. If that was the case, then the ranch was in big trouble.

"Everything look good?" Ken asked, and Jesse realized he'd been waiting for him to pull out his checkbook.

"Yep, all good," Jesse said.

Paying the account down would put a dent in his savings, but most of it was money he'd saved from his quarterly payments. Seemed only right to tip it back into the ranch if it was in trouble.

And his gut was telling him it was.

Ken added the new fencing supplies onto the total and Jesse wrote out the check and handed it over.

"Tell Jed we appreciate the business, as always. And apologize to him for yesterday. I can only do what the computer tells me it's okay to do," the other man said with an embarrassed shrug.

Clearly it had been an uncomfortable conversation between him and Jed yesterday.

"Will do," Jesse said.

He nodded goodbye then headed out to the yard to load

up his truck.

If he and Jed had been different kinds of brothers, he'd have cornered Jed and demanded he tell him what was going on. He couldn't do that, though, so this was the next best thing. He'd bought enough wire and rebar to finish upgrading the main fence, which should protect their feed supplies for the coming winter. He knew Jed wouldn't be happy about Jesse covering the cost, but he figured his brother was smart enough not to look a gift horse in the mouth.

And with a bit of luck he wouldn't find out Jesse had paid off his store account until Jesse was long gone.

Jed's pride would take a hit initially, but Jesse hoped his brother would eventually appreciate what he'd done—or at least take advantage of the renewed line of credit to take care of some outstanding maintenance issues around the ranch.

It didn't matter if he was pissed off with Jesse, as long as paying down the account took some of the pressure off.

The truck loaded up, Jesse climbed behind the wheel and headed for home.

Chapter Seventeen

CJ HALF EXPECTED Jesse to make some joke about her being a sleepyhead when she woke, or to simply pounce on her the way he had every morning so far, but he didn't say a word and when she rolled over she discovered why—the bed was empty. She sat up and glanced toward the bathroom, but the sliding door was open, and there was no sound of anyone moving around.

She flopped back onto her pillow, aware of a sense of disappointment. Making love to him in the mornings had swiftly become her favorite way to start the day. She loved the sleep-warm smell of his skin and the roughness of his whiskers, and she especially loved how eager and urgent he was.

But not today, apparently.

Someone's getting a little spoiled.

Indeed.

She checked the time on her phone and saw it was just after seven. Definitely time to get up. Thanks to the lack of supplies there was no fencing to do today, but she was sure

289

there'd be something else she could lend a hand to—there was always work to be done on a ranch.

She was about to slide out of bed when she saw Jesse had left her a note on the counter near the bed: *Gone to town, back soon. J.*

That explained that, then.

She had a quick shower, smiling every time little flashes from last night came back to her. She'd had such a good time going out for dinner with Jesse, and it had been hotter than hot making out with him in his truck. All the fun of teen nostalgia with the perks of being an adult thrown in.

And then he'd made the night perfect by telling her he didn't want to let her go at the end of the week. The memory was so sweet she closed her eyes, savoring it.

He'd been braver than her. She'd been busy protecting herself, trying to guard her heart, telling herself not to invest too much and that she didn't need this in her life right now—and Jesse had just put it out there, no bullshit or games.

One of the many reasons she was so besotted with him.

The only faint, far-off cloud on her horizon was the tickle of unease she felt every time she thought about their disagreement regarding Jed. She'd pushed a little, stuck her toe into deep waters, and he'd locked down, tight. It worried her a little, how firmly he'd held her at arm's length. Especially when he was prepared to be so open about his other feelings.

But surely that would change, now that they'd committed to each other. Surely now they'd both admitted this was no fling, that this was real, he'd feel safe enough to talk about what was clearly a deep wound where his brother—his family—was concerned.

CJ stilled in the shower, warm water sliding over her skin, a frown on her face. Then she shook off the shadow of worry. Last night had been amazing. She refused to be a glass-half-empty person, not today.

She finished her shower, then dressed in her work clothes and headed up to the house. Sierra looked up from where she was eating toast at the table as CJ entered the kitchen.

"Morning. Coffee's fresh, and I made bread last night and it's pretty damn fine, if I do say so myself."

"Yum. I'm going to miss your cooking when I go," CJ said, pouring herself a cup of coffee before walking across to top Sierra's up. She'd learned over the last few days that Jesse's sister was a caffeine fiend, never passing up a chance to mainline more.

"Guess you'll just have to come stay again," Sierra said with an arched look.

"Guess I will," CJ said.

Sierra put down the piece of toast she was holding. "Okay, I want to say something, and it's probably going to come out sounding weird. But here goes—whatever you did to Jesse, please keep doing it, because I haven't seen him this happy in years. Plus I really like you. In fact, I might have a lady crush. Hope that's okay."

CJ nearly snorted coffee out her nose when Sierra tacked on the last part of her speech. "I really like you, too. And I didn't do anything to Jesse. Apart from the, um, obvious."

"Well, I guess you should just keep doing that, because this is the longest he's stayed home since he left, and it's been really, really nice having him here," Sierra said.

"How long does he normally stay?" CJ asked.

"Forty-eight hours, max. Every time. And then he's out of here. So we're at an all-time record right now. Almost clocking up a full week."

Her tone was light, but her eyes were sad.

CJ hesitated, but she and Jesse had committed to each other last night and she needed some background to guide her. She sat at the table, nursing her coffee cup between both hands.

"What's the problem between him and Jed?" she asked boldly.

Sierra sighed. "You noticed that?" she asked dryly.

"Just a little."

"When Jesse was eighteen, Jed kicked him out," Sierra said.

"Ah," CJ said. She hadn't anticipated that. She'd thought maybe there'd been some dispute over managing the ranch, hence Jesse's reluctance to tackle Jed regarding any financial problems the ranch might be experiencing.

"Mom and Dad had only been dead a year. It was a horrible time. Casey disappeared into himself. I cried so much I was pretty much permanently dehydrated. Jed threw himself into managing this place. And Jesse…Jesse took it hardest out of all of us, I think. He was so unhappy, and he never seemed to want to be here. He was always out with friends from the football team, coming home stinking of beer and weed. He was messing up at school, too, and they told him he wouldn't graduate if he didn't get his crap together. Of course, Jesse took that as a challenge and played up even more. Jed tried to talk sense into him, but mostly they just yelled at each other."

Sierra looked down at her coffee.

"Things came to a head when Jed finally convinced me to have a birthday party. It had been just over a year since they'd been gone, and we were all starting to get used to the sadness. I knew Jed wanted me to be happy, so I said yes. Had a couple of friends over to stay the night. And Jesse rolled up, drunk as a skunk, being loud and obnoxious. Jed told him to go to bed, Jesse took offence, and wound up punching Jed in the face."

"Oh, wow," CJ said. She'd seen her brothers scuffle over the years, but they'd never had an all-out fight where they'd thrown punches meant to truly hurt and maim. "You must have been terrified."

"It was awful. Jed just stood there, didn't put his fists up. Casey got between them. Jesse looked devastated, as though he couldn't believe what he'd just done. The next morning,

Jed talked to him out in the barn. I don't know exactly what went down between them. Jed told us that he gave him an ultimatum—shape up or ship out, because Jed had his hands full with everything else and didn't have the time to carry Jesse as well. Anyway, Jesse came up to the house afterward and started throwing stuff into a bag. Then he drove off, and we didn't hear from him for months."

Sierra's eyes were shiny with tears at the memory and CJ reached across to squeeze her forearm.

"Sorry for bringing back bad memories."

"I'm fine. It's just I know those two idiots love each other like crazy. Jed was sick with worry after Jesse left. Used to stay up late, searching around on the Internet, trying to find some clue where he was. He'd ring Jesse's friends, ask if anyone had heard from him. When Jesse finally called, Jed walked outside and when he came back his eyes were all red." Sierra shook her head, her mouth twisting with frustration. "Why do men always try to hide their soft side? It drives me nuts."

"Because they get told they have to be tough all the time," CJ said. She'd seen it with her brothers, heard her father telling them to suck it up and toughen up.

"Well, the world could do with more softness as far as I'm concerned. I'm over the tough-guy shit."

"So Jesse obviously came home again at some point?"

"Only because I harassed his ass. Called him every week, cried on the phone, begged him to please come home for

Christmas. And he finally agreed. I thought the two of them would sort their crap out if they could just be in the same room. It had been four years since Jesse left by then. He was working as a pickup rider with the rodeo, hadn't started riding saddle bronc yet. Jed was older; everything was more settled here with the ranch. I figured they'd be able to talk calmly and put it behind them. But they didn't talk at all, as far as I can tell. Not about anything important. It was like they were strangers, they were so polite and careful with each other. Unless Jed said anything big brotherly, then Jesse's back would go up so fast… And it's never really moved on from there, even though Jesse has been home half a dozen times since then."

CJ nodded. She'd seen Jesse bristle, and she'd witnessed Jed's regret that he couldn't seem to get it right with his younger brother.

"Thanks for filling me in. I've been wondering, and Jesse doesn't want to talk about it."

"If I could lock them in a room, I feel in my heart that they could work it out, but they're both so freaking stubborn and stupid… It drives me nuts," Sierra said.

CJ considered the other woman, mulling over what she'd seen of the two brothers, thinking about the way Jesse had gone into hard shutdown mode yesterday when she'd dared to probe a little. Whatever had gone down between him and Jed, Jesse had taken it into his soul.

The sound of booted feet had them both looking toward

the door as Jed entered. He looked tired, even though it was first thing in the morning, but he gave them both a small smile.

"Morning, ladies."

"Morning," CJ said, fighting the urge to squirm in her seat. There was no way Jed could know they'd been talking about him, but she felt guilty just the same.

She didn't regret asking Sierra to fill her in, though. She needed to know what was going on with Jesse if she was going to be with him.

Sierra cleared their plates and left to have a shower and CJ was about to ask what was on the agenda for the day when the sound of a pickup pulling up outside drew Jed's gaze to the window.

"Where's Jesse been this early?" he asked.

"He left a note saying he was going into town. Not sure why," CJ said.

Jed's gaze narrowed, his focus on whatever was going on out in the yard and CJ watched as his face got tight and hard.

"*What the fuck*," he said under his breath, the words only audible because the kitchen was so quiet. Then he turned on his heel and strode for the front door.

After a moment's shock, CJ pushed to her feet and followed him, exiting to the front porch just as Jed approached Jesse by his pickup in the yard.

"What's all this?" Jed asked, and CJ realized Jesse was

unpacking more fencing wire.

That was why he'd gone into town—to collect and pay for the supplies he suspected his brother couldn't afford. No doubt he'd been operating on the old "easier to apologize than ask permission" maxim, but by the looks of it, Jed was not thrilled about Jesse going behind his back.

"Figured we could get the fencing finished while CJ and I are here to help," Jesse said.

He shot a look at his brother, and even from fifteen feet away CJ could see the challenge in his eyes. He was daring Jed to make an issue of it, daring him to throw the subject of the ranch's finances on the table.

Jed eyed his brother, his jaw working. Then his gaze went to the rolls of wire, the lengths of rebar hanging out the back of the pickup's bed.

"I've got a meeting in town this morning," he finally said. "You'll have to get started without me."

Then he turned and walked back into the house, eyes downcast as he passed CJ. She joined Jesse at the back of the truck.

"That went well," she said dryly.

"Better than I expected, to be honest," Jesse said, one corner of his mouth tilted slightly. "Wait till he finds out I paid off the account."

"Was it bad?" she asked.

"Bad enough." He hefted another bale of wire and headed for the barn.

Leaving CJ standing blinking in the early morning sunshine, astonished at the brevity of the exchange.

That was it? That was all the information he was going to give her? A few crumbs, even though she was stuck in the middle of all this drama and he'd told her last night he wanted a future with her?

She started to go after him, then stopped in her tracks when she saw Casey was in the barn, dealing with the horses. She'd never been a fan of public scenes, and that's what this would become if she tried to talk to Jesse about this now, in front of Casey.

She would wait till later to tackle him. After all, this was a tangle eleven years in the making. Twelve years, if she counted from when the Carmodys' parents had died. And CJ's gut told her that she should, that today's unhappiness had its roots in the tragedy of the past.

Did anyone ever get over such a sudden, devastating loss? She didn't think so, especially when it happened during a formative period in a person's life. And Jesse had had that loss compounded by being kicked out of home a year later, consequently losing the rest of his family. Was it any wonder he had big walls keeping the world at bay when it came to this stuff?

Packing her frustration and concern away, she pulled on her yellow leather work gloves and turned to grab a bundle of rebar.

It took them ten minutes to load the trailer with the new

supplies, then Jesse went inside to change into his work gear while she and Casey added all the necessary tools to the haul.

They were just saddling the horses when Sierra and Jesse joined them, and a few minutes later they were on the move, Casey once again in charge of the four-wheeler. CJ kept sneaking looks at Jesse, trying to discern something—anything—from his neutral expression.

He was good at covering his thoughts and feelings, though, and she was glad when they arrived at the section of fence where they'd stopped work yesterday so she could concentrate on something concrete. There was only so much spinning of mental wheels that one person could do.

Maybe it was the fresh air or the warmth of the sun, but after an hour or so she felt her shoulders relax, and Jesse became more playful, teasing his sister and goading Casey into a competition to see who could drive the rebar into the fence post the fastest. They'd just finished lunch and were lazing in the grass when the sound of an approaching horse came to them on the breeze.

Jed, CJ guessed, come to pitch in now that his morning appointment was dealt with. She wondered if they'd left any sandwiches for him and stood to go check the cooler, dusting off the rear of her jeans. Which was when she caught sight of Jed's face as he approached.

She'd never truly understood the term "thunderous" before today. Jed looked as though he was on the verge of exploding, his face rigid with suppressed emotion, his eyes glinting dangerously.

Exactly like a storm about to break.

She took a step toward Jesse, instinctively wanting to protect him, but he was already standing, his gaze on his older brother. Braced for what was coming.

Maybe it was her imagination, but it felt as though the world held its breath as Jed came to a halt and dismounted. Throwing Pedro's reins over the horse's head, he jerked his chin toward Jesse.

"We need to talk."

Jesse simply nodded, following Jed with measured steps when the other man walked out into the field. CJ watched, anxiety a knot in her belly, her gaze never leaving Jesse's tall figure.

This moment felt dangerous, loaded, even though she didn't fully understand what was going on. All she knew was that these two men had problems they refused to confront or talk about—and right now, one of them was aching for a fight.

"YOU WANT TO tell me why the Big Z just emailed me a receipt for payment in full of my store account?" Jed demanded the moment the two of them were far enough away not to be heard. His chin was high, his face taut.

Jesse was pretty sure he'd never seen his brother so angry.

"I saw a problem, I had the solution. I took care of it,"

Jesse said, making a point of keeping his tone calm. He'd anticipated some version of this conversation once Jed got wind of what he'd done—he'd just hoped they'd be having it later rather than sooner, preferably down a phone line instead of face to face.

"You didn't think I might have something to say about that? That I might have a fucking opinion about my brother paying my debts?" Jed asked.

"That debt belongs to all of us."

Jed took a step forward. "I run this ranch. I decide what gets paid, and when."

"Even if it means we can't finish the fencing?"

"You think that's the priority around here, Jesse? You think if I had ten thousand to spare I'd choose to sink it into an account I can pay off once we send our next stock shipment to market?"

"How would I fucking know? You treat ranch business like it's top secret. How the hell am I supposed to know anything about this place?" Jesse asked, his temper finally getting the better of him.

"You walked away. You don't get to stick your nose in whenever you feel like it."

Jesse's whole body got hot at his brother's mischaracterization of their shared history. "Oh, yeah, I just walked away."

"I gave you a choice, and you took the easy way out because you didn't have the balls to stay."

It was a version of the truth and shame curled through Jesse. He looked away from his brother's angry glare, momentarily unable to hold his eye.

"Here," Jed said, and Jesse saw there was a slip of paper in his outstretched hand.

It took him a second to recognize it was a check.

"I don't want that."

"Take it," Jed said.

"You need it. Don't pretend you don't."

Jed stepped closer and stuffed the check into the chest pocket of Jesse's shirt, the movement sharp and aggressive.

"I don't want your fucking money."

Jed turned and started walking back to where he'd left Pedro. Jesse pulled the check from his pocket and stared at his brother's slanted handwriting. He tore the check into halves, then quarters, and let them fall to the ground.

Jed mounted his horse, said something to Casey, then took off in the direction of the house, Pedro stretched into a full gallop. Jesse could feel CJ watching him, and he willed her to keep her distance. He needed a moment to find his feet and he turned away, hoping CJ and his siblings would take the hint.

You didn't have the balls to stay.

The accusation ricocheted around his mind, tearing away the polite pretense they'd all helped construct over the past decade and more.

Because his brother was right—Jesse *had* left because he

couldn't face his family anymore. Because he couldn't handle looking into their eyes and seeing their pain and grief and knowing that it was all his fault.

He took a few steps forward, physically trying to move away from all the shit swirling around in his head and gut. It didn't make any difference—his brother's words still echoed in his head.

He shouldn't have tried to help. Shouldn't have gotten involved. It had been a mistake, just like staying longer than a few days and offering to help out with the fencing had been a mistake.

Jed didn't want him here.

And who could blame him?

Not Jesse. He'd recognized eleven years ago that his presence was a burden his siblings shouldn't have to bear. Casey and Sierra might not admit it, but it was easier for all of them when he wasn't around. Jesse didn't doubt for a moment that they loved him—but a part of them had to hate him, too, after what he'd done.

Going away and staying away had been the last good thing he could do for them.

The thought brought clarity, settling the maelstrom in his mind.

If he'd stuck to his own rules, none of this would have happened. But it wasn't too late to fix his mistake. He made some mental calculations as he stared into the distance.

If he and CJ left this afternoon, they could make it to

Helena by nightfall. There was a place he could stable Major on the outskirts of town, and he and CJ could find somewhere nice to stay and live it up for the final few days before the rodeo in Great Falls. He started to pull out his phone, then remembered there was no signal out here.

Fine. He'd have to wait till they got back home and he could tap into the ranch's Wi-Fi to solidify his plans. The important thing was that he had a plan, that he wouldn't have to sit across the kitchen table tonight and look at his brother and remember the contempt in his face and voice as Jed stuffed the check into Jesse's pocket.

I don't want your fucking money.

At least they both knew where they stood now. No more games, no more polite bullshit.

The thought brought a burning heat to the backs of his eyes and he had to blink a few times before he had a grip on himself.

When he was confident he had himself under control, he glanced across and saw Sierra was watching him, a frown on her face, while Casey and CJ had started working on the next fence post. Squaring his shoulders, he started walking, the long grass whipping at his jeans. When he was close enough to be heard, he held up a hand and caught his sister's eye.

"I don't want to talk about it," he warned.

Sierra opened her mouth, anger and concern flashing in her green eyes. Then she seemed to think twice about whatever she was going to say and shut her mouth with an audible click. He moved past her, pulling his work gloves back on before hefting the sledgehammer and joining CJ and Casey at the fence post.

He heard his sister mutter a four-letter word, then she joined them, taking the drill from CJ when she was finished boring out the fence post. CJ passed a piece of rebar to Casey, who was balanced on an A-frame ladder. Once Casey had guided the metal rod down into the fence post, Jesse passed up the sledgehammer and Casey pounded the metal into the hole until it was well and truly embedded.

No one said a word as they worked. He caught CJ studying him, her gaze troubled, but he simply gave her a tight smile and picked up the drill to move it to the next fence post. He'd barely taken a step before Sierra lost the battle to bite her tongue.

"Come on, Jesse, this is bullshit. Will you please tell us what's going on?"

"It's nothing you need to worry about," Jesse said.

"Right. You and Jed looking like you're about to start pounding on each other is nothing to worry about," Sierra scoffed.

"That's between me and Jed."

"Was it something to do with you coming back with more fencing supplies this morning?" Sierra asked.

"Which part of 'I don't want to talk about it' do you not get?" Jesse said.

"Stop trying to shut me down. Something is clearly going on. You're upset, Jed's upset."

Jesse could feel the last of his patience draining away. He

already felt raw after what Jed had said, and he was not about to offer himself up to Sierra for sisterly interrogation.

"For God's sake, can you just leave it?" he snapped.

It came out more harshly than he'd it meant to and Sierra flinched. Then, because she was Sierra, she came out fighting.

"You know, I have had it up to *here* with you and Jed and the taciturn cowboy schtick," she said. "Why on earth don't you just freaking sit down and talk to each other instead of acting like the world will fall apart if you talked about how you feel for a change?"

He glared at his boots, counting to ten as he tried to keep a grip on his temper.

"Leave it, Sierra," Casey said, and Jesse shot his brother a grateful look.

"I'm sick of leaving it. This family needs to start talking, and we're going to start right now," Sierra said stubbornly, her gaze not leaving Jesse's face.

Jesse returned her stare for a long beat, then tossed the drill onto the grass at his sister's feet. He caught CJ's eye. "I'll see you back at the house."

He crossed to Major, caught up his reins and stuck his foot in the stirrup to lever himself into the saddle. Sierra stood shaking her head, hands on her hips, as he turned the horse and headed for home.

The sooner he got out of here, the better. For all of them.

Chapter Eighteen

THERE WAS A long silence after Jesse's departure. Then Sierra let out a string of four-letter words that would put a merchant marine to shame.

CJ shifted uneasily, feeling very much the stranger in the midst of all this family turmoil. Every inch of her wanted to go after Jesse, but she'd committed to helping with the fencing and it went against the grain to simply abandon Casey and Sierra.

Casey make a noise in the back of his throat and turned away.

"Don't tell me you agree with him?" Sierra asked, incredulous.

"You're not going to nag him into doing what you want," Casey said.

"You and I both know if I don't nag nothing will ever change," Sierra said. "You really want to spend Christmas every year wondering what excuse Jesse will come up with for not coming home?"

Casey frowned. "They need to sort it out for themselves."

"They've had eleven years. My patience is officially worn out," Sierra said.

CJ went to collect the drill from the long grass, an action that drew the attention of both Carmodys.

"Sorry," Sierra said after a brief moment, a sheepish expression on her face.

"You don't need to apologize," CJ said. She glanced at the fence. "We should finish this run, don't you think?"

Casey went to collect the fencing mesh, while Sierra picked up the wire cutters. The three of them worked with quiet efficiency to stretch wire across the three fence posts they'd just extended. When they were done, Casey started packing gear into the trailer.

"No point pretending we're going to get much done now," he said.

CJ shot him an appreciative look, wondering if he could sense how eager she was to go after Jesse.

She helped pack away the rest of the equipment, feeling a stab of sympathy every time she caught sight of Sierra's unhappy face. CJ had just spent a year grappling with her father's inability to communicate his true feelings; she knew exactly how frustrating and confusing it was to be shut out when it was obvious serious shit was going down.

Once the tractor was loaded, she and Sierra mounted their horses and pointed them homeward. Impatience ate at CJ and she itched to urge her horse into a gallop, but she told herself Jesse wasn't going anywhere.

Still, she was relieved when she spotted the house in the distance, and even more relieved when they rode into the yard. Sierra stretched out a hand for CJ's reins as they dismounted outside the barn.

"Go. I can take care of the horses."

"I can't let you do that," CJ said. Taking care of her own mount had been drummed into her from a young age.

"Go talk to Jesse. Seriously," Sierra said.

After a beat, CJ handed her reins over. "Thank you."

She walked quickly around the side of the barn and along the path. The door was open to the Airstream and her shoulders dropped an inch or so.

It was only then that she realized she'd half expected Jesse not to be here when she got back.

He was sitting on the bed when she ducked into the trailer but came to his feet the moment he saw her.

"Sorry for taking off like that. Sierra was driving me crazy," he said.

"Are you okay?" She moved forward, wanting to be close.

The moment she laid hands on him she could feel the tension vibrating through him.

"Sure." He kissed her briefly, not quite holding her eye as he drew back. "Listen, I was thinking that you deserve some R and R after all this ranch work. A couple of days' rest to make sure you're ready to kick ass at Great Falls. If we leave before three, we can make Helena in time for dinner. There's a bed and breakfast place in town I read about, supposed to be really nice. Then we can head up to Great Falls on Friday."

If her hand hadn't still been resting on his chest, she wouldn't have felt the way his body grew hard with tension as he waited for her response. She studied his face for a moment, trying to understand what was happening.

"Okay. You want to go, we can go," she said.

The pec muscle beneath her hands softened with relief.

"But I want to know why," CJ added.

Instantly he was tense again.

"Didn't you hear what I just said?" he asked, taking a step backward and ending the physical contact between them.

"You didn't give me a single reason why, Jesse. You just said you didn't want to be here."

"Isn't that enough?"

It would be so easy to give in, to say yes and follow him to Helena and let all of this slide into the past but her gut told her that if they were to have any kind of future together she owed it to both of them to stand her ground.

"You said last night that you want to have a future with me, that you want this to be about more than a few fun nights, but you won't even give me a hint about what's going on with you and Jed, or why you want to go early."

"Jed was pissed about me paying off the account. He said his piece; I said mine. I don't want to hang around anymore."

It all sounded so reasonable, so matter-of-fact.

"Why won't you talk to me?" she asked quietly.

He stared at her, a muscle flickering in his jaw. "I don't know what you want me to say. Things are fucked between me and Jed. He doesn't want me here. You've seen what it's like. Me being home doesn't make anyone happy."

"I don't believe that for a second," CJ said.

"Look, none of this will even matter when we're gone from here, okay? So why beat a dead horse?"

"Because it matters to you."

Her words made him flinch, and pain flashed in his eyes.

CJ moved closer. "If you could see your face right now… It kills me, Jesse. Please trust me with this. I promise I won't let you down."

He stared at her. She could see he was equal parts tempted and terrified and her chest got tight. She reached out to catch his hand, squeezing it wordlessly, her eyes burning with unshed tears.

She cared so much for this man, wanted so much for him to deal with whatever ghosts haunted him.

"You don't understand," he said.

"Help me to," she said.

He swallowed audibly, then fixed his gaze on their joined hands.

"It's my fault my parents are dead. It's my fault they died that night."

It was so not what she'd been expecting that for a moment CJ couldn't think. Then she blinked and her brain came back online.

"I don't understand. Were you driving?" she asked, confused.

Neither Jesse nor Sierra had ever mentioned that detail when they talked about their parents' deaths.

"I was in town, getting into trouble with some guys from school. My folks were coming into town to pick me up from the sheriff's office."

CJ chose her words carefully, aware she was navigating sensitive territory. "You think it was your fault because they were coming to pick you up?"

Jesse stared at her as though he couldn't fathom why she'd even need to ask that question.

"It *was* my fault, CJ. They would never have been on that road if it hadn't been for me. They'd still be alive. Jed wouldn't have had to give up his whole life. Everything would be different."

The conviction in his voice, the certainty, sent a chill down her spine and she understood this was the gospel he lived his life by. Every day, Jesse Carmody woke up with the belief that his parents' premature death was his fault, that the destruction of his family as he knew it, of his brother's future, was at his door.

The realization made her want to weep for him. Twelve years he'd been carrying this burden around with him.

"Jesse, that accident could have happened anytime. How

many times a week did they drive into town? Ten? Twenty?"

"They were on the road that night because of me. *Because of me*," he said, striking his chest with his fist.

"Why did they crash? Tell me what went wrong," she said, hoping if he gave her enough details she'd be able to make him see the fallacy of his belief.

"It doesn't matter."

"Yes, it does. Did they hit ice? Did a deer run across the road? Was there a pothole or some other problem? Because none of those things could possibly be your fault, Jesse."

"I don't know all the details." He half-turned away from her, desperate to be done with this conversation. "There was ice on the road. I think. They died when they had a head-on collision with another car."

"I'm sorry. That's horrible. But you weren't behind the wheel of that other car."

"Look, I appreciate what you're trying to do, but you can't change the past, CJ. It is what it is."

CJ moved closer. She studied his face for a long moment, determined to find a way to get through to him. She could see the defeat in his eyes, the absolute acceptance of his own culpability, and she racked her brain for counter arguments.

He stared down at her, his mouth stretching into a humorless smile.

"See? There's nothing you can say. Now do you see why I want to go?"

Something he'd said earlier sprang to mind then: *Me be-*

ing home doesn't make anyone happy. She closed her eyes as the true meaning behind his words hit her. Not only did Jesse blame himself, he believed his siblings did, too.

Suddenly everything fell into place—his refusal to tackle Jed head-on about any financial difficulties the ranch might be having, his few and far between visits home when it was clear he loved being here, his confusion whenever Jed praised him or acted with affection.

"Jesus, Jesse," she said.

For a moment she felt overwhelmed by the thought of all the pain this man carried around with him. It was monumental, epic. Biblical.

And she understood in a flash of insight that there was nothing she could say or do to convince him he was wrong. This wasn't something she could do for him. This was something Jesse needed to hash out with his family. Only they could set him free.

"Where's your bag?" Jesse asked.

"You need to talk to Jed. You need to talk to all of them, tell them what you just told me."

He spotted the duffel Sierra had given her and threw it on the bed. A couple of her tops were folded on the kitchen counter and he tossed them into the bag. She caught his arm, forcing him to look at her.

"Did you hear me?"

"You think it's news to them? You think they don't know?" he asked.

That was exactly what she thought. But what chance did she have of convincing him of that when he'd absorbed his own guilt into his very blood and bone?

"You want us to go? I'll come with you—but first you have to talk to Jed," she bargained.

"He said his piece today. I don't need to hear more." He said it firmly, flatly, shutting the door on further conversation.

"What's the worst thing any of them could say to you?" she challenged.

He stared at her, his face pale. "Nothing that I haven't said to myself a million times over."

"So why not talk to them?"

"Because then I'd have their voices in my head as well as my own."

Her chest was so tight with emotion she could barely breathe as she stared at him. She didn't know whether to hold him or shake him.

"Are you coming with me or not?" he asked.

"Not like this," she said, playing her final card. "I care for you too much to help you run away from this."

She saw the surprise in his eyes. He hadn't expected her to say no. Not when push came to shove. She held her breath, waiting for his response. Hoping that standing her ground might be the push he needed to confront the past.

"Then I guess I'll see you in Great Falls."

His words landed like lead weights in her belly, and before she could react, he leaned forward and planted a single, hard kiss on her lips. Then he was ducking out through the doorway, and she was standing alone in the trailer.

For a moment she stood frozen in place, overwhelmed by what she'd just learned, and by the depth of the wound Jesse carried. Everything she'd said to him, every tactic she'd tried in the last ten minutes, felt woefully inadequate. She had no idea what to try next, how to best offer him support and comfort. All she knew was that she cared, to the depths of her being, that he was okay.

Taking a deep, calming breath, she tried to think of what to do next. She figured she had a few minutes up her sleeve while Jesse hitched his trailer and settled Major inside it. Enough time to clear her head and come up with a game plan.

Then she heard the sound of a truck starting up.

Alarmed, she spun toward the door. She broke into a run as she exited the trailer, and when she rounded the barn she was just in time to see Jesse's truck disappear down the drive.

He must have hitched the trailer before he came to speak to her, ready to make a quick exit. He'd been that desperate to get out of here.

And suddenly, she understood what she had to do.

She headed for the house, her stride long. She took the steps to the porch two at a time. She slammed into the house, her gaze going straight to Jed's closed office door.

She didn't bother to knock—there was no time for niceties.

"Jesse's leaving. You need to go after him," she said as she flung the door open.

Jed looked up from the computer screen, his expression tight and closed off.

"If he wants to go, he should go," he said. "It's not my place to stop him."

CJ stared at him, frustrated and urgent in equal measure. Jed had no idea what was at stake, but telling him would be a betrayal of Jesse's most heartfelt confidence. She knew without asking that Jesse had never told another soul what he'd told her today, and she could not—would not—breach that trust.

"He's upset. I'm worried about him driving when he's so worked up. You need to go after him," she said.

Jed returned his gaze to the computer screen, so self-contained she wanted to scream.

"He knows how to handle himself," he said, his fingers tapping away at the keyboard as he returned to his work.

CJ acted before she could think about it, stepping forward and slapping the keyboard away with so much force it slid off the edge of the desk with a plastic clatter.

"Go after your brother. He needs you," she said, tears springing to her eyes.

Jed looked at her, his face pale, and she knew she'd finally gotten through to him.

"Please. If you leave now you can still catch him."

JESSE WAS ONLY a couple of miles up the road when he felt the trailer pull heavily to the right, dragging him toward the edge of the road. Thankfully he wasn't going too fast and could easily correct. He tested the steering, confirming there was an odd drag to the right, and signaled to pull over. He climbed out of the truck and went to inspect the trailer. Sure enough, one of the two rear tires had blown on the right side.

"Shit." He kicked the offending tire, the emotions in his chest vibrating behind his sternum, wanting out.

He just wanted to be gone from here. Was it so much to ask?

He grabbed the jack and tire iron from the back of the pickup. The trailer carried a spare bolted beneath the rear, and he took that off and rolled it to where he'd left the jack. Kneeling in the gravel and dust, he felt for the jack point under the trailer, cursing when he touched sharp metal and nicked his fingers. Sucking the blood off, he tried again, more carefully this time, and finally located the jack point. Sliding the jack beneath it, he started to pump the handle.

Then he realized he'd forgotten to loosen the nuts while the tire was on the ground, a rookie's mistake and one that should have been beneath him. One of the first things his father had taught him about cars was how to change a tire, making Jesse rotate all four tires on the family pickup to prove he'd learned the lesson.

He could hear his father's voice in his head as he lowered the jack down. *Gotta loosen the nuts on the ground, but not all the way, Jesse boy. Make gravity work for you, not against you.*

His voice was so clear in Jesse's head, low and with a hint of gravel, tinged with the underlying good humor that had characterized his father, and suddenly everything in front of him was blurry and he couldn't seem to hold back the bubble of emotion rising in his throat.

His head bowed and his shoulders curved inward as a soundless sob racked him. Hunched forward, he gave himself over to the rush of emotion, powerless against its strength, unable to do anything except ride the wave.

It was all so fucked. He was so fucked. He'd walked out on CJ and his family. He'd let everyone down.

"I'm so sorry, Dad," he whispered. "God, I'm so fucking sorry. I wish I could take it back. More than anything I wish I could. I miss you so fucking much…"

But his father wasn't there to hear his words of regret, because he'd died twelve years ago when he and Jesse's mom had been driving into town to pick up Jesse from the sheriff's office.

If Jesse hadn't gotten messy drinking stolen beers with his football buddies and broken into the school gym that night, his parents would still be alive. They wouldn't have been on the road when Gideon Tate hit black ice and lost control of his SUV, sliding across the line and hitting Jesse's dad's pickup head-on. They wouldn't have died instantly as the windshield shattered and the car crumpled.

And he was never, ever going to be able to correct his mistake or make it up to his parents or his siblings for what he'd done because death didn't offer second chances.

One night, one stupid, dumb, careless act, and he'd destroyed his whole family.

Was it any wonder he didn't want to come home, why he couldn't stay? He'd changed all their lives forever, and they all knew it, and for years Jesse had known that the best thing he could do was give them the gift of his absence so they didn't have to look at him every day.

There was so much grief filling his chest it hurt, and he couldn't seem to get a grip on his tears. His shoulders shuddered and he sucked in air, fighting for control.

The sound of a car coming registered and he was glad he was shielded from the road by the trailer. Still, he used his forearm to try to wipe his face.

Then he heard the car slowing.

He turned his head and felt a dull thud of recognition as a dark blue Ford pickup pulled in behind his rig. The door opened, and Jed got out.

"What happened? You get a blowout?" his brother asked, walking toward him.

Then he caught sight of Jesse's tear-ravaged face and stopped. There was so much shock in his eyes, so much uncertainty, and to his shame Jesse felt the tears coming again. He turned his head away.

"I got it," he said, but he was pretty sure he wasn't fooling anyone with his croaky voice.

"What's going on, Jesse?" Jed said, drawing closer. Then Jesse felt the warm weight of his brother's hand on his shoulder as Jed hunkered down beside him.

The gentle tenderness in the gesture and the concern in his brother's voice were too much and Jesse couldn't hold back the words he'd kept inside him for twelve years.

"I'm sorry. I should have said this to you years ago. If it hadn't been for me, they would never have been on the road that night. I know it, and I know you're the one who's had to carry everything because of my fuckup. I'm sorry. For all of it. I'm really fucking sorry."

"Jesus, Jesse. *Fuck.*"

There was a thud, and Jesse turned his head to find his brother sitting on his ass beside him, his face pale with shock.

"You've been carrying *this* around for years? Are you fucking kidding me?" Jed said. "You are not responsible for Mom and Dad dying. You hear me? It was an accident."

"We both know they wouldn't have been on the road into town if they hadn't been coming to pick me up. If I hadn't fucked up."

Jed shook his head. "No. No way. Jesse… God… If I'd known this was what you thought… We should have talked about this years ago."

"What's to talk about? It's pretty simple. I was a screwup,

and Mom and Dad were on the road that night because of me."

"No. I read the accident report, Jesse. There was ice on the road. And Mom's airbag didn't deploy properly. That's why they died."

"Don't try and let me off the hook. They wouldn't have been anywhere near Gideon Tate when he lost control of his car if it hadn't been for me."

Jed shook his head again, the movement fierce and determined.

"No, wrong. Listen up, okay, because this is important. The day before the accident, Mae's mom broke her leg."

Jesse frowned. Jed almost never talked about his ex, Mae Berringer, the girl he'd been crazy in love with through senior year of high school and the first year of college.

"Mae was worried about her mom because she was on her own, worried she wouldn't be able to cope once they sent her home from the hospital. Mae wanted to come home to look after her, even though we were in the middle of exams. So the next day, when Mae's mother got released from the hospital, I asked Mom to look in on her, make sure she had everything she needed so I could reassure Mae. Mom being Mom, she made a couple of casseroles to take over, and when the call came from the sheriff's office about you, she and Dad decided to kill two birds with one stone. Instead of going straight into town, they went to the Berringers' place first."

Jed's gaze never left Jesse's face. "They spent ten minutes there, then got back in the car and headed into Marietta. So, let me ask you—was it *my* fault they died, because I asked them to look in on Lucy Berringer?"

"It's not the same thing."

"If they hadn't made that detour, they would have been halfway to town when Gideon Tate hit that ice. Miles away. But because of me, they were there, at that exact moment."

Jesse stared at his brother. His own guilt was so well established in his own mind, it was hard for him to think about what his brother was suggesting. But Jed was right— ten minutes either way and their parents would be alive.

But not for a moment did Jesse think that made their deaths Jed's fault.

The implications for what that might mean for Jesse's own guilt were nothing short of mind-blowing and for a moment Jesse could do nothing but sit and breathe and try to get his head around it.

"Let me tell you something else about that night," Jed said, almost as though he could read Jesse's thoughts. "You know I told you about Mom's airbag not deploying? I found a notice from the dealer in Dad's files when I was trying to get on top of everything, letting Dad know the airbags needed to be replaced because of a recall. But Dad never got around to making an appointment." Again, Jed paused, letting the detail sink in. "Does that make it Dad's fault she died, because his bag deployed and hers didn't?"

Jesse stared at his brother, the question sitting in the silence between them.

Would his mom still be alive if his father had acted on the recall? Jesse's best guess was probably not, because their father's airbag had worked as intended and he'd still died. The odds were good it would have gone the same way for their mother.

And yet.

"It was an accident," Jed said quietly. "Wrong place, wrong time. No one's fault. Or, if you prefer, everyone's fault. Yours, mine, Dad's, Gideon Tate's, the car company, the contractor who graded that bit of road, the tire manufacturer… You can't keep hauling this around with you, Jesse. It's not your burden to carry."

Jesse heard his brother's words, and they made sense. Still, it took him a moment to process. Took him a moment to feel his chest muscles relax, for his hands to unclench from where he'd been gripping his knees. A rush of overwhelming emotion burned its way up the back of his throat, and he bowed his head.

It was hard to keep a grip on the grief and relief, guilt and gratitude—it was all so tangled up inside him. For years he'd hated himself for that night. Hated what he'd done to his family. But maybe, if it wasn't his fault, he could let some of that go now.

Maybe he could allow himself to be a real part of the family again.

Jed didn't say a word, just let him duck his head and deal with it. When Jesse finally felt able to look up again, he saw Jed's eyes were swimming, too.

"While we're clearing up the past…I should never have told you to leave that day," Jed said. "I've been trying to say this to you for years. I was sinking like a rock, trying to cope, and I overreacted like an idiot. I hate that you still don't feel like you can come home, and that that day is always between us. Most of all I'm sorry I let you down when you needed me the most."

There were no words, so Jesse simply grabbed his brother in a fierce embrace. They hugged so hard Jesse felt his shoulders pop, and still he couldn't let Jed go. Quiet and solid, determined and honorable, his brother was a thoroughly decent human being, and the thought that Jed had been kicking his own ass all these years over what had happened between them killed Jesse.

"You have never let me down. *Never*," he said, his voice gruff with emotion.

"Same goes for you. Always."

They broke apart. For a moment Jesse didn't know where to look. He felt raw. His eyes hurt. His chest hurt.

Then all of a sudden reality seemed to push in on him and he realized he and his brother were sitting in the dirt and gravel on the side of the road, bawling like kids. It was such an absurd visual, so completely at odds with the image he'd spent years projecting—Jesse Carmody, tough-guy bronc rider—he barked out a laugh.

Jed looked startled for a moment, then his mouth twitched into a smile, too.

"Guess we could have found a better place to do this," he said.

Jesse cocked his head as a thought hit him. "Were you coming after me?"

"CJ sent me after you. Almost dragged me out of my chair with her bare hands."

"Yeah?" Jesse used the back of his hand to wipe his eyes. "I shouldn't have gone behind your back at the store," he said.

"I shouldn't have blown up at you." Jed glanced back toward his truck. "You were just trying to help. I can see that now."

Jesse glanced at his brother's grim face. "How bad is it? Bad enough to lose the ranch?"

Jed's head whipped back round and he frowned. "Not that bad. Not yet."

"Here's an idea—why don't you tell me, Casey and Sierra what's going on and we can all pitch in?"

Jed was already shaking his head before Jesse had finished talking and Jesse gave him an exasperated look.

"Why should you always be the one to carry the load all the time? Last time I looked, we were all adults. You don't have to protect us anymore. We're equal shareholders in the property. This is on all of us, not just you."

"I'm the one who fucked it up. I should be the one who

fixes it," Jed said stubbornly.

Jesse grinned, suddenly able to see so much of himself in his brother's self-defeating behavior. "Man, we Carmodys are a bunch of stubborn sons of bitches, aren't we? Unless you emptied the ranch account and put it all on a horse called Lucky at the Kentucky Derby, I'm pretty sure you're not responsible for the fact that ranching is one of the toughest gigs on earth. Share the pain, Jed. Four heads are better than one."

Jed stared at him for a long beat, then he gave a single decisive nod. "All right. If you think it'll make a difference."

"I do." He glanced at the flat tire and abandoned jack. "Why don't you fill me in while I fix this thing? Then we can take it from there."

Again Jed nodded, and Jesse rolled to his knees and started winding the jack down.

"Don't really know where to start," Jed said.

A quick sideway glance revealed his brother's eyes were downcast. This was as hard for him as talking about their parents had been for Jesse.

"At the beginning is usually a good place. I promise not to laugh at the really dumb parts."

Jed crack a smile then, and for the first time in twelve years Jesse looked at him and saw a friend and not the brother he'd let down.

Seemed it was a day of revelations. Good ones, mostly.

Reaching for the cross brace, he got to work on the wheel nuts, and his brother started talking.

Chapter Nineteen

CJ SAT ON the porch steps with Sierra, itchy with dread and doubt.

She should have gone after Jesse herself. Better yet, she should have gone with him when he asked, instead of using her presence as a bargaining chip, or barred the door and refused to let him out of the Airstream.

In all three scenarios, she would not be sitting here, worried sick about him, about the way he'd looked when he left her and what that might mean for him and for them.

Sierra's hand landed in the middle of her back, a warm, reassuring weight. "Jed will chase him down, don't worry. He's the most tenacious of us Carmodys."

CJ nodded, unable to speak. Sierra had no idea what was going down with Jesse; she'd just assumed Jesse taking off was a continuation of the argument he and Jed had out in the field earlier. It wasn't CJ's place to share Jesse's pain with her, even though she knew with absolute certainty that this family needed to shed light on its dark corners. Jesse had to tell his own story, in his own time.

If he wanted to. If Jed caught him. If Jesse told him what he'd been carrying around with him all these years and Jed could convince him to let go of his guilt.

CJ closed her eyes, feeling sick with worry—which was when she heard the faint sound of a car engine. She opened her eyes and stood, her gaze narrowed on the bend in the drive, trying not to hope too hard.

Jed's blue pickup appeared around the bend, and her heart sank when she saw Jesse wasn't following him.

Almost immediately she started making plans in her head. Jesse was heading for Great Falls. He'd mentioned Helena—maybe he'd still go there. If she hit the road now, maybe she'd be able to find him.

Then Jesse's truck rounded the bend, the trailer rocking as he navigated the rutted road, and relief rushed up inside her like a fountain, flooding every part of her.

"Pretty sure he didn't just forget his phone charger," Sierra said.

CJ smiled faintly, too busy trying to catch a glimpse of Jesse's face through the windshield to respond.

Jesse's truck came to a halt and he climbed out at the same time Jed exited his pickup. Jed glanced at the trailer, then across to where CJ and Sierra were standing on the porch steps.

"I'll take care of Major," he said.

"Thanks, man," Jesse said, and CJ bit her lip as the two men exchanged a quick man-hug.

Then Jesse glanced across to where she was standing and started walking, and she saw he'd been crying, and that there was something different about the way he was holding himself as he approached her.

He seemed…lighter. More at ease with himself.

She was aware of Sierra slipping discreetly away as he stopped in front of her.

"Before you say anything, I need to do this," she said, and she put her arms around him and held him to her, trying to convey all her care and compassion in the wordless gesture.

He looked so raw, like he'd been to hell and back.

His arms came around her, and they simply stood quietly for several moments, giving and receiving comfort. After a beat she released him and he took a small step back.

"Thanks for sending Jed after me," he said.

"Took some doing. You Carmodys are stubborn."

"Tell me about it."

CJ reached out and brushed the hair at his temples. "You talked?"

She knew they had, could see the shift in him, but she wanted to have it confirmed.

"Yeah."

"And?"

"Turns out there were some things I didn't know about that night."

CJ listened as he explained about the stop his parents had

made on the way into town, and the recall notice Jed had found among their parents' papers. She could see he was still feeling his way, getting his head around what he'd learned, but the fundamental message had sunk in: he wasn't to blame. He could forgive himself. He could let himself be part of the family again.

The thought made her well up again. When she'd first met him, Jesse Carmody had seemed cooler than Cool Hand Luke, rough and rugged. But there'd always been a gentleness in him, a generosity, an awareness of others, and the knowledge that he'd denied himself his family for so long, when they were so clearly important to him, was painful to her.

She wanted him to be happy. She wanted him to be whole.

And suddenly the words were in her mouth, unstoppable, necessary.

"I love you," she said.

His eyes lit up, and her chest felt warm and tight with emotion.

"I love you, too, Cassidy Jane," he said.

He kissed her, the full length of his body pressed to the full length of hers, a deep, soulful kiss that felt like a promise.

When they drew apart she framed his face with her hands, gliding her thumbs gently over the lines beside his beautiful eyes, her touch tender and careful. This man had become incredibly precious to her in a very short time, but she didn't have a single doubt about her feelings for him.

"Thank you for trusting me," she said. "I'm so glad you talked to your brother. I'm so glad you can let go of that terrible thing."

He pressed his cheek into her palm. "Thanks for not kicking me in the teeth after I was dumb enough to walk away from you."

She smiled. "Thanks for coming back. For wanting us enough to face your demons."

Because she understood now how terrifying that had been for him, and how far he'd had to travel to get to the place they were right now.

"Demons, huh? Thought I was just a bit fucked up."

"No way. You're perfect. The perfect, definitive Jesse Carmody. The man who made me love him, even though all I had in my head was saddle bronc and leaderboards."

"You make me sound pretty impressive," Jesse said, pretending to give it some thought.

"You are. In and out of bed." She kissed him, savoring the taste of him, the feel of his lips against hers. His arms closed more tightly around her, and she let him take them deeper.

She had no illusions about what had happened today. She didn't think Jesse was suddenly going to shed the pain and guilt he'd been carrying with him all of his adult life like a snake sheds its skin. But she could see the new lightness in him, and she'd seen the way he and Jed had hugged out in the yard, and she'd looked into his eyes as he told her his story, and she had great faith that he—they—were going to get there.

They were going to make this work.

So when he took her by the hand and led her toward the trailer, she went with him willingly, happily, eagerly, because this was the man who'd won her heart, and she was the woman who'd won his, and this was the start of their happy every after.

IT WAS NEARLY seven by the time Jesse had finished hashing over the details of the ranch's current financial situation with his siblings. They'd been sitting around the table for an hour and a half, looking at spreadsheets, discussing various issues, proposing changes and ideas.

Getting Jed to agree to have a family conference had taken some work, but Jesse had finally made him see sense. His brother was used to doing things a certain way and to keeping his own counsel, but eventually he'd agreed to a sit-down meeting with Casey and Sierra.

The last few hours hadn't been fun, not by a long shot. But at least they now all understood the scope of the problem. A couple years ago, the ranch—Jed—had taken on more debt in order to increase the herd and replace the barn roof. It had seemed like a smart idea at the time. Then he'd been hit by low beef prices, a hike in interest rates, a couple of bad calving seasons, and the loss of winter feed to foraging deer and elk. And things had gotten tough.

For months now Jed had been robbing Peter to pay Paul, juggling funds, scrimping where he could, cutting costs altogether where he had to—and none of them had had a clue.

"I still can't believe you haven't paid yourself a wage for five months," Sierra said, sitting back with her arms crossed over her chest.

She'd surprised Jesse with her reaction to the revelation the ranch was in trouble. He'd expected her to be mouthy and upset, but she'd been quiet, taking notes, looking up things on her laptop, digesting everything. Then he'd remembered she was twenty-six now, and that she'd done better at school than any of them. He'd only been surprised because he didn't know her very well anymore.

That was something he planned to rectify, now that he and Jed had sorted themselves out. He had years to catch up on with his family. He wanted to watch Casey captivate the crowd again with his music, and he wanted to know more about Sierra's flying, and most of all he wanted to give his older brother the room and space to have dreams of his own again.

"It wasn't a big deal," Jed said. "It's not like I don't have everything I need here."

"Jesus, that's the saddest thing I ever heard," Casey said, and they all laughed.

Jesse looked at the legal pad in front of him, deciding it was time to summarize.

"Okay, we've all agreed to tipping some of our individual savings into the pot. Sierra and Casey are going to take a wage cut, and no one gets any quarterly payments. And we're going to take a look at all our processes to see where we can be more economical."

"I'm going to see if we can negotiate down our vet fees," Sierra piped up. "Don't forget that."

"And I'm taking over the accounting from Jed," Casey said.

They'd all agreed that Jed could no longer carry the administrative load of the ranch on his own. Jed kept twitching every time a task was farmed out to one of his siblings, but Jesse was pretty sure he wasn't imagining the relief in his brother's eyes.

They had a long row to hoe, and more than a few hurdles to face, but Jesse was confident they could save the ranch if they all pulled together. Like their father always said, Carmodys were good improvisers.

A noise on the porch made him look at his watch and he saw it was seven on the dot. The sound of the front door opening and closing echoed through the house, and seconds later CJ appeared in the kitchen doorway, a stack of pizza boxes in her arms. She looked beautiful, tall and strong, her dark hair flowing over her shoulders. Her eyes met his the moment she entered, and he saw the warmth and love and need in her.

"Oh, man, I am so ready for this," Casey said, rubbing his hands together.

CJ slid the boxes onto the kitchen bench. "I forgot to ask what you all like, so I just got anchovies on everything."

She said it with an utterly straight face, and Jesse grinned as his siblings fought to hide their dismay.

"Kidding, guys. I'm not a sadist," CJ said.

"Thank God," Sierra said. "I would have tried to choke it down for you, CJ, but I wouldn't have liked it."

Sierra jumped up to grab plates and napkins while Casey sorted out beers and Jed cleared the table. Jesse took advantage of their distraction to slip an arm around CJ's waist and pull her close. She smiled, her gaze soft on him, and he felt the twin pull of his love and lust for her. He was the luckiest man on earth, and he knew it. Hopefully that awareness would go some way to making him worthy of CJ at some point in the future, but for now he would just live with the knowledge that he'd lucked out big-time when he managed to convince her to fall in love with him.

"People are about to eat, if you don't mind," Sierra said, nudging them out of the way before flipping the lid open on a pizza box. "Save the public displays of affection for when we don't need to digest."

Her brow furrowed in concentration, she picked out the perfect slice.

"Sorry, Squirrel. Didn't mean to ruin your appetite," Jesse said, then he swiped the slice from his sister's hand and took a big bite.

"*Hey.* You rat," she said.

"What can I say? Snoozers are losers," he said.

"So true," CJ said, swiping the slice from him and taking a huge bite herself.

Sierra cackled with laughter. "I love you, CJ."

"Me, too," Casey said, hands full with his own mammoth slice. "This pizza is amazing."

"I love you, too, CJ, because you're the best fence builder I know," Jed chimed in.

CJ was laughing, utterly in her element. Jesse held up both hands in protest.

"Hang on a minute. I'm the one who loves CJ. She's all mine, and the rest of you can back the hell off."

The rest of the meal proceeded in much the same vein, and once the pizza boxes had been crushed and the table cleared, he and CJ went to sit on the porch to watch the stars.

They each nursed a beer, and he tucked her under his arm as they sat in silence, soaking in the clear, cool air and gazing at the night sky.

"How did it go with you guys? Did you work out a plan of attack?" CJ asked after a while.

"Yeah, we hammered something out." He'd filled CJ in on the details of the ranch's problems before the family meeting, and she'd volunteered to go into town to get dinner for them and leave them to talk in private.

"You think it's going to be okay?" she asked.

"I don't know. Nothing's guaranteed, right? But we've got some ideas. I think we're in with a strong chance."

"Come on, all you stubborn Carmodys pulling in the same direction? Pfft," CJ said, waving a hand dismissively. "You've totally got this."

"You happy to keep coming back here when we can to pitch in? Won't be a lot of wages to throw around until we're more solvent, but we'll have food and lodging taken care of."

"Baby, we won't need wages, we'll have prize money. We'll be rolling in it."

He knew her bravado was for comic effect, but there wasn't a doubt in his mind that CJ was going to make her mark in the world of pro rodeo.

He was going to enjoy the hell out of going along for the ride, too. Maybe he'd even give her a run for her money every now and then, steal a few prizes out from under her nose.

"What?" she said, giving him a look. "Why are you staring at me like that? Have I got a beer moustache?"

"Yes," he lied. "Let me take care of it."

He kissed her, loving the small happy sound she made and the way her body melted against his. After a moment they pulled apart, sharing a smile before they resumed their star watching.

Sitting on the porch steps, the love of his life against his side, Jesse realized he was experiencing a perfect moment. He tried to catalog it all so he could capture the memory perfectly—the taste of beer, the warmth of her body, the brilliant blue-black of the night sky. Then it hit him that this was just the beginning for them, that there would be hundreds, thousands of moments like this in their life together. If they were lucky.

He smiled and pressed a kiss to the top of CJ's head. He had the feeling they were going to be *very* lucky. After all, they'd found each other, hadn't they?

Raising his beer to his mouth, he swallowed a mouthful and went back to watching the heavens above with the woman he loved.

The End

The 79th Copper Mountain Rodeo

Available now at your favorite online retailer!

More books by Sarah Mayberry

Tanner
The American Extreme Bull Riders Tour series

Almost a Bride
The Great Wedding Giveaway series

Make-Believe Wedding
The Great Wedding Giveaway series

Bound to the Bachelor
The Bachelor Auction series

His Christmas Gift

Available now at your favorite online retailer!

About the Author

Sarah Mayberry is the award winning, best selling author of more than 30 books. She lives by the bay in Melbourne with her husband and a small, furry Cavoodle called Max. When she isn't writing romance, Sarah writes scripts for television as well as working on other film and TV projects. She loves to cook, knows she should tend to her garden more, and considers curling up with a good book the height of luxury.

Visit her website at www.sarahmayberry.com

Thank you for reading

The Cowboy Meets His Match

If you enjoyed this book, you can find more from all our great authors at TulePublishing.com, or from your favorite online retailer.

TULE
PUBLISHING

Printed in Great Britain
by Amazon

34047276R00199